LUNER

A GOOD GUYS NOVEL

JAMIE SCHLOSSER

Loner
Copyright © 2021 Jamie Schlosser

All rights reserved.

This novel is for your enjoyment only and may not be reproduced, distributed, or transmitted without permission from the author except for brief quotations in a book review. Please do not participate in or encourage piracy of copyrighted materials in violation of the author's rights. Purchase only authorized editions.

This novel is a work of fiction. All names, characters, places, and events are a product of the author's imagination. Any resemblance to actual people, living or dead, or to locations or incidents, is coincidental.

Due to language and sexual content, this book is intended for readers 18 and older.

Cover design: More Than Words Graphic Design
Cover Model: Lucas Loyola
Photographer: Wander Aguiar
Formatting: Champagne Book Design
Proofreading: Deaton Author Services

DEDICATION

To Adalyn and Everly.
I hope you always love yourselves as much as I love you.

PROLOGUE

She was just supposed to be a job I turned down.

I've been picky about my clients before, and when I was approached by a man with ties to the mafia in search of his daughter, my immediate answer was no. His personal private investigator had recently died under mysterious circumstances, and I didn't want to meet the same fate.

Then I saw Rosalie's picture.

I should've walked away.

I didn't.

CHAPTER 1

Rosalie

The last of the fireworks burst in the dark sky over the trees in the distance, and I watch the sparks die away. If I close my eyes, I can almost imagine the cheers and other happy sounds from Maryville.

Parties and celebrations are happening right now.

Without me.

Underneath one more explosion, people are laughing, kissing, and making plans to raise hell together later.

The white lights fizzle out.

And then it's done.

Quiet.

Dark.

If I sniff the air coming through my cracked window really deeply, I can smell food from the festival. Fried, sweet, delicious food.

My stomach rumbles, but as I release the grip on the curtain, my appetite turns to disappointment, weighing heavily in my gut.

I've never been to a firework show up close before, or pigged out on greasy treats until I can't eat another bite, and it's likely I never will.

Unless I take matters into my own hands.

Unless I defy my mother, the one person who's always been there for me. The only person who's ever loved me.

The person who smothers me until I feel like I'm suffocating.

Conflicting feelings about my mom wage war inside me as I look over my shoulder. My eyes go to the Hello Kitty backpack shoved underneath my bed. My grab-and-go bag. It's been packed with the essentials for three days. Hidden by a few teddy bears surrounding it, it blends in with the rest of the childish décor of my bedroom.

My four-poster twin bed has a frilly pink canopy. The slanted ceilings above it are covered with clouds and angels—something I'm proud of because I painted it myself. There's a bookcase next to my computer desk. It's stocked with my favorite novels and every edition of *Teen Magazine* from the past six years. The pages are weathered, and the spines are worn from reading them so many times.

Next to that is my favorite area. My easel stands proudly, holding acrylic paints and brushes in the storage bins attached to it.

Countless colorful canvases litter the room. Some are mounted around my window, but this attic doesn't have enough wall space for every painting I've done. The most recent artworks are stacked in the corner. All of them are of faraway places. Forests, mountains, and monuments like Mount Rushmore.

Places I'll only get to touch with a brush.

Unless I leave. I just haven't decided if I have the guts to do it yet.

Mom thinks keeping me here is for the best. She says I'm sick. Too crazy to fit in with other people. That I wouldn't even know how to act in a crowd.

Maybe she's right, but I won't find out for sure if I never try.

Sighing, I'm about to turn away from the window, but movement by the hedges outside grabs my attention.

I blink at the shadows, wondering if my eyes are playing tricks on me again. Maybe it's a coyote or a racoon. Living this far from town, it's not uncommon to see wildlife roaming our lawn.

Or maybe it's him.

Preston.

The new groundskeeper is easy on the eyes. The first time I saw him, I felt like an electrical shockwave traveled through my entire body. I swear my heart raced for hours after a glimpse of him chopping wood, with his muscles rippling under his black T-shirt.

Admittedly, I'm a total creep when it comes to him.

I've spent the last two months discreetly staring at him whenever I can.

I wonder what it would be like to have a relationship with someone like Preston. Sometimes I imagine he's mine, and he's just outside doing some work before coming back in all sweaty. He'd pull me into the shower with him and tell me how much he missed me, how he can't stand to be away from me for another second.

I know, I'm delusional.

My mom would probably freak out and fire Preston if she knew I paid so much attention to a man. An older man, judging by the gray peppering his dark hair at the temples. And the hired help, no less.

I continue squinting through the glass for a few more seconds, but I see nothing unusual.

Just for the hell of it, I start unbuttoning my nightgown. Trying to be sexy like the girls in the magazines, tilt my head to the side and let my long hair fall over my shoulder as I reveal my chest one inch at a time.

Baring my small breasts, I do a sultry pout as I stare at my reflection in the glass, and I imagine Preston's out there, watching me. Rubbing my finger over the exposed skin of my upper chest, I notice how pale it is. In the moonlight, I'm almost translucent. I need bronzer. Even better, actual sunlight.

My pout turns to a frown as I graze my flat stomach. I have no curves. My clavicle and ribs stick out, but maybe they wouldn't if I ate more. I try to, but everything tastes like chalk. Even the turkey feast we made for Thanksgiving dinner tonight was bland and unappealing.

Mother tells me it's the mental illness. Depression makes people lose their appetite.

Well, I think anyone would be depressed if they had to spend their entire life stuck in the same house. The scenery never changes. Every day is the same as the day before. It's the same sounds and smells. The *tick, tick, ticking* of the grandfather clock. The stuffy air.

My senses need variety, damn it.

Ashamed of my bony body and my pathetic attempt to be desirable, I cover myself.

No one's lurking around at night, especially not Preston. The guy's a saint. The few times I've managed to convince my mother to let me out of this house recently for some fresh air, I purposely sought him out.

Once, I found him in the detached garage meticulously organizing his tools. Another day he was raking leaves from the quarter mile lane to our house. It became obvious very quickly that I was bothering him because he wouldn't even look my way.

His responses to my questions were mostly grunts before he mumbled an excuse about needing to go somewhere else. Somewhere away from me, doing whatever it is he does for fall cleanup.

Guess Mother gave him the same warning she told all the other employees over the years: stay away from Rosalie or else you're gone.

It's a wonder she let me get close enough to talk to him at all. She was probably testing him, and he passed with flying colors.

Turning away from the window, I tell myself I just need to accept the fact that I'm alone. That another year of my life has almost expired, and the world keeps spinning without me in it.

I've never understood why some people would wish for invisibility as their superpower. I know what it's like to not be seen, and it sucks major balls.

A ping from my laptop snuffs out any heavy feelings, and I rush over to check the screen.

JessaBelle2002: Happy early birthday! The big 18 is just hours away! Did you do anything fun tonight?

RosieDoll528: Sorta. The nearest town had a firework show for their annual Thanksgiving festival. I watched from my window.

JessaBelle2002: Oh. Not in a partying mood, huh?

RosieDoll528: Even if I was, I couldn't go.

JessaBelle2002: Why? You STILL grounded? Damn, girl. What did you do to get into so much trouble? It's been weeks.

It's been a lot longer than that.

Twirling a lock of hair around my finger, I think about how to answer her innocent question.

Jessa and I have been friends on Solitaire Slam for a couple months now. When my mom set me up with the game last year, she figured it was a one-player game. She didn't realize there's a chat feature. All along, she's had no idea I can talk to people from anywhere in the world.

I was a good little daughter for a while. I blindly followed her rules, ignoring message requests. Then a spunky girl started blowing up my inbox. Jessa broke me down with questions about makeup advice, of all things.

As if I knew anything about that. I didn't then, and I still suck at it now, even after practicing every day since I got my cosmetic collection in the mail several weeks ago. I've found that I enjoy painting my face. It's like a blank canvas. I can change myself into someone different. Someone better. Although, most of the time, I'm a little too heavy handed with the stuff, and I end up looking like a clown.

At least I have someone to commiserate with. Jessa's specialty is hair, but makeup is something we're learning together.

Like me, she's homeschooled, so she understands what it is to be isolated. I'm not sure she knows the meaning of the word like I do, though. She's still allowed to have friends. Go out. Meet people.

Over time, our friendship has developed effortlessly. At this point, Jessa knows me better than anyone else ever has—besides my mom, of course. I've told her superficial stuff, like my favorite books and my art hobby. We talk about movies and music. She even knows about my obsession with true crime documentaries and podcasts.

I take credit for the fact that I got Jessa hooked on Harlee Verona's videos. Harlee's a beauty influencer who posts a few times a week. Since social media sites are blocked on my laptop, I have to look her up on YouTube, and luckily, my mom hasn't forbidden me from that website yet. Sometimes Harlee talks about new fashion trends or Hollywood scandals, but my favorite episodes are when she tells tales about serial killers. At the end of every video, she gives out a life hack or a safety tip. Like how to escape from the trunk of a car, should you ever find yourself stuck in one.

My mother frowns upon rated R stuff with violence and sex, but who needs movies when you have real stories? They're surprisingly educational. It's amazing what you can learn about crime when you watch shows about murderers. Stalking, weapons, hard drugs, forensics, DNA, evading the police, capture, prison.

Oddly enough, my mom doesn't mind that I watch them. If anything, she likes that they scare me. "See, Rosalie?" she'll say. "The world is a horrible, horrible place."

I'm smart enough to know you never fully trust someone on the internet, so I've held back my deepest secret from Jessa. Sure, she's nice and she's sent several pictures of herself to prove she's not a creep, but maybe she isn't really a seventeen-year-old girl from Florida. Maybe she's a middle-aged man from New York.

Either way, I need this friendship like I need air, so I've chosen to believe she is who she says she is while hiding the ugliest part of myself.

She doesn't know I'm sick, and I'd like to keep it that way.

Deciding not to respond to her question, my finger goes to the mousepad as I move a few cards around. I'm about to finish the game when a notification pops up with a chime.

I have a new message request from Jimbo6969. Clicking the icon, I open my inbox, and it takes me a second to figure out what I'm looking at. Covering my mouth, I make a noise of disgust.

The video features a closeup of a guy exposing himself. It's just a five-second clip of him pulling his camo-print underwear down to reveal a penis buried in a lot of hair, but it keeps playing over and over again on a loop.

Gross.

JessaBelle2002: Hello? You still there?

RosieDoll528: Yeah, I'm here. I just got my first ever dick pic. Or video, in this case.

JessaBelle2002: EW. Forward it to me.

RosieDoll528: Why?

JessaBelle2002: Just do it.

Well, if she really wants to see this mess, who am I to stop her? I send it her way. Maybe we can laugh about it. Plus, there's nothing like a floppy dick to distract someone and change the subject.

JessaBelle2002: Omg, he's not even hard. It looks like a drunk guy falling out of the back of a cab.

I laugh.

See? She's funny. This is another reason why I keep her around.

RosieDoll528: LOL. Well, I've never seen a drunk guy fall out of a cab.

Or a penis for that matter.

JessaBelle2002: Trust me. They're both flaccid and clumsy. So, what did you do to get put on lockdown for so long?

Ugh. So much for that subject change.

Should I tell her the truth and risk losing my one and only friend?

Sometimes when I'm talking to Jessa, I forget I've been locked in this attic for the majority of the last six months. On this side of the screen, I can be anyone I want. I can pretend I'm not an emotionally troubled, mentally unstable captive in my own home.

I used to have free roam of the house until something my mom calls 'the incident.'

The incident being, I might've stolen some of her happy pills from her nightstand and accidentally overdosed. I didn't want to die—I just wanted to feel good. And I did feel good for a few minutes until I got really sleepy and passed out next to the grandfather clock in the hallway on the second floor. I remember staring up at it, watching the arms go round and round the Roman numerals as darkness closed in. Instead of annoying me, the *tick, tick, ticking* made me happy. Giddy, even. Hearing that sound is the last thing I can recall from that day.

Waking up in the hospital wasn't scary. It was worth it. I got to meet people. Even with my mother hovering every time the nurses came in, it was fun. There was noise and life.

But during the days I was away, Mom had a heavy-duty lock installed on my bedroom door so I couldn't leave the attic unsupervised. Now she's always watching me. Always breathing down my neck.

I've been trying to gain back her trust ever since, but so far, she won't budge on the new arrangement. I get to go down to the dining room for meals. If I beg enough, she'll let me go outside for about fifteen minutes at a time. Bedtime is at seven, at which point, I'm locked in here until the next morning.

Fridays are still cleaning days, and I think the only reason my mother includes me in the activities is because she needs the help. I've actually started to look forward to polishing floors and dusting just so I can do something different with my hands. How sad is that?

To sum it up, my life is hell.

Oh, to hell with it. Friendship is nothing without honesty.

RosieDoll528: I can't leave. Ever.

JessaBelle2002: What, like you're grounded for life? Lol.

RosieDoll528: I guess you could say that, but there's a reason. I'm bat-shit crazy. Like, legit looney tunes.

JessaBelle2002: You're kidding, right?

RosieDoll528: Nope. I have to stay in my house for my

own good. And the good of everyone else. It was either that, or a mental institution.

Yes, my mother has threatened to have me committed several times. It's her go-to when I'm being particularly difficult. I'm not sure if she'd follow through with it, but sometimes she's unpredictable. She's just as crazy as I am—*thanks, genetics*—and I worry she'd have us put in the same psych ward together.

JessaBelle2002: I don't believe it. You don't seem crazy.

RosieDoll528: That's because I'm medicated.

Yeah, I have my own happy pills now. Mom made sure I got some, though she controls my dose.

She doesn't know I've been biting my pills in half for several weeks and stowing the leftovers away. Not so I can overdose again; just in case I decide to run away. That way, I'll still have some medicine with me until I can get settled somewhere else.

I like my pills. I need them. They make me somewhat normal.

Staring at the screen, I wait a full minute as I wring my hands. No response from Jessa.

I let out a humorless chuckle.

What did I expect? She's probably in the process of blocking me right now.

Regret filters in as I get back to my card game. I shouldn't have said all that. I could've made up any lie. How would Jessa know the difference?

But I'm allergic to lying—no joke.

I literally have a physical reaction to being untruthful. My heart starts to race, and I break out in a sweat. My skin gets red and splotchy on my chest and neck. The worst part? The sneezing.

My mom sees that as proof that there's something unnatural about me. Something sinister and dark. She used to tell me I had a demon inside of me. I'm not sure if I believe in demons, but I do know there's something off with my brain.

I'm just wired wrong.

A ping makes my eyes dart to the conversation box.

JessaBelle2002: What's wrong with you?

I flinch. Well, at least she's direct.

RosieDoll528: It's an extreme anxiety disorder. If I don't take my meds, I have bad nightmares and I wake up screaming. Sometimes I sleepwalk. Other times I'll be awake for days.

JessaBelle2002: Insomnia and anxiety? A lot of people have those issues, and they still function in society just fine.

RosieDoll528: This is different. I don't know how to explain it.

JessaBelle2002: Don't you get lonely?

RosieDoll528: All the time.

JessaBelle2002: Do you ever get visitors?

RosieDoll528: Unless you count my doctor who does house calls, no.

JessaBelle2002: So you literally only see your mom?

RosieDoll528: Pretty much.

An image of Preston flashes in my mind. The way sweat trickles down the back of his neck, soaking his T-shirt while he brings the ax down on the logs. The way his gloved hands grasp the wooden handle. The way his ass flexes in his dirty jeans.

I rub a hand down my face, then check my desk mirror to make sure I didn't smudge my makeup. It's fine, but my lips need a touch up. Unzipping my floral makeup pouch, I dig around for my pink lip gloss.

I wonder if Preston would like red better… Would he kiss it off? Smear it across my face?

Damn it.

These uninvited thoughts and fantasies about him just won't stop.

All I'm doing is torturing myself.

My mom has made it clear that no one would ever want me. It's the same reason why she's single. That's why my father left her. Left us both and never looked back.

JessaBelle2002: What about when you were little?

RosieDoll528: I've always been here. Only here.

JessaBelle2002: Doctors don't usually diagnose small children with mental illnesses. It's very rare.

RosieDoll528: I guess I'm just a rare case, then. It was bad enough that my mom thought I needed to stay home. She means well, but it doesn't stop me from hating her a little. That's bad, right? Hating my own mom?

JessaBelle2002: Not when she's abusing you. She can't keep you trapped forever.

RosieDoll528: She can try.

JessaBelle2002: It sounds like you could use a vacation. You'll be a legal adult tomorrow. Come down to Florida.

RosieDoll528: Oh, my mom would definitely never allow that.

JessaBelle2002: I wasn't suggesting you ask her permission.

Jessa's line of thinking isn't too far from my own. She's

hinted at a real-life meeting before, but it always seemed like a hypothetical suggestion. Something in the future.

Now… she's talking about *now*.

I give my backpack another glance as temptation mounts.

RosieDoll528: How would I get there?

JessaBelle2002: I take it you don't know how to drive?

RosieDoll528: Nope.

JessaBelle2002: I can get you a train ticket. It'll take you a couple days to get down here, but it'll be worth it. We can hang out at my parents' beach house. Go to Disney World. Swim in the ocean…

I shudder. She doesn't realize it, but she just provoked one of my worst nightmares.

RosieDoll528: No swimming. Just looking at the water would be fine for me. From a distance. A good distance.

JessaBelle2002: Does that mean you'll actually do it?? You'll come here? DO IT.

Paralyzed with want and indecision, I sit completely still with my fists balled in my lap.

JessaBelle2002: DO IT DO IT DO IT.

JessaBelle2002: Seriously, Rosie Doll. There's no reason why your life should be on hold. It should've started the day you were born.

She's right. I've been caged for far too long.

Nibbling the inside of my lip until I taste blood, I blink as I seriously contemplate the offer. It'd be very generous of her, taking me in like that.

But if I leave here, I can never come back.

I wouldn't want to.

That means I'll have to figure out how to take care of myself.

Other than getting out of the house, I hadn't thought too far ahead about my next steps in life. Jessa's hospitality would be appreciated for as long as she's willing to give it. I could use that time to form some plans, then I could go off on my own.

RosieDoll528: Are you sure you're not a serial killer? Lol.

JessaBelle2002: Are you sure you wouldn't be into that sort of thing?

RosieDoll528: *eye roll* That sounds like something a serial killer would say.

A picture comes through of Jessa making a silly face. She's in pink pajamas with princess crowns all over it, and her blue-streaked blond hair is tied up into two pigtail buns.

RosieDoll528: You're kind of a dork. I like it. I'm glad you're my friend.

JessaBelle2002: And I'm glad you're mine. So? Vacay? Are you for real about coming here? Because seriously, just tell me when you're leaving, and I'll get you that ticket.

Can I do this? I can. I will.

My heart pumps overtime as I type out my response.

RosieDoll528: Yes. I'll wait until midnight, then I'll sneak out.

JessaBelle2002: OMG. Yay! I'm so happy right now.

JessaBelle2002: Wait, will you be able to get out without getting caught?

Swiveling in my chair, I look at the bathroom. Past the open door, there's an old laundry chute. It's a tight metal shaft that goes all the way from the attic to the basement, with little openings at each floor on the way down.

I know from personal experience that I can fit inside.

On nights when I couldn't sleep—restless from boredom and high on my meds—I've been brave enough to wiggle down the chute and poke around in the basement or creep through the house. Getting back up that way is a bitch and a half, but it can be done from the second floor.

But I won't have to come back this time.

My fantasy is about to become reality.

CHAPTER 2

Ethan / Preston / Jessa Belle 2002

I'm a man of many identities. I've changed my alias so many times, names are meaningless.

Fitting, since I was born as a nobody. Unwanted. Abandoned like useless trash.

Twenty-seven years ago, someone gave birth to me somewhere. Probably in an alleyway or a bathroom. Then they put me in a plastic bag and placed me in a pile of garbage to die. I was found by a homeless man who took me to the hospital. The story made national news, and families all over the country filled out applications to take me in.

It should've been happily ever after from there.

It wasn't.

Suffering from fetal alcohol syndrome, I was a difficult infant. Unhealthy and fussy. Cried constantly. I had delayed speech as a toddler. I bounced around a lot of foster homes and the names I got called in most of them weren't nice. *Hey, stupid* was common.

Only, I wasn't stupid. I was just quiet. Observant. I liked to watch people. To figure them out. To memorize their tells when they're lying or when they're about to lose their temper. Call it self-preservation if you want.

As I got older, I got really into puzzles. At four, I was working with 1000+ piece puzzles. I only owned one, so I'd put it together, take it apart, repeat. One time, an older kid at a home I was staying in stole a piece and ate it. Fucking ate it. Chewed it up right in front of me. I had a tantrum for days. I couldn't deal with how angry it made me that I'd never be able to complete that puzzle again. That fit of rage got me transferred to another foster home.

After that, I was labeled a problem kid. Eventually, I was diagnosed with ADD, OCD, and some doctors said I was on the spectrum.

To this day, I'm not sure if they were right. My mind just works differently than some. I notice small details, such as the missing piece of a puzzle. I become obsessed with finding a way to complete it. Fix it. When I can't, it bothers me.

It's what makes me so good at my job. I like solving mysteries.

Maybe if I'd just been loved, I would've turned out closer to normal. I might've developed better, healthier. Maybe I wouldn't have been so mad.

Then again, maybe not. Guess I'll never know.

Once I reached adulthood, I didn't want to be Edmond Smith, the dumpster baby of Detroit. So I changed my first name to Ethan, and I enlisted in the Marines. Because of my high test score, I made it into Intelligence. I wish I could say I joined because I'm a patriot, but it wasn't about that. I needed stability, an income, and a place to live. It was good for me. During my time in the service, I honed my tech skills, got a college degree in business management, and grew from an angry teenager to a decent man.

After I got out, I started a freelance private investigator business. As Ethan Smith, I worked in the adoption world for several years, connecting adult children with their biological parents, and vice versa. Some wanted closure. Some wanted a relationship. Some didn't get the answers they were seeking.

No matter the outcome, it was noble work. I took pride in it, and I had personal reasons for being so invested. I figured I'd never find out who my parents are, but that didn't mean I couldn't help others do the same.

And I was satisfied with my life until a few months ago.

Everything changed when Ivan Belov contacted me and flipped my entire world with just one picture—a photo of the most beautiful, sad, lonely girl I've ever seen. If love at first sight exists, it happened to me that day. For some reason, a part of me recognized Rosalie as my destiny.

Now I find myself as Preston Walker, the reclusive groundskeeper on the Pearsons' twenty-six-acre estate.

I'm not sure I recognize who I've become since committing to this job.

I used to think I knew who I was. I thought I'd built a secure, stable life. One based on morals.

That's the problem with being on high ground—the farther the fall. In the past couple months, I've broken just about every ethical code I have.

I gave up everything for this project. My apartment. My business. Contact with people I consider family.

Oh, yeah, and I'm catfishing a teenage girl. Might as well throw my dignity out the window, too.

Tonight's no different than every other night.

Me, out here. Making sure Rosalie's okay.

Her, in there. Wishing she were somewhere else.

Spying on her is my new normal.

Hiding in the shadows, I watch the third story of the old Victorian mansion. As always, the light is on, and the dark iron bars over the window look like slashes through her freedom, or tally marks of her captivity.

In my line of work, I've seen a lot of messy family shit. Babies who were put up for adoption because they were the product of rape or incest. Mothers and fathers who never wanted to be found by the kids they gave away. Kids who were bitterly disappointed when they learned their relatives had died, and they'd never have the connection they craved.

But I've met a lot of heartwarming situations, too. Sweet reunions with parents who'd been looking for their kids for decades. Kids who embraced their biological relatives without hesitation.

Rosalie won't have any of those outcomes. Her history is a tangled web of lies, deceit, and tragedy.

When Ivan first called me and said his daughter had been abducted, I told him to contact the proper authorities. I prided myself on keeping my business legit and legal, minus a few computer hackings when I'd gotten desperate for sealed adoption records.

Then Ivan started telling me one of the saddest stories I've ever heard. About twenty years ago, he knocked up a stripper. The woman took off without telling him about his baby, and by the time he found out he had a daughter, the little girl was gone.

Like, face-on-a-milk-carton gone.

The baby, who went by the name of Melody back then, ended up in the foster care system after her mom overdosed on heroin and died. Things were looking up for Melody after a few years, though. She got adopted by a great family at the age of three. However, Melody went missing during a camping trip a few months after that.

Breaking news and an Amber alert later, Ivan realized who she was. Because the resemblance between him and the girl on the TV was striking. Still is. White-blond hair, a cleft in their chin, and brilliant eyes of two different colors are just a few features they share. Rosalie's right is blue, and her left is green. Just like Ivan. After tracking her origin, it led him back to the woman he'd had a fling with, and it confirmed that he wasn't alone in this world, but his daughter was nowhere to be found.

There was a lot of speculation about little Melody's disappearance, but her body was never recovered. The only evidence left behind was a red shoe in the river near the campsite.

Now it's just a cold case.

To his credit, Ivan never stopped looking. As a mafia boss, his reach is limitless, lawless, and without a budget. His first step was to cast a wide net, throwing donations at schools and other organizations in Detroit where a child might show up. He rubbed the right elbows and made the right friends.

Determined to find his daughter by any means necessary, he put a detective on his payroll. Years passed with nothing, but the big break finally came when a teenage girl got airlifted to a hospital in the city earlier this year. She fit the age and description of Melody, and the director of the hospital happened to be married to Ivan's detective—which I doubt was a coincidence. Ivan is always strategic when it comes to the people he surrounds himself with, and it paid off.

After a nurse took a strand of Rosalie's hair along with a discreet picture, her true identity couldn't be denied.

Rosalie is Melody.

How she ended up with Loralee Pearson? No one really knows, but I have strong suspicions because I've done some extensive digging on Loralee's past. Back during her twenties and thirties, she was a junkie with a trust fund. She had no responsibilities and a seemingly endless pool of money to fuel her addiction. Her record shows a pattern of hospitalizations due to overdoses and a couple arrests for drug possession. Then, a little over two decades ago, she gave birth to a stillborn baby girl.

There's nothing on her after that.

Most would think she cleaned up her act and settled down. And she sort of did, but she didn't do it alone.

Somehow, she ended up with Rosalie.

After learning Rosalie's identity, I should've gone straight to my FBI contact. Jen Harding has been working on Michigan missing children's cases for more than two decades, and I know it would mean a lot to her to be able to solve this mystery.

But what would happen to Rosalie after that? She'd get tossed back to a family she doesn't remember. To people who loved her when she was a toddler but know nothing about who she is now.

No, I need to be the one to save her. Her future is bleak unless I do something about it. Right now, I feel like I'm holding the key to her life—a good life—and all she has to do is let go of her prison.

Every day she's in that house, she's in danger. She already ended up in the hospital on suicide watch once.

I don't believe Rosalie's insane. Psychologically abused? Definitely. Traumatized? Hell, yeah. But anyone with her life would be.

My one condition with Ivan is that Rosalie has to leave on her own terms. Originally, he wanted me to break in and take her, but kidnapping isn't part of my job description. I told him I'd help her get out, even convince her to run, but I wouldn't take her against her will.

I figure if she has a friend on the outside, she's more likely to take the leap, and I'll be here to help her when she escapes.

Back to why I'm catfishing her. Through Solitaire Slam, I've infiltrated her life.

Obviously, getting close to her as myself would never have worked. Loralee would fire my ass so fast if she thought I had any interest in Rosalie.

The hired help doesn't last long around here, and I think that's a strategic move on Loralee's part. Keep the turnover rolling, so no one is here long enough to get the full picture. Which means my time is limited.

During my research, I found out one of their maids tried to report Loralee to Child Protective Services seven years ago, but the woman was here illegally, and she was suddenly deported. Another man who used to deliver groceries started a rumor in town that the house was haunted after seeing a 'very pale girl' lingering in the attic window. All that did was make people want to stay away even more. Their last groundskeeper asked too many questions—that tidbit was directly from Loralee's mouth during the interview, and the message was clear: stay silent.

People have tried to help. The system failed.

A text comes through on my phone.

Ivan: I need the daily progress report.

No change, I lie. **Will touch base with you tomorrow**.

Ivan: I'm getting impatient.

You and me both, buddy.

By tomorrow, hopefully I'll be with Rosalie. Because it sounds like my subtle persuasions are working.

RosieDoll528: Are you sure you're not a serial killer? Lol.

JessaBelle2002: Are you sure you wouldn't be into that sort of thing?

RosieDoll528: *eye roll* That sounds like something a serial killer would say.

Shit. I'm being creepy.

Scrolling through my phone, I choose a picture from my past and send it through. I take a second to stare at it, and grief hits me as if ten years hasn't gone by since Krystal left this world. My guilt over the way she died still hangs over me. I wasn't there when she needed me. I couldn't save her.

I'll be damned if I let that happen again with Rosalie.

Channeling my inner Krystal, I send a cool and collected, yet persuasive, message. Then I hold my breath as I wait for the answer I need.

RosieDoll528: Yes. I'll wait until midnight, then I'll sneak out.

I can't believe my eyes. Heart pounding, I read her message a few times just to make sure I'm not imagining it.

"She's really gonna fucking do it," I whisper to myself while typing.

JessaBelle2002: OMG. Yay! I'm so happy right now.

I look at the house. More like a fortress, really. A long time ago, the wooden siding was painted pink and purple, but the color has faded so much it's almost gray. There are bars on most of the windows. Cameras with motion sensors are mounted over the front door, pointing in three different directions. I know for a fact the back patio door has been nailed shut, making it impossible to get out that way.

Unless Rosalie has a better idea, I'm going to have to step in. Deactivate the cameras. Hack into their alarm system to shut it off. Revisit my lock-picking skills.

JessaBelle2002: Wait, will you be able to get out without getting caught?

RosieDoll528: Yep. I have a whole plan in place.

JessaBelle2002: What plan?

RosieDoll528: The laundry chute will take me down to the basement. I'll climb out of a window down there. Easy peasy.

The laundry chute? This girl isn't playing around. I never would've thought of that, but it's fucking smart.

JessaBelle2002: Is that safe?

RosieDoll528: Oh, yeah. I've done it lots of times. That's the thing about being stuck in the same house your whole life. You get to know the place really well. Every fortress has a weak spot, and I've had nothing but time to figure it out.

JessaBelle2002: You diabolical genius.

RosieDoll528: *hair flip* Thanks. So, you'll be able to get me a train ticket?

JessaBelle2002: Yeah.

RosieDoll528: How?

She's probably worried about money. Little does she know, she doesn't need to be concerned because this is an imaginary train ticket. I'll be intercepting her as soon as she comes out of the house, and we'll be taking a car I have stashed in a storage garage in the nearby town.

Quickly thinking about how I'd actually do it if a train were the plan, my fingers fly over my keys.

JessaBelle2002: I'll pretend I'm your parent, buy it under your name, and say you'll be traveling as a minor.

RosieDoll528: No, I mean, don't you need to know where I live? Michigan is a big state. You don't know what station I'm going to…

Fuck. I'm so excited this is finally happening, I'm letting my cover slip.

JessaBelle2002: Lol I was just about to ask that, silly.

RosieDoll528: Maryville. I Googled, and there's only one train station. It'll be quite a hike for me to get there, but I can do it.

With trembling fingers, I give her the number to my burner phone, telling her to call me once she's on her way. Rosalie says a quick goodbye with a bunch of funny emojis before signing off.

I kind of want to scold her for being so trusting.

I could be anyone. Obviously, I'm not who she thinks I am, and I suspect she's going to be pissed when she finds out. Which will be sooner rather than later.

Glancing at the time, I realize I have less than two hours to get my shit packed and make sure I'm in position.

Slowly backing away, I press my lit-up phone screen to my thundering chest and look at Rosalie's window one more time, wondering if she's going to make another appearance tonight.

My dick twitches at all the memories of seeing her up there. Sometimes she prances around naked, flaunting her perky breasts and rosy nipples. Other times, she stands in front of the window topless, like she's daring me to look.

I'm not a pervert or a pedophile like Jimbo6969 probably is.

See, Rosalie's not as young as she thinks. Tomorrow isn't her birthday and she's not going to be eighteen. In reality, she turned nineteen back in September. Loralee must've underestimated Rosalie's age when she took her, and she assigned her the birth date of her stillborn child.

Speaking of Jimbo6969, he needs to learn a lesson. Anonymously forwarding his video to Jen Harding sounds like a good idea, and I do just that, smiling with satisfaction when the email goes through. I'll consider it my good deed for the day. Solitaire Slam attracts a lot of minors, with its bright colors and hyper techno music.

Also, I hate the idea of anyone else hitting on Rosalie. She might be an adult, but that fucker tried to corrupt my girl with his limp dick.

And that's what I've come to think of her as—my girl. It

doesn't matter if it's not true. My heart refuses to receive that memo.

It's been a long time since I wanted to claim something for my own. Growing up, nothing was permanent. Possessions came and went, just like parental figures and friends.

But I want Rosalie so bad I can barely stand it. Of course, maybe I'm just fooling myself thinking she'd want me back, but a guy can hope.

Even if it means crossing Ivan.

Yeah, he paid me fifty-thousand in cash up front, and I'll get the other half *if* I deliver Rosalie to him.

And that's a big if, because I want what's best for her. Is that Ivan? I'm skeptical.

That detective Ivan hired? He ended up dead in a shallow grave after he discovered Rosalie's location. Some hikers found him in the forest with half of his skull blown off. If that's what loyalty earns someone, I don't want to find out what betrayal will get me.

A few seconds later, blond hair comes into view in the window, along with sparkling eyes. Rosalie's irises are so light, they almost look like they're glowing. A beacon in the night.

My lighthouse.

That puzzle I had when I was a kid… it was of a lighthouse on a rocky shore. And the colors I remember most were blue and green, just like her eyes.

I almost scoff when I see the frilly white nightgown she's wearing. Her mother dresses her like an old-fashioned doll.

No, not her mother. I have to stop thinking that way.

That woman might be the only parent Rosalie remembers, but Loralee Pearson is a liar, a criminal, and a fraud. A cheapskate, too.

For a millionaire, she sure does pinch her pennies.

She doesn't pay me enough to take care of this property

year-round, and she makes me work with old basic tools instead of investing in a fucking leaf blower or some shit. To make things worse, she recently added grocery shopping to my list of duties. I've considered a lot of different careers for myself, but a personal shopper was never one of them.

My living arrangements leave a lot to be desired, too. The guest suite above the detached garage is half-finished and roach infested. Sometimes the water heater goes out. The mini fridge isn't big enough to store food to last a week, and a plug-in hot plate is all I've got to cook with.

Of course, I'm not here for the accommodations. I don't mind the small space, the unpainted drywall, the bugs, or even the cold showers.

I have one purpose and one purpose only—make sure Rosalie gets away from this hellhole. My only mission is her safety and freedom.

The pretty girl tilts her head to the side and starts using her reflection in the glass to braid her hair. My fingers itch to touch the silky strands she's weaving with her delicate fingers.

I want to be the one braiding it. Twisting it. Tying it.

After securing it with a band, she raises her arms and smooths some flyaway hairs from her face. The action causes the thin fabric of her gown to stretch across her breasts, putting the outline of her nipples on display.

Off-key humming comes from the cracked window, and as Rosalie sways, she sings the saddest, loneliest rendition of happy birthday I've ever heard.

She won't be alone for much longer.

Soon, we'll be together.

CHAPTER 3

Rosalie

Leaning against my door, I press my ear to the wood and listen as the grandfather clock chimes eleven times.

"Come on," I whisper, antsy to get the show on the road.

Talking to myself is a bad habit, but I can't help it. It's a consequence of being isolated for so long. Or a blessing. I can play out entire conversations with myself and no one. That's a talent, right?

Less than a minute later, I hear the shuffling of footsteps, the creak of a door, and the click of a lock.

Right on time.

In about five minutes, my mom will be popping her pills and falling into a deep sleep for at least six hours. Give or take a little bit.

It's enough time for me to get to the train station before she wakes up.

Nerves make my hands shake as I rush over to yank my backpack out from under my bed. Unzipping it, I spy my fanny pack inside. My leftover medication is in there, and I raise tonight's pill to my teeth to bite it in half.

Swallowing, I consider taking the whole thing.

Tonight might be a full-dose kind of night.

There's a risk versus benefit to think about. My pills make

me sleepy, and that's not helpful when I need to be up all night. On the other hand, I need to be calm enough to focus.

Half a pill, I decide, stashing the rest away with my other extras. I can't afford to be sluggish.

A cold breeze blows through my window as I quickly get dressed in jeans and a sweatshirt, reminding me my good winter coat is in the closet downstairs next to the front door. I won't be able to get to it with how creaky the floorboards are.

Well, it looks like I'll be freezing my butt off.

After layering on a second sweatshirt, I rush around the room to grab a few last-minute essentials. My toothbrush, a handful of underwear, and some socks. I cram my makeup bag into the front pouch of my backpack. Grabbing a couple of bottles of water from my mini-fridge, I slide them into the side pockets. By the time I stuff my laptop in with everything else, the zipper is practically busting at the seams.

I look at the little laundry chute door.

Shit.

I can't get down to the basement with my bag. All the times I practiced before, it was without any cumbersome objects weighing me down.

If I drop the backpack first, my laptop might break, and I can't let that happen. It's my line of communication to Jessa.

Getting an idea, I look to my closet and walk over to the open doors. All my dresses and nightgowns are hung neatly, sorted by color.

Trailing my fingers over the cotton and lace, I experience an annoying stab of guilt. My mom made all of these for me with her own hands. When I asked her how she did it, she said she made them with love.

Well, these are going to be of use to me now.

Rapidly pulling each one off the hangers, I gather a huge heap in my arms. Then I waddle through the bathroom door, go over to the laundry chute, and stuff them inside. I let go of the pile and listen to the fabric softly swish four floors down. That should at least provide a soft landing.

Next, I push my backpack through the door and quietly mutter prayers for my laptop's safety as it whizzes down. Several seconds later, I hear a soft thud echo back at me.

Okay. This is it. My moment.

I stare into the darkness of the chute.

Can I really do this?

"You have to. What's the worst thing that can happen? You get caught sneaking out and end up right back here. If you don't at least try, you'll die here someday."

That's the worst-case scenario. My mom isn't immortal. At some point, she's going to die, and I'll be left alone here, stuck in this house by myself. By then, half of my life could be wasted already.

Leaning against the wall, I scan the bathroom of my prison one more time.

The small space is cramped with the slanted ceilings. The tallest part is barely high enough to accommodate for the standup shower. The floral wallpaper is faded and peeling in some spots.

A light wooziness filters through my head as the medicine starts to take effect.

I take a freeing breath. My muscles relax. My brain and body sync up in perfect harmony.

There's no pain.

Worries slip away.

What I love most about being medicated is the fact that I feel more myself this way. I feel right. The world is right. Everything is… right.

Even the guilt I was experiencing just minutes before is muted to a dull, easily ignorable buzz.

Yes, my mother will be lost without me, but she made this bed we're in together.

Out of the two of us, she's the crazier one for sure. Sometimes I wonder if she likes the fact that she passed her mental illness down to me, because at least then she's not alone.

She's tried so hard to give me whatever I want, within reason. I have a television, DVDs, and multiple streaming networks. I have my laptop and access to the internet. Sure, she likes to check my browser history occasionally. Which is why I've gotten good at erasing it.

Admittedly, manipulating her is a talent I've developed. Once I realized throwing a really loud God-awful fit would get me what I want, I started having tantrums.

I'm not proud of it.

But.

A girl's gotta do what a girl's gotta do, and my mom won't listen unless I make it impossible for her to ignore me.

Last Christmas, she bought me a treadmill after I trashed the dining room because she wouldn't let me go for runs around our property. I broke a bunch of plates before she started making promises to placate me. The machine was a compromise.

A similar incident got me some casual clothes. That time, I didn't break anything, but I did go streaking through the house as naked as the day I was born. The next week, I got yoga pants, jeans, sports bras, T-shirts, and hoodies delivered to our door. I'd been fed up with the stupid dresses she makes me wear for a long time, and she finally said that I could wear whatever I want as long as I do it in my room.

It's not enough.

As much as she's tried to make me happy, she can't.

Because the things I desperately want in life need to be done out there. Out in the world. With other people and places.

Unzipping the fanny pack on my waist, I fish around in the pouch for a folded piece of paper.

My bucket list.

Learn to wing eyeliner
Eat an entire pizza
Kiss someone
Get married
Be a mom
Be a basic bitch

The last one is the ultimate goal. I want to be painfully normal. I want the minivan and the suburbs. The messy bun and leggings. The ridiculously expensive Starbucks lattes everyone makes videos about.

Reading over my list gives me the motivation I need to start folding myself into the chute.

My mom's had me backed into a corner for years. It was only a matter of time until I snapped.

I have a life to live, and it sure as hell won't happen here.

CHAPTER 4

Rosalie

Sweat trickles down my temple as I wiggle. My knees are tucked up to my chest, and I use my thigh muscles, pushing against the metal walls to keep myself from falling too fast. I passed the second-floor eight feet ago, so I know I'm coming up to the office bathroom.

When I feel the swinging wooden flap with my shoe below me, I push it outward, wiggle some more, and hook my legs over the ledge. With some maneuvering, I'm able to get through the little door without making a noise.

My feet touch down on black and white checkered tiles. Moonlight comes through the bathroom window, casting a glow over the clawfoot tub. There's a wicker chest of drawers next to the pedestal sink, and I rummage around in it until I find a small flashlight.

I click it on, and a dim yellow circle appears on the pink wall in front of me.

Over my heavy breathing, I listen for any warning signs in the house. No creaks or footsteps. Except for the ticking clock, everything's quiet.

Tiptoeing over the wooden threshold of the office, I go to the bulky antique desk, crouch down behind it, and slowly push the heavy leather chair out of the way. Two false drawers hide the old safe. It's two feet tall, fireproof, and weighs a shit ton.

The combination isn't hard. I figured it out years ago when I still had free roaming privileges in the house.

Sticking the flashlight in my mouth, I point it at the dial and turn it until I land on the numbers that make up my birthday.

Click.

Just like that, I'm in.

The solid door swings open with a quiet squeak from the rusty hinges.

Stacks of cash are piled inside. I haven't counted all of it, but I estimate the amount has to be up in the millions. Mom doesn't trust banks. Apparently, she shouldn't trust me either.

I pick up a wad of fifties. The bills are bound together, and I quickly count a thousand dollars in the bunch. I take ten. Then I take five more, stuffing all the money into my bursting fanny pack.

"Think of it as your inheritance," I rationalize. "She won't even miss it."

But she'll miss you.

Damn it.

The guilt is back.

My finger bumps into the little plastic baggie, and without giving it too much thought, I dig out another half pill. Looks like it's a full-dose kind of night after all. I need a little something extra to douse my nerves.

After swallowing it down dry, I continue my little pep talk. "It's her fault for holding on too tight. If she would've given me a little more freedom…"

I still would've left. Eventually, anyway. That's what people do when they grow up. They go to college. Get jobs. Make friends and have families of their own.

I don't care if I have to go to ten different doctors to find the right dose with my medicine. Maybe add in another drug to balance me out. I'll even go to therapy or group meetings. Anything to be sane enough for society.

Before I close the door of the safe, I rummage around inside one more time.

I don't see my birth certificate anywhere. My mother clutched that thing like her life depended on it the entire time I was in the hospital, and I have no idea where she stashed it. I suppose I don't need it, so I give up after a couple minutes of searching.

There's a familiar wooden box next to the bills. It holds a gun. I'm not super familiar with firearms. Whether it's loaded or not is a mystery, and I don't intend to find out. Sure, having a weapon when I'm traveling alone would probably be smart, but I'm likely to end up shooting myself in the foot.

Next to the box, there's a green velvet sack. It holds rubies, emeralds, and other jewels my mom collected in her youth during adventures when she was a bit of a hippie. Every shiny object marks a special place, and there's a story to go along with each one. Some were gifts from the men she used to date. Others are souvenirs she picked up from random cities.

I envy her for that—for the fact that she had years of drifting around the country with endless spontaneity and no direction.

When I was little, she used to let me play with her treasures while she told me stories about them by the fireplace. Every memory she had always turned into some sort of cautionary tale. She molded her glory days into warnings about the dangers of the world, and at the time, I believed her. That was before we started butting heads. Back then, I was okay with it just being the two of us.

Then I got older, and I started wanting more.

I started wanting to make my own mistakes.

The clock starts chiming, telling me I need to go, so I close the safe. I shove the flashlight into my fanny pack, zipping it as I go back to the laundry chute and climb inside.

The rest of the way down is easy. Instead of folding my legs up against my body, I let them extend downward.

Using the rubber on the bottom of my shoes, I press my feet against the metal to slow my descent. It makes little squeaks, which I'm hyperaware of, so I decide to free fall to the bottom.

Like a slide, the tunnel starts to curve and flatten out.

I get ejected onto my pile of clothes. The landing is ungraceful—I roll to the side and end up with my face squished against the cold, musty concrete, but I'm not hurt.

Sitting up, I brush myself off.

"That wasn't so bad." I can't believe I'm almost out of here.

My backpack is a couple feet away, and after checking on my laptop to make sure it didn't get busted, I zero in on the old red toolbox.

Inside, there's a variety of rusty tools. I'll need them because the windows down here are sealed shut, which is the only reason they're not hooked up to our alarm system—no one is supposed to be able to get in or out.

It's going to take some effort to get one open. During a previous practice trip to the basement, I scraped away some of the sealant, but I'm going to have to remove the entire pane to get out of here.

After collecting what I need, I drag a sturdy-looking wooden crate over to the window and step up onto it. Then I get to work, hammering the chisel around the outside and dismantling the crank with the screwdriver.

"Got it," I whisper excitedly as the entire window loosens in my hands.

The air coming in is colder than I thought it'd be, and my fingers almost instantly go numb. I'm not even outside yet, and I'm already shivering.

This is going to suck.

As I carefully set the window on the floor, I notice the trail I've left behind. The pile of clothes, the tools, the crate.

Evidence.

Well, my mother won't have any trouble guessing exactly how I got out.

Not much I can do about that now.

I push my backpack outside, then I hoist myself up.

It's more difficult than it looks.

Since the opening is only about fifteen inches tall and two feet wide, I don't have much room to struggle, and I end up flailing with my body half in and half out.

But I don't give up. I didn't make it this far to get stuck with my face in the dirt.

Digging my fingers into the soft earth, I claw and climb. I like it. I haven't played in the mud in years, and I enjoy the way it cakes under my nails.

I keep going until my butt is out.

Once I crawl to the grass, I drag my backpack over to me and collapse on my back.

I'm not in shape for this, but I feel good.

Alive.

My lungs work overtime, pulling in the crisp night air and exhaling in visible foggy puffs. At least the sky is clear. It's been so long since I've seen the stars from somewhere other than my window.

A feeling of hope and happiness comes over me. I know that's partly the medicine's doing, but I don't care. Blissed out, I close my eyes and run my fingers over the cool green blades of our lawn.

Snap.

A twig somewhere to my right breaks, and I don't have to be an expert to know it didn't happen naturally.

Someone's out here with me. Or maybe some*thing*.

I'm actually hoping it's a wild animal and not my mother, because I'd rather take my chances with a bear than her.

It could be a totally harmless deer.

Either way, I need to haul ass.

Rolling over, I grab the strap on my backpack.

Just as I stand, the air changes. I feel a presence behind me, and before I have a chance to run, an arm wraps around my middle while a gloved hand clamps over my mouth.

For a second, I assume it's my mom, but she doesn't wear gloves. Also, the person feels big and strong, like they're surrounding me. They must be at least a foot taller than I am.

I start to struggle, but their face lowers next to mine, and I feel something rough and prickly on my jaw. Facial hair. I've never felt a beard before, but I know that's what it is.

Definitely not Mom.

My mother has often talked about being a target for people who want things from her. That's why security is so important. Honestly, I always thought she was just being paranoid with the alarm system and the surveillance cameras.

"Don't scream," a deep raspy voice whispers in my ear. I draw in a breath through my nose to do just that when his hold on me tightens. "I'm serious, Rosalie. Don't, or else you're never getting out of here."

I try to say, "How do you know my name?" but it comes out all muffled under his hand.

"If I let you go, do you promise to be quiet?"

I give a nod.

He hesitates, like he's not sure if he should believe me or not.

I'm not sure if he should either.

I realize if I wake my mom, my entire plan is blown. But

that's better than getting robbed, raped, brutally murdered, or any combination of the three.

I don't want to end up being featured in my own documentary. While I love watching them, I'd rather not be on one myself.

My attacker doesn't remove his hand from my face or his arm from my body, but he does loosen his grip a fraction. There's a warmth coming from him, and there's a sudden softness to his touch.

And it doesn't feel like I'm trapped. It's more like I'm being… held.

Surprising sensations suddenly arise. Pleasant ones.

Standing here, locked together, my body starts reacting in a disconcerting way.

The smell of leather, citrus, and spice invade my nose. Cold wind blows, and my nipples pucker beneath the constricting sports bra. The man's fingers move to my wrist, and his thumb rubs up and down in a soothing way inside the cuffs of my two sweatshirts.

My stomach tumbles until it feels like it lands between my legs. Against my own will, I relax, my body melting into his. There's a firmness to his chest and arms. Like he works out. I have the overwhelming urge to let my head fall back and feel his scruff on my cheek again.

If I didn't think there was something wrong with me before, I definitely do now. I'm as crazy as they come.

Because seriously, the first time a man ever touches me, I turn into a simpering idiot.

I shouldn't be enjoying this.

The robber-slash-rapist stiffens. "Did you just say something about enjoying this?"

Shit. Did I say that out loud? And does he have to sound so smug about it?

Great. Now he's going to think I'm inviting his sexual

advances. Isn't that how these stories go? People love to say *she asked for it*.

My eyes go to the basement window. That stupid little window. It was supposed to be my way to freedom. Instead, it delivered me into the hands of a probable serial killer.

Slowly, he slides his hand away from my mouth, and I breathe deeply because I suddenly feel like I'm oxygen deprived.

"If you're looking for money," I pant quietly, "I have some. You can take it."

"I don't want your money."

So I was right about his intentions. If he doesn't want cash, then he must want me.

Well, I promised I'd be quiet if he let me go. I didn't promise I wouldn't run.

As soon as his hold on me slackens enough that I have room to move my arms, I do my best to elbow him in the ribs. He grunts, and I use his momentary surprise take off for the trees. With only a half-moon above us, it'll be dark in there. If I can make it to a bush or something, I can hide.

It's a longshot, but it's a chance.

As I dash across the lawn, I can hear my attacker gaining on me. Aside from my treadmill jogs, my small stature is accustomed to a sedentary lifestyle, and I'm no match for someone with long legs who works out regularly.

But right now, I don't care about that.

In fact, I don't care about much of anything at the moment.

My medicine is in full-swing, hushing the fear I know I should be feeling.

Cool air kisses my cheeks, and wind blows through my hair. The burn in my lungs and legs is just a quiet echo of pain that feels more like a nice heat. I'm outside, where I can see the sky and the stars.

Free.

It's exhilarating.

For a second, I numbly consider the possibility of death, and a strange acceptance falls over me. I'm being chased by someone who might want to kill me, but this is the most fun I've had in years.

Not bad for a last life experience.

At least I won't die in my cage.

CHAPTER 5

Preston

Little thing is stronger than she looks. She might've bruised one of my ribs. Pain radiates through my right side as I try to catch up to her.

Her legs are pumping surprisingly fast, but I'm right on her tail. I could reach for her and end this game now, but I won't. Can't crush her hopes and dreams just yet. I want to let her think she's got a chance of outrunning me.

A melodic giggle floats up on a breeze, and my feet falter.

Is she… laughing?

There it is again.

She is. She's fucking laughing. Who does that when they're terrified?

I didn't mean to scare her, but shit, there's no good way to approach someone like that in the middle of the night. Worst case scenario, she might've screamed loud enough to wake Loralee, and I couldn't let that happen.

She's almost to the tree line, so I decide to go for it. Three long strides bring me close enough to grab her. I circle her with my arms, and she lets out an outraged shriek.

As I tackle her, I spin us so my back hits the ground, and I absorb most of the impact.

"Let me go, you robber-slash-rapist," Rosalie growls, kicking with all her might.

"What did I tell you about being quiet?" I hook my legs over hers to stop her thrashing, but Rosalie takes me by surprise again.

In a swift move I don't see coming, she whacks me in the crotch.

My stomach tenses, I wheeze, and I bite the inside of my lip to stop myself from groaning in pain.

Taking advantage of the damage she's done, Rosalie slips from my hold like she's coated with butter and rolls to the side.

Cupping my poor balls, I sit up, ready to tell her who I am, but suddenly, she's behind me. Her arm goes around my neck and she squeezes.

Ah. A chokehold. A poorly executed one, but I'm impressed. And surprisingly turned on.

You wouldn't think I could still get it up after getting punched in the nuts, but all this wrestling and body contact is giving my dick the wrong message.

I've denied myself human touch for a long time. Tonight's the most physical contact I've had with someone in ten years.

I could quickly become addicted to it, even if she is trying to knock me out.

Getting to my feet, I stand, taking Rosalie up with me. She's light. Too light. I hadn't realized how little she weighs until just now. I'm almost afraid to be too rough with her.

Gently, I try to pry her arms away while swinging her this way and that, but she won't let go of my neck. With her feet dangling a half a foot off the ground, she holds on tight, refusing to succumb to my efforts to shake her off.

We don't have time for this nonsense.

All right. Time to try a different tactic.

Staggering, I make it seem like I'm getting dizzy before dropping to my knees. I fling my arms out, feigning a pathetic attempt at grabbing her off my back. After a few seconds, I slump to the ground, face first.

A few seconds pass before Rosalie slowly removes her arm.

"Shit," she gasps, getting to her feet. "I did it. I actually did it. Oh, God, he looks dead. Is he dead? What if I killed him?"

She nudges me with her foot, and I hold my breath while staying limp. Whimpering, she starts pacing and continues talking to herself.

"*I'm* the murderer. *I* am. No. No, no, no." Her shoes crunch over the autumn leaves. "It was self-defense. No one could blame me for it. But I can't just leave him here. If I run now, I'll definitely look guilty." The pacing stops. "Damn it."

The fretting is entertaining as fuck, and it takes everything I have not to laugh.

Grasping my jacket, Rosalie begins pulling my arm to turn me over. It's not easy for her—I'm a big dude. I've always been tall, but in recent months, with nothing to do other than manual labor and exercise, I've packed on some muscle.

With a final grunt, Rosalie gets me onto my back.

She lets out a choked sound when she sees my face in the moonlight. "Preston?"

I should probably end the ruse now, but this is too much fun. I give no response, allowing her to believe she's ended my life as I stay completely still. My lungs are burning from lack of oxygen, and my lips twitch from holding back a grin, but I want to see what Rosalie's going to do.

"Okay, okay," she says breathlessly. "I can fix this." Her fingers flit over my chest before she puts a hand under my neck. She tilts my head back and pinches my nose. "Just like the movies. Here goes nothing."

CPR? Is she seriously going to try to revive me? After I scared the shit out of her and chased her down like a madman?

Yeah. She is.

Peeking through one eye, I see her shadowed face coming closer. Right before her lips descend on mine, I spring up and grab her shoulders. She lets out a frightened squeal, and I flip us so I'm on top.

"Hi," I simply say.

Her face is outraged as she scowls fiercely at me.

"You—you let me think you died?" she asks incredulously. "What kind of a sicko are you?"

Fight mode takes over again, and her body bucks against mine. I like it. A little too much. Every movement equals friction, and my cock is already straining in my pants.

"Shh," I hush, pressing a finger over my mouth while glancing up at Loralee's bedroom window.

Although Rosalie calms a little, she's still quietly seething when she hisses, "What the hell are you doing lurking around in the middle of the night like a homicidal ninja?" Her features morph to anger and betrayal. "Did my mom hire you to watch me? Is that why you're really here? To be her guard dog? Listen, I can pay you. Maybe not more than she will, but it's something. Just take the cash and look the other way."

"I don't want your money," I say for the second time.

"Then what do you want?" She gyrates again, reminding me of how close we are. How I'm on top of her and we're pressed together in an intimate way.

Goddamn, she feels good. Soft. Warm.

The temperature is dropping fast, and it's so cold our breath fogs up the space between us. Being this close, I can smell the floral scent of her shampoo. Roses. Of course.

Reluctantly, I push away, removing myself from her as I get to my feet. "I'm here to help you."

Sitting up, Rosalie squints skeptically through lashes coated with at least three layers of mascara. "Help me?"

"Run away," I clarify.

"Who says I'm running away?"

I give her a look before eyeing her fanny pack. "No need to deny it."

She doesn't trust me. That much is obvious when she lies, "No. I'm just going for a—" Wrinkles appear on her nose. "—A nighttime stroll." *Sneeze*.

"Really," I deadpan. "Is that something you do often?"

"Yeah."

"Why is it I've never seen you walking around at night before?"

"Maybe because you weren't paying attention." *Sneeze. Sneeze.*

"I'm always paying attention." When her nose twitches again, I start to get concerned. "What's wrong? You sick?"

"Must be." *Sneeze*. "Guess I should go back in. It's chilly." She starts to scramble to her feet.

I'm too impatient for these delays. Going into this, I knew it would be difficult to convince her to go with me. Naturally, she's not going to go willingly with a stranger.

But we have a very narrow timeframe to work with, and she's determined to waste it with protests.

I know what will get her to stop. "Cut the crap, Rosie Doll."

At the nickname, she freezes and falls back onto her butt.

Her eyes narrow.

Her nostrils flare as she connects the catfishing dots.

"Jessa? I knew it!" she exclaims, too loud for my liking. "I knew you were an old dude."

"Hey." I'm insulted. "Old dude?"

"What are you, forty?"

I gawk at her. "Try twenty-seven."

"What's up with your gray hairs?" Her eyes roam my temples where I have more salt than pepper.

"It's called premature graying. Started when I was sixteen."

I shake my head. "That's beside the point. We're getting off topic."

"No, I think we're very much on topic." With a whole lot of attitude, Rosalie plants her elbows on her knees. "Jessa's real. I've seen her. How do I know you didn't hack my account? Maybe you read our conversations tonight. Maybe you're just impersonating her to get close to me."

Poor girl. She's in denial. She doesn't want to believe her friend never existed.

"Ask me some questions only Jessa would know," I challenge.

Rosalie haughtily raises her chin. "What's your favorite color?"

"I'm wearing it." I gesture to my clothes—the leather jacket, hoodie, jeans, and boots. All black.

"What's your favorite band?"

"R.E.M."

"What's *my* favorite band?"

"That's a trick question. You have favorite songs," I specify. "But only one at a time. You listen to it over and over again until you're sick of it. Right now you're stuck on "Letting the Cables Sleep" by Bush because you're exploring the wonderful world of 90's alternative music. You're probably almost done with it, though, because it's been on repeat for the past four days. Before that, you were on an 80's kick. Jefferson Starship. When we first started talking, you'd been listening to "Something Just Like This" by Coldplay. How am I doing?"

As I've been spilling such exact details only "Jessa" would know, Rosalie's eyes have gotten wider and wider. No one could make that shit up, and conversations on Solitaire Slam disappear after twenty-four hours, so it's not like I could've just snooped in her account once. I have seven weeks of facts about this girl if she needs me to keep going.

"Listen." Crouching down to her level, I look Rosalie in

the eye. "I understand you feel betrayed because I'm not who you think I am."

"No shit."

"I'm not really a groundskeeper, either. I've been undercover."

Confusion flattens her pretty lips. "Undercover for what?"

"For you. I was hired to help you get out."

"I don't understand. Hired by who?"

"Your father."

Rosalie blinks. "I don't have a father."

"You do. DNA doesn't lie. You match a man in Detroit. I have the papers in my wallet to prove it, and I'll show you as soon as we can get away from here."

"Where's your badge?" she asks. "If you really are a detective, then you'll have proof of that, too."

"I don't work for an agency or the police. I'm self-employed."

She scoffs. "Of course you are."

"And I'd show you a business card, but I don't have anything linking me to my old identity. I couldn't while I'm here. It's too risky."

"So Preston isn't your real name?"

"For now, it is."

"Obviously, it's not Jessa." Hurt coats her words. "I trusted you. I've never had a friend before… but I liked you. I thought you were real."

I swallow hard. "I am real."

"This whole thing was a bad idea." Wetness gathers in Rosalie's eyes, and I hate that I'm the one who put those tears there. "God, I'm so stupid."

"Hey, you're not stupid. Don't talk about yourself like that."

"Gullible, then." She sounds so defeated. "I fell for one of the oldest tricks in the book. My mom told me the world is full of disappointment. I haven't even left my yard yet and my heart is already broken."

Man, she's fucking killing me.

I hitch my chin toward the third floor. "You really wanna go back to that?"

Drawing in a deep breath, Rosalie takes a second to consider it as her eyes ping around the only home she remembers.

I glance at where she left her backpack by the house. "If we're going to go, it has to be now. I'll show you all my IDs. I'll tell you about every different alias I have, all my secrets… if you'll just come with me."

I back up, giving her the choice to run as far away from me as she can.

She glances at the woods. Then her eyes land on me. "I don't know what to do. I'm confused and hurt. I don't know the difference between what's true and false. I feel like I'm stuck on a swinging pendulum, and I need you to tell me something real to make it stop."

"Something real? It's not safe for you in there. I know that much, Rosie Doll."

She looks away. "Don't call me that. And so what you're saying is, it's safer with you? With my supposed father? You think I want to go live with someone I've never met? Why does everyone always want to make my decisions? Am I not allowed to call the shots, ever? This is my life!" she whisper-yells, ripping some grass up and tossing it into the air.

She's right, which is why Ivan's plan has never sat right with me. I took this job with every intention of following through with his wishes. I just wanted to release this girl from her prison.

Then my interest turned to obsession, and my obsession morphed into something deeper.

Now I care about Rosalie.

Too much.

If anything, I'm relieved that she doesn't want to go to Ivan.

"All right." I hold my hands out in a placating gesture. "You're right, okay?"

She's still sitting at my feet, looking so fragile and beautiful. Her oversized clothing swallows her petite frame, and I want to fatten her up a little. Put a healthy glow on her skin and a happy sparkle in her eyes.

I extend an arm to help her up. After hesitating for a couple seconds, she decides to take it. Her fingers slide against my gloves, and I wish we were skin on skin. Just the thought of it sends shivers up my spine.

"Rosalie, I'm going to go get your backpack," I tell her firmly once she's standing, and I let go of her hand. "Then we're going to walk through the woods together. We'll get to the property line, then we'll get into town where I have a car. I'll take you anywhere you want to go. I'll even let you ditch me once I know you're somewhere safe."

"Really?" She doesn't believe me, raising an eyebrow and tapping her cute little foot.

"Well, if I'm being honest, I'm hoping you'll let me tag along with you for a while. Let me make sure you're okay in the long run."

In fact, I'm counting on it. She needs me. And I need her.

"Why would you want to do that?"

"Because you're my best friend," I quietly admit. "Getting to know you these past couple months has been the best time of my life. You want something real? Well, there it is."

Before Rosalie has a chance to return the sentiment or reject it, I turn away from her and start across the grass. While I retrieve her things, she stays in place, patiently and curiously waiting for me.

As soon as I get back to her, I slide my jacket off and drape it around her shoulders.

"What are you doing?" Her eyelids get heavy with satisfaction as the warmth engulfs her, but she's eyeing my hoodie as if it's offensive. "You're going to freeze."

"I'll be fine." I zip the leather up to her chin. "A hike in the cold is nothing compared to what I went through at boot camp."

"Boot camp? You're military?"

I nod. "Marines."

"So you have to live by some code of honor or something?" There's hope in her question, like being in the military automatically makes me more trustworthy.

I wish.

"If there's anything you need to know about the world," I say, "it's that we're all human. Doctors, police, soldiers. People make mistakes. They lie. They cheat. It's just a fact of life."

Glancing to the woods, I note the way the thick tree trunks and spindly branches cloak the area in shadows. We can't use a flashlight until we're farther away, but I've become familiar with the area. Not far from here, I've cleared a path, which will make the journey faster.

I hold out my hand to Rosalie. We're about to venture into the wilderness together, and it's best that we hold onto each other so we don't get separated.

Suddenly, Rosalie slaps my palm.

I look at her.

She stares back. "What? You were asking for a high-five, right? Or I guess it's a low-five. No?" She reads my silence as a bad thing and starts to squirm awkwardly. "Oh, you wanted a handshake. Oops."

Damn, she's adorable.

When her fingers clasp mine, I maintain a tight grip. "We need to hold hands."

Her face pinches with confusion. "Why?"

"It's too easy to get lost in the woods at night. We have to stick together."

"You want to hold my hand?" she asks slowly, like she doesn't believe me.

Or like she finds the suggestion repulsive.

I can't tell which.

"It's for the sake of safety." I lace my gloved fingers with hers. "I'm not trying to do anything ungentlemanly. We just need to do things my way until we're far away from here, because that's how we're going to—"

Survive.

I don't want to finish the sentence because it might scare Rosalie. In truth, she should be scared. I'm betraying the mafia to give her what she wants, but I'll shoulder the burden of that knowledge for the both of us.

"Going to what?" she prods.

"I just don't want to lose you," I simply say, gently tugging her along.

She has no idea how much I mean those words.

CHAPTER 6

Rosalie

I can't believe I'm with Preston right now. The guy I've been fantasizing about. And we're *holding hands*. Even though the flashlight is on now, I haven't let go. He hasn't either.

I never noticed it before tonight, but Preston has the cutest little gap between his two front teeth. The tiny imperfection makes him look younger, offsetting the gray hair and making his age more believable.

He also has nice skin. The parts that aren't covered by his beard are smooth and tan.

And his eyes. It's too dark to see now, but before, when we were less than two feet apart, I noticed how thick his lashes are around his brown eyes. With some mascara, they'd look fake, and I wonder if he ever uses Maybelline like he said in our chats.

I shake my head at myself.

I'm still thinking of him as Jessa. A little stab shoots through my heart as I mourn the loss of the friend I thought I had. I told her things. Personal, private things.

Him. I told *him*.

God, we talked about boys. I told him I've never kissed anyone before. How humiliating.

Although right now I'm sort of longing for the chatty girl I thought Preston was, because this silence is unnerving.

Now that I have a person with me—someone who isn't my

mother—all I want to do is pepper him with questions and talk about anything and everything.

It feels like we've been walking forever. Really, it's probably only been twenty minutes or so, but the rhythmic sounds around us are driving me mad. Feet crunching on a bed of dried leaves, the chirp of insects, and the wind whistling in the branches above us.

"So, about my… father," I say, my voice at normal volume since we're pretty far from the house.

"What about him?"

"What's his name?"

"Ivan Belov."

Doesn't ring any bells. Searching my deepest memories, I try to think of a time when my mom ever mentioned someone named Ivan, but I come up with nothing. "What's he like?"

"Russian, bossy, and used to getting his way."

"Well, if he wanted to see me so badly, why didn't he just go through the court system like everyone else?"

"The situation is complicated," Preston says carefully. "And Ivan's not exactly on the right side of the law."

"What does that mean?"

"He's in the mafia."

"Well, shit." I didn't hit the lottery with my parentage. "And how much did he pay you? What am I worth?"

"Fifty thousand dollars."

"Wow." Compared to what my mom has stashed away, that's not a ton, but it's still a large amount.

"That's half upfront," Preston clarifies. "I'll get the other half if I complete the mission."

A total of a hundred thousand dollars, and all he has to do is deliver me to some man I've never met. Obviously, deception is something Preston is good at. He had me fooled with silly emojis and pictures of a teenage girl. A pretty one, at that.

Who is that girl? She's someone. Maybe he lifted her pictures from a stranger's social media. Or maybe it's an ex-girlfriend.

Jealousy and suspicion cut through the pleasant buzz of my medicine. I glance at our joined hands, then at Preston's profile.

No one in their right mind would give up an extra fifty thousand dollars for a crazy chick. Worry creeps in, and I start to wonder if I made a huge mistake by accepting his invitation.

"Won't my father be mad if you don't take me to him?" I inquire, keeping my tone casual.

"Not your problem," Preston grunts.

"It'll be my problem if he comes after you while we're still together."

"You let me worry about that, Rosie Doll."

"I thought you agreed not to call me that anymore."

"I did no such thing." He looks over at me. "And so far tonight, you've called me a robber-slash-rapist, an old dude, and a liar. And what else? A homicidal ninja?"

True.

I sigh, not liking how we're dancing around a topic. I've never been good at keeping my worries bottled up, and I can't hold back any longer.

"Am I your prisoner? Are you planning to go through with the job? I wouldn't blame you if you are. That's a lot of money to give up for someone. I just want you to tell me so I know what to expect."

The glow from the flashlight's aimed at the ground, and it gives just enough light to read Preston's tender expression as he looks at me. "I've made mistakes, Rosalie. Mistakes I can never take back. But one thing I can promise? I'll do whatever it takes to make sure you're safe. I won't leave you. In fact, nothing could keep me from you."

"Not unless I want you to go away, right?"

He works his jaw and agrees, "Not unless you want me to go away."

What a noble speech. Either this guy's good with words, or he's being completely transparent. I just don't know him well enough to tell the difference, but I want to believe everything he says.

Not just because he's Jessa—the person I've looked forward to talking to every single day. But because he's the man from outside, the one I've lusted over for months.

As we continue on the path, my palm gets sweaty, and I'm kind of glad he's got gloves on so he can't feel how clammy I am.

I'm just nervous and excited, and I wonder if I'm the only one feeling the electric tension between us. Our contact keeps sending continuous jolts up my arm, making my heart flutter.

"So what's the plan, then?" I ask, sounding a bit winded. "Was all that stuff you said about Florida bullshit?"

"No. That really is where I want to take you eventually."

"You know, I'm pretty sure it's a federal offense to kidnap someone and take them across state lines."

Preston gives me a funny look. "You watch too many murder shows. It's not kidnapping if you're willing."

He's right. And I am willing. Unfortunately, he's my best bet. I don't know how to travel or where I'm going. Since Jessa doesn't exist, I need him for the time being. "You have family down there or something?"

"Nah. We won't stay there long either. I figure we can take a boat to Costa Rica."

At the mention of water, I almost trip, but Preston's there to steady me. "A boat? No. No, we can't do that."

"Why not? You can't stay in the States. It'd be too easy for you to be found. People will be looking for us—"

"No," I cut him off. It doesn't matter what his reasons are.

Getting on a boat is a hard pass, so I tell him, "I don't do large bodies of water. Or small ones, for that matter. No, thanks."

"It's not optional."

Out of everything that's happened since I crawled through that little window, thinking about being on the ocean is the worst. I'd be completely vulnerable.

All my nightmares come rushing in.

Cold water. Suffocation. Flailing helplessly.

"Hey, you're shaking." Preston's deep voice is soft and gentle as he stops and turns toward me. He shines the flashlight up toward my face. "You still cold?"

"No," I say honestly, leaving out the fact that I'm shivering from fear. I don't want him to know about my stupid phobia, so I play it off like immediate dangers are my concern. "What if we get attacked by a wolf out here?"

He cocks his head at the sudden change of topic. It's the only indication that I've thrown him for a loop. "I have my fishing knife."

"You're going to take on a vicious animal with a fishing knife?"

"I don't think there are many wolves in this area anyway."

"Could be a bear. Bobcats can be aggressive."

"We'll be alright." Just like when he was pretending to be Jessa, he doesn't get deterred from our earlier conversation, because he jumps back to our travel plans. "We need to get as far away from here as possible. Once Loralee realizes we're both gone, she'll be looking for us. She has enough money to hire a hundred private investigators. She'll dig up anything she can on the Preston Walker who's been working for her, which isn't much other than the basics that come up during a routine background check."

I let out a bittersweet laugh because I'm obviously not the only one he's got fooled. He passed my mother's requirements, which means he's really good at what he does. "Who the hell are you?"

"Before this, I was Ethan Smith." He gets to walking again, and he pulls me along with him.

"That still doesn't answer my question." I might be naïve, but I see right through his evasiveness.

Suddenly, a new sound breaks through the symphony of night. Among the chirping bugs and rustling leaves, I hear trickling and sloshing.

Water.

Reaching over to grab Preston's wrist, I make him point the flashlight ahead. I see a wooden bridge over a shadowed area where the ground falls off. My hand trembles so much I can't keep holding onto Preston. When I let him go, the light drops back to the ground at our feet, but darkness won't change what's ahead.

Stepping backward, I gulp. "I didn't know there's a river out here."

Preston scans the area with the light and supplies, "It's a creek, not a river."

I let out an anguished noise. "Might as well be the same thing. I can't cross it. We have to go back."

Preston pins me with a stare. "What are you talking about?"

"I'm afraid of water, okay? Terrified. I can't even take baths because I can't stand the feeling of being in it." Turning away, I mutter to myself, "Maybe Mom knew I could never run away. If our property is surrounded by a creek, then she knew all along I never had a chance."

Pins and needles all over my skin. So cold. Can't breathe.

Someone starts shaking my shoulders. I'm being jostled around, and it takes me a second to remember where I am and who I'm with.

"Rosalie, look at me," Preston orders, and I do as he says. "Do you trust me?"

"No," I reply without hesitation.

He chuckles, like he already knew that answer was coming. "Someday, I hope you will. Okay, here's how this is going to work. You're gonna close your eyes, cover your ears, and count to thirty. Just thirty seconds."

"You've got to be kidding."

"Nope."

I chew my lower lip. "What are you going to do?"

"Don't worry about it. All you have to do is keep counting."

He's crazier than I am if he thinks this is going to work. He's literally asking for blind trust. Still, I don't have many choices.

"You can rely on me, Rosie," Preston says vehemently. "Go on. Be my good girl."

My good girl.

He gives me an encouraging nod, and I'm surprised to realize how badly I want his approval. I want to hear him say I'm his good girl again.

I cover my ears and close my eyes.

My voice sounds loud in my head as I begin to count, "One… Two…" I feel an arm go around my shoulders and another hooks under my knees. "Three." I'm lifted up, cradled against Preston's torso. "Four… Five…"

I can feel us moving forward, and my throat gets tight.

"Keep counting." Preston's muffled command makes its way to my ears.

"Six, seven, eight, nine…" To hell with doing it slow. I want to get to thirty as soon as possible, so the numbers fly from my mouth, one right after the other.

Before I can utter twenty-five, my legs are being lowered.

Whimpering, my palms leave my head and I wrap my arms around Preston's neck. I don't even care that I'm climbing him like a demented kitten in a tree. I keep my feet suspended in the air and cry, "Don't drop me in!"

"I'm not," he soothes. "Look. Open your eyes."

I peek through an eyelid. Ahead, there's a break in the trees, and I see a road. Moonlight reflects off the dark pavement. I glance down.

Solid ground.

The sound of the water is behind us now. "We're over the bridge. We made it."

Refusing to look back, I slide down Preston's body and stand on my own.

My lips curl up with a goofy grin. He has no idea what he's done for me. He treated me like I'm brave. Like he believes in me. No one has ever done that. If I'd been with my mother, she would've played off my fear and told me I'm not capable of such things.

"Did I do good?" I ask, craving Preston's praise one more time.

He smiles down at me softly. "Yeah, baby, you did really good."

Baby.

God. That's better than 'good girl.' I might melt right here.

Now that I'm no longer paralyzed by fear, I throw myself at Preston and hug him. Grateful, I beam up at his handsome face.

I can't stop smiling. My expression is fueled by pride for getting through my fear and relief that we don't have to do it again.

And also because I'm happy to have Preston with me. I literally couldn't have made it this far without him.

He smiles back, and the sight of that cute gap causes a flipping sensation in my gut. "Told you I wouldn't let anything happen to you."

"Yeah, because I'm worth a lot of money," I scoff, joking.

His amusement fades and his look turns intense. "Rosie, you're not a job to me. If I'm being honest, you never were, and I don't give a damn about the money."

CHAPTER 7

Preston

"You doing okay?" I steal a glance at Rosalie.

Her steps are sluggish, and her eyelids are drooping. "Uh huh."

That's the same response she's given the past few times I've asked, but it's obvious she's not going to be able to hike much longer.

To avoid being seen on the road, we stayed in the woods until we came to a field. Unfortunately, the dirt's soft out here, and it's a lot more work getting through it than walking on firm ground.

We're both dirty, cold, and exhausted.

Good thing we're almost to our destination.

Sunrise is probably an hour away, and Maryville looms in the distance against the gray horizon. Luckily, the storage center where my car is stashed is on this side of the town.

"There." I point ahead to the vast expanse of the orange and white buildings. "We're almost outta here."

"Good," Rosalie simply says, her normal talkativeness absent.

"Put your hood up," I tell her, doing the same to shadow my face. "There are surveillance cameras in the parking lot. Best we're not recognized."

"Okay," she responds, obeying me.

Rosalie's compliant when she's tired. When she's scared, too.

Back at the creek, Rosalie was frozen. It's been a long time since I've seen someone that terrified. Her eyes went distant as if she were having flashbacks. She'd told 'Jessa' she's not a fan of water, but I didn't realize how bad it was until we had to cross that bridge.

I don't know the source of her fear.

Aside from the time she was hospitalized six months ago, she's got no medical records. No history of checkups, vaccinations, or medications for illnesses. Whoever the 'doctor' is that does house calls, I suspect he's a fraud. Probably Loralee's drug dealer or something.

Suddenly, Rosalie stumbles a little, and it's a good thing we're still holding hands because she'd bite the dust if I weren't here to keep her upright. She squeezes me tight as she regains her balance.

And that's how we arrive at unit number thirty-four—holding hands like runaway lovers.

I like it.

I don't want to let her go yet, so I fumble with my keys in one hand, unlock the handle, and slide the garage door up.

Rosalie's the one to break our contact first, walking forward to run her fingers over the sleek black paint on the 1977 mustang.

My baby. I splurged on it a few years ago. Paid cash for it. I don't spoil myself often—or ever—but this is my dream vehicle.

Damn, I'm gonna miss this car.

I go around to the trunk and pop it open. Scanning my supplies, I take stock of my disguises. I'm going to have to change my appearance, but I'm not sure which direction I'm going with it. I have temporary tattoos, fake piercings, and flannel. I could go the grungy hipster route. Then again, it's been a while since I've worn my suit and tie.

Rummaging through the space, I move a box of hats and

hair dye to the side and pull out two garment bags. I unzip the plastic and sniff the clothes. A little musty, but not too bad. Nothing a good airing out can't fix.

Rosalie quietly approaches. "What are you doing?"

I glance at her dirt-streaked face. "We're going to be changing identities for a while, and probably more than once."

"You've got this all figured out."

I can't tell if she's impressed or appalled by my preparedness, so I shrug. "It's what I do."

"Your job," she says flatly. "Right."

After slamming the trunk, I move into her personal space and lightly grip her chin. "What did I say about my job?"

Blue and green stare up at me. "That I'm not part of it?"

"That's right. You're not a job. You're my Rosie Doll."

"Your good girl?" she asks hesitantly.

My cock stiffens.

"Damn right." I split a grin, and I can't help noticing her lips trembling with the desire to smile. "So, the plan." Moving past her, I open the passenger side, get into the glove compartment, and hold up an old burner cell. "I'll destroy my current phone and use this one instead. Then when we get a few hours away, I'll swap my car for something less recognizable."

"You're getting rid of this?" Enamored with the shininess, Rosalie rubs the hood.

"It's just a car," I grunt out regretfully. "Ivan knows I drive this. We need to be untraceable."

Rosalie pins me with a curious look. "You're really not kidding about me not being a job. You're giving up so much for me." There's a heavy pause. "Why?"

Ignoring the question pertaining to my unhealthy obsession with her, I change the subject and let her hot-pink backpack slide off my shoulder. "Do you have any electronics in here?"

"Yeah." She nods slowly, taking it from me. "My laptop."

"We need to dump it on our way out of town."

"But—but—"

"No offense, but if I can ditch my sweet ride, then you can lose the computer. I'll buy you a new one."

Rosalie lowers her sad gaze to the concrete. "I guess I'm just attached to it for sentimental reasons. For a long time, it was my only window to the world. Plus, I met Jessa on there."

I spread my arms before letting them fall to my sides. "I'm right here. I know I'm not who you thought I was, but I'm still the same person on the inside."

Glancing up, she squints. "You knew things. Girl things. How?"

During my time catfishing Rosalie, I tried to stick to the truth as much as possible. I might've lied about my identity, but everything else, all the little things that make me who I am, are actual facts. My knowledge about girly shit helped me pass as a female, but that's part of me, too. Part of my past.

"Another story for another time."

"Fine. Be all mysterious. I'll just warn you that I plan to use this road trip to interrogate you. I can be very annoying. You'll spill all your secrets." She turns her nose up as she folds herself into the car, setting her bag on the floor between her legs.

I chuckle. "I look forward to it."

CHAPTER 8

Rosalie

I give the crowbar an incredulous look as Preston puts it in my hands. "You want me to smash it?"

"To pieces," he confirms. "Lots of 'em."

My poor laptop's sitting on the leaf-covered ground, all lonely and shit. It's dumb to think of an electronic device as having feelings, but I feel bad for it. "Can't we just leave it here? Maybe someone will find it and give it a home."

Preston laughs. "It's not a puppy. We don't have much time." Lifting his wrist, he looks at his watch. "When does your mom usually wake up?"

"Around six, but she won't come get me for breakfast until eight."

"Do it," he urges. "We gotta go."

"Pushy," I grumble, even though I know he's right.

We stopped on a deserted country road on the other side of Maryville. The same creek we crossed earlier runs this way, and after I do some damage to my laptop, Preston plans to toss it into the water. He already destroyed his cell phone and did the same with it.

Placing my feet shoulder-length apart, I grip the metal bar like a bat. Then I let it come down on the sleek black device. There's no force behind my action. It barely leaves a crack, but I wince at the damage.

"What's wrong?" Preston asks, his lips twitching with amusement. "Never destroyed anything before?"

"No, I have."

"Really?" The skepticism in his tone makes me bristle.

"As a matter of fact, yes. I suffer from…" I struggle to find the right words. "Uncontrollable fits of rage. I've slammed doors so hard they split down the middle. I once tipped over a China cabinet and broke every dish. Expensive stuff, too. Limited edition from England." It sounds like I'm bragging, but the truth is, I'm ashamed of my inability to control myself.

Preston doesn't look like he's judging me when he asks, "Why'd you do it?"

"I wanted to go to school. I wanted to go to the mall and to the movies and to have friends. I just wanted out of my fucking room. Lots of reasons. Take your pick."

"But she wouldn't let you," Preston concludes.

"She said I was too crazy," I admit, my voice small with shame. "And then when I got violent, all I did was prove her right."

"She was gaslighting you. Putting you in situations that would make anyone go mad, then punishing you for it. Think about that when you use the crowbar."

He's right. For a long time, I've tried to be normal, hoping my mom would see that I'm a good person. No matter what I did—or what I didn't do—it never made a difference.

I think about the endless days and nights in that house. The *tick tick ticking* of the clock. I remember how as I got older, instead of gaining the independence I was entitled to, she just withheld it from me.

"I bet I could tell you something that would really piss you off," Preston pipes up, sounding a bit sad.

I'm so tired of being out of the loop.

"Tell me," I demand.

"Today isn't your birthday." He blows out a breath. "And you're not eighteen."

My mouth hangs open as I blink at him. "W-what?"

He scratches his jaw, and he looks like he feels sorry for me when he replies, "Rosalie, you turned nineteen two months ago. On September 25th."

Suddenly dizzy, I sway on my feet. "That can't be true."

Preston's hand goes to my shoulder to steady me. "It is. I swear it. I'll tell you more once we get to a safe location." He gives me an apologetic squeeze. "You just have the right to know how old you are."

"Why would she do that? Why would she lie to me about my age?" The realization makes me sick. "Oh my God. She wanted to keep me younger."

One of the first memories I have is of my third birthday party. It was just my mom and me at the house, but she'd rented a traveling petting zoo for the day. I got to ride ponies, feed goats, and hold rabbits.

I've always wondered why I'm able to recall a day so clearly when I was just a toddler. But now I know I wasn't three at the time. I was four—more than a year older than I thought I was.

And I started puberty early. Once I began reading teenage magazines, there were a lot of articles on menstruation, and I realized getting my period at ten years old wasn't so common. I used to mentally curse my body for robbing me of an extra one or two period-free years. But if Preston's right, then I was right on schedule.

This time, when I use the crowbar, I mean business. Grunting, I swing it with as much force as I can muster. Over and over again, I hit the laptop, relishing in every crunch and crack.

By the time I land the last blow, I'm out of breath and sweating. I don't even realize I'm crying until Preston's in front of me, wiping my cheeks with his thumbs.

His brown eyes are so warm and concerned as he gently cradles my face in his hands.

Feeling defeated and deflated, I let the heavy metal drop from my hand.

"Come here." Wrapping his arms around me, Preston pulls my face to his chest. "I'm sorry. Maybe I should've eased you into that a little better."

"I don't know how you ease anyone into finding out something like that."

"Yeah. I'm trying to be careful about how much I tell you. I don't want it to be too much for you."

"There's more?" The question comes out muffled against his shirt.

"Unfortunately, yes."

Preston's right to hold back. He seems to know my limits more than I do, and honestly, I'm not sure how much more I can handle. I've been awake for too long. My muscles are tired and shaky. I'm hungry and cold.

I just want a break from it all.

Tilting my face up, I zero in on Preston's lips. "Kiss me."

His fingers spasm against the back of my neck, pressing me closer. "You're vulnerable right now. You're dealing with some shit—"

"Exactly. So make it better for me."

The confident mask I'm wearing wants to fall, but I don't let it. I realize I'm putting myself out there and risking rejection, but I have reasons for wanting a kiss. My mother made me feel as if no one would ever want me. I need to prove her wrong. Plus…

"It's something I have to cross off my bucket list anyway," I add, trying to make it sound like it's not a big deal.

Preston skeptically twists his mouth in the most adorable way. "Are you sure you want it to be me? An old dude?"

"You're not that old." I playfully push at his chest, and I'm shocked when I feel how fast his heart's beating.

It's like a marching band under my fingers.

Could he want me, too? Has he thought about me as more than the pathetic girl who needs rescuing?

And I think about his question. Would I be asking to be kissed if he were someone else?

I've spent years dreaming of intimacy, but it was always a faceless person.

My fantasies became clearer when Preston showed up on our property. Suddenly, the person had dark scruff on a defined jaw. Gray hair mixed in with black.

So, yeah, I'm sure, and I'm glad Preston and Jessa are one in the same. Really, I'm getting two for one here.

Whatever this guy's real name is, it doesn't matter. A name doesn't define a person.

"I don't want anyone else," I tell him seriously, silently begging him to come closer.

His face lowers, and his tone is teasing when he says, "You don't know anyone else."

"It wouldn't matter." Shaking my head, I grasp at the strings on his hoodie. "Right now, I just want you."

Without warning or finesse, his mouth slams into mine. And I do mean slams. Our lips don't just collide—they crash.

My eyes go wide. In movies, people always close their eyes when they kiss, but I'm so taken aback by the passion exploding from this man that I don't even have enough sense to reciprocate.

"Kiss me back, Rosie," Preston murmurs against my mouth, sliding his fingers into my hair and running his thumbs across my cheeks.

Unsure of what I'm doing, I begin to respond, following his rhythm and mimicking what he does when he roughly massages my lips with his. The hard press of his mouth doesn't ease up when he his tongue demands entry, and I have no choice but to open for him.

And ohhh. When his tongue swipes against mine, I turn to mush as a burst of heat comes from my heart. My cheeks get warm. My icy fingers regain some feeling.

Now I close my eyes.

The world goes dark as I let Preston lead with bruising nips and sucks, and I just *feel* him.

Every sensation is new. From the scrape of his facial hair against my skin to the way his teeth occasionally dig into my bottom lip before he draws it into his mouth.

My pulse is going haywire. My knees are weak. I can't get enough air.

I feel sticky inside my panties, and there's an insistent throb between my legs.

The next time Preston's tongue sweeps into my mouth, I suck on it.

He groans low, like a cornered animal.

Without disconnecting the kiss, his hands go to my waist and he walks me backward. I'm stopped when my back meets a tree, and he uses the fact that I'm trapped to go even deeper. To push his body against mine.

Something hard pokes me in the stomach, and I gasp. When the sharp sound slips out, it slices through the moment, bringing us both back to reality.

We don't have time for this, and we both know it.

Panting, Preston buries his face by my neck. His hot breath is nice against my cold skin, and I want his kisses there, too.

"Sorry," he whispers. "Sorry, sorry, sorry."

"Why are you apologizing?" I lift my fingers to my lips, touching them lightly. They feel hot and swollen.

Preston pulls back and studies my face. His gaze darts around as if he's searching for an injury.

"Did I hurt you?" He smooths some of my flyaway strands from my forehead, tucking them behind my ears.

"No," I reply honestly. "Actually, I wouldn't mind doing it again."

Preston opens his mouth like he wants to say something. But he shuts it again and steps back. "We should get going."

Just like that, he saunters away, bending down to collect the remains of my laptop.

CHAPTER 9

Preston

Pushing down on the pedal, I accelerate up to a reasonable amount past the speed limit.

We need distance.

I've been driving west for the past three hours. Soon, we'll go south, but there's somewhere I want to see first.

Along the coast of Lake Michigan, there's a string of lighthouses. Now that I know how much Rosalie hates water, getting close is out of the question, but we can drive by the one that's on the way to our next stop.

I have another storage unit in a touristy town near the last lighthouse by the Indiana border. I chose the place on purpose because the town is too small to have a heavy law enforcement presence but big enough to pass through without getting odd looks. There, we'll check in to an inconspicuous motel, eat, sleep, and change our clothes before we get back on the road.

By now, Loralee has woken up. She's noticed Rosalie is gone. I can imagine her running around the house, finding the trail of Rosalie's escape. She'll go out to the garage and find me gone as well.

I'm not sure what she'll do after that. It's not like she can go to the police and tell them the child she kidnapped all those years ago ran away.

Then there's Ivan. He probably won't be aware of my

deceit until tonight's check-in when he finds out my phone is disconnected.

Honestly, I'm a little worried about how he's going to react. I won't breathe easier until we're out of Michigan.

Fortunately, I've got it all planned out. In fact, my backup plan has a backup plan.

What makes me so good at my job is that going unnoticed is second nature for me. I've been ignored my entire life. Blending in is easy.

Rosalie? Not so much.

I glance over at her sleeping form in the passenger seat.

I've seen her in daylight before because of the couple times she approached me while I was working. But then, I barely looked at her. Didn't want to make it obvious that I was interested.

Having her up close like this, it just makes me realize how gorgeous she is.

She's stunning, with her straight nose, her high cheekbones, and the cleft in her chin. She's got the kind of face that can stop people in their tracks.

And that could be a problem.

She lets out a light snore. Shifting, she mutters something unintelligible.

Damn, she's cute.

She's snuggled up under my jacket, and I like that she probably smells like me now. Her head's leaning against the door, and her hood is halfway off, revealing her gorgeous light strands that are still tied together in a long braid.

Although she got dirty and sweaty during our hike, her face is still all done up. Thick eyelashes coated with black mascara are fanned out on her upper cheeks. Her lips are a deep pink—I think I kissed the lipstick off her, but the color remains, probably because she's chapped from the cold or from our hot make out session.

My body's still buzzing from that kiss.

Last time I had any physical gratification with someone, I was a reckless, selfish teenager. I'd been afraid I would be clumsy and out of practice with Rosalie. At first, I was. I literally mauled the girl.

I'm sporting a semi just thinking about it.

When I remember what it felt like to have her pinned up against that tree, I ache, and not just in my pants. There's a weird hollow feeling in my chest.

Putting my eyes back on the interstate, I rub at my sternum while trying to figure out why I'm hurting. It's a pain I haven't experienced since I was a kid, back when I wanted a family more than anything.

Longing. That's what it is. A yearning so intense it causes a physical sensation in your heart because you can't go on living without it.

I'm so fucked.

From the very beginning, I felt a pull to Rosalie when I saw her picture. Then we had a connection as soon as we started chatting online.

But this is different.

This is worse.

It's better.

It's amazing and terrifying all at once.

I like her. Like, really like her. She's stubborn and determined as hell. She's equal parts intelligent and gullible. I'm sure she'll be inquisitive and curious once she gets enough sleep.

The interrogation she threatened me with failed miserably. All the questions she claimed she'd throw at me after we got on the road never happened. After toying with the radio and settling on a classic rock station, she rested her head on the door. She was zonked out before we were two miles from the small town.

I'm glad for the reprieve, because I don't know all the answers to the questions she'll ask. Most of what I'm assuming about her past is an educated guess. Her life is like a puzzle, and I don't have all the pieces.

Dropping that bomb on her about her birthday was a risky move, though it delivered my intended effect. Rosalie's got some pent-up rage. She's traumatized in ways she doesn't even realize.

Someday, I'll dig until I find out exactly what happened in her past. Until then, I just want to be with her. I want to show her the world isn't always terrible, and that she has a place in it. She belongs.

She can belong with me.

CHAPTER 10

Rosalie

I wake to a loud sound. When I open my eyes, it's dark and I'm still in the car. Outside, there are walls surrounding us, like the entire vehicle is enclosed in some kind of concrete capsule.

Startled, I try to sit up straighter, but the seat belt strap goes taut across my chest and shoulder. A shriek bursts from me when I look to my left and see an unfamiliar man in the driver's seat.

"Shh. It's me." Preston takes off his black-rimmed glasses.

I blink at him. "You look totally different."

"Good." He runs a hand over his freshly shaved jaw.

His usually messy hair is slicked down and parted on the side. The dark-blue suit he's wearing fits him well, and the white shirt underneath is unbuttoned at the top to complete a business-casual style.

He's gone from rugged laborer to wealthy nerd. Both looks suit him, but I'm a little sad at the loss of the facial hair. I liked the way it made my face tingle when I kissed him.

As I lay my palm over my racing heart, I'm disoriented and confused. I don't feel like I know the person next to me, and I need a true fact to ground me. "Tell me something real."

"My eyes are actually blue," Preston says. "I had colored contacts in before."

That's what's throwing me off. His eyes. Though I have to admit, his natural color is kind of beautiful.

I look down at my dirty jeans. "Do I need a disguise, too?"

"Yes."

Digesting the new information, I observe our surroundings. When I look behind us, I realize we're under the shade of another storage garage. Parked outside, there's a gray sedan.

I point at it. "Is that what we'll be driving instead?"

"Yep." Preston lovingly rubs the steering wheel of the spiffy car.

I feel bad that we're leaving it here. "Preston—"

"It's Kent Jones now." He holds up an ID to prove it before handing me my own.

"Sarah Jones?" I'm shocked because my picture is on it.

Scrutinizing my face in the little square, I try to figure out if it's been photoshopped. I'm staring blankly at the camera, unsmiling. My hair is down and a bit stringy.

But sure as shit, it's me.

How did someone get a current picture of me?

Then I notice the material around my neck. It's light blue with darker blue dots on it. "Is that a hospital gown? I was in the hospital about six months ago. Did someone take my picture there?"

"Yes." Preston gives me a look I can't decipher.

It's not one of his tender stares. He almost looks scared. Or apprehensive. Like he's... judging me?

I don't have much—if any—experience with someone else's expressions. I can't read him. Whatever his face is doing, I'm not a fan.

"What?" I say defensively, frantically smoothing my braid. "Is my hair being weird?"

"Rosalie, we need to talk about why you were in the hospital," he states. "Suicide isn't the answer. No matter how bad it is, there's another solution. Sometimes being strong and patient is what it takes. If you hang on, at least you'll have a chance to make your life better. If you die, it won't get better—it'll just end. You have to promise me you won't hurt yourself ever again."

My mouth is opening and closing like a fish. "I—I didn't try to kill myself."

Preston tilts his head like he doesn't believe me. "You overdosed, baby."

"Not on purpose." Humiliation over the whole ordeal comes back full force, and it's even more embarrassing that Preston, of all people, knows about my misstep. "I was dumb, okay? Yeah, I took some of my mom's pills, but I didn't know how much was too much. It was an accident. And why the hell are you looking through my hospital records? Does my privacy mean nothing? That's—that's personal, damn it."

I'm worked up now, my chest expanding with quick breaths.

Placing a calming hand on my shoulder, Preston explains, "The hospitalization happened before I was involved. I only know about it because Ivan told me, and the records labeled you as suicidal. I'm sorry. I shouldn't have assumed."

Preston's sincere apology and willingness to concede takes the wind right out of my sails. I'm not used to someone being so… rational. My mother never admits she's wrong, and she's never said she's sorry for anything. Ever.

It's a totally new experience and strangely validating.

"It's okay," I tell Preston as the anger drains out of me. "I know it looks bad, but I really didn't mean to hurt myself."

"I believe you." That's new, too—someone taking what I say at face value.

I cover Preston's fingers with mine. "Are all men as good as you?"

"No. Absolutely not, but I'm flattered that you think I'm good."

"My father—is he good? Does he love me?"

"Rosalie, it's—he—" Preston's response is stilted, as if he doesn't know how to answer. "I would like to think he cares, but I can't speak for Ivan's feelings."

"Am I horrible for leaving without giving him a chance?" I try to put myself in the shoes of a man who just wants to know his daughter. A man who's paying a buttload to get to me.

"No. He's a dangerous man who doesn't just bend the law—he flat out breaks it. Besides, this is your life, right? You can do whatever the hell you want. You call the shots." Preston affectionately pinches my chin. "Got it, Sarah Jones?"

Nodding, I glance at the ID I'm still holding. "So we're supposed to be siblings?"

He gives me a wolfish grin. "Husband and wife."

My eyes go wide before a frown overtakes my mouth. "Oh."

Preston huffs out a laugh. "Try not to sound so disappointed next time, Mrs. Jones. A man's ego can only take so much. Here, this might make you feel better."

Picking up my left hand, he slides a solitaire diamond ring on to my finger. The band is white gold, and the gem sparkles, even in the low lighting.

I hold up my hand to admire my new accessory, but I can't wipe the forlorn expression from my face. "Is this real?"

"The ring is, but the marriage isn't, okay?" Preston's tone is reassuring.

He's misreading me. I'm not upset because of the temporary identity switch or the fact that we have to pretend to be a couple.

I'm sad because the ring, the marriage, the life we're pretending to have—it's something I desperately want, but it's fake.

Maybe our kiss didn't mean all that much to him. I mean,

I basically threw myself at him. What was he supposed to do? Turn me down? Yeah, right.

He's probably got a girlfriend somewhere. Or a wife. As I remember the pictures of the girl he sent me when he was posing as Jessa, jealousy burns hot inside me, flaring in my stomach and turning my cheeks red.

"Hey," Preston says softly, moving his head to catch my stare. "What's going on?"

"I just don't like the name," I fib, feeling the stinging in my nose already. "That's all." *Sneeze, sneeze.*

His eyes narrow. "What's wrong?"

"Nothing." *Sneeze.*

"You have allergies or something? I have antihistamines in the trunk with the rest of our stuff."

"No, I'm fine." I put a hand on his arm to stop him from getting out of the car. "Really."

He studies me for a second as if he senses my deceit.

Then, like he can see right through me, his face morphs to a curious expression. "It's a tell."

"What?"

"The sneezing. It's your tell. Do you always sneeze when you lie?"

How the hell did he figure me out so fast?

Instead of denying it, I look at anything but him when I reply, "I'm weird, okay? I've been doing it for as long as I can remember. It's like an anti-superpower."

"I think it's adorable," he says sincerely, and I turn my head his way. "And kind of handy for me because I'll always know if you're not being honest."

I make a face. "Well, good for you. At least you don't think I'm possessed."

A wrinkle appears on his forehead, and his lips quirk up like he thinks I'm messing around. "Like, by a demon?"

Serious, I hold his eyes and nod.

Any remnant of a smile drops from his sexy mouth. "Loralee's done a number on you. Made you think there's something wrong with you."

His conclusion is correct, but I just shrug.

He leans into my space and cups my face with his big hand. "You're perfect. Do you understand me?" I don't know about that, so I start to shrug again, but Preston's fingers tighten against the back of my neck. "I mean it. Say it."

"Say what?"

"That you're perfect."

"But I'm not."

"You are to me. We're not getting out of this car until you say it."

Ugh. Fine. "I'm perfect." *Sneeze*. My hand goes up to my nose. "See? Even my body knows I'm not."

Giving me a sad smile, Preston rubs my cheek with his thumb. "That's something we're going to work on. Let's go. We've got to get you into your disguise." He slips away from me, and I follow his lead, locking and shutting my door after I'm out of the car. I trail over to the open trunk of the Mustang as Preston continues, "One makeover, coming right up."

"A makeover?" That sounds fun. My lifted mood doesn't last long, though. Because Preston holds up a lumpy, flesh-colored bodysuit of some sort. "What the hell is that?"

The grimace I receive reflects my own. "A pregnancy suit."

"You better be telling me that's for you," I half-joke.

Preston doesn't laugh. "No one will be searching for a pregnant woman and her husband. Sorry, it's pretty heavy." He tests the weight by lifting it a few times.

When he hands it over, I almost drop it. Because, damn, he's not kidding. "I'm supposed to walk around with this on? I'll be waddling like a penguin."

"Exactly. We need it to look real."

Holding it over my front, I imagine how it'll look once it's under my clothes. My shirt will stretch over the rounded stomach. I'll be able to rub it and rest my hands on it.

Yeah, it'll be pretty convincing. And that's just another prick of disappointment. Another item on my list that's going to be purely pretend.

"I know this sucks, okay? But it's just temporary." Preston picks up a baggy cream-colored sweater. "Here's a maternity shirt. I've got clean jeans for you, too."

After I accept all the stuff from him, I go to the dark back corner of the storage unit. I wrestle myself into everything while Preston has his back turned, and when I'm done, I look down at myself.

Just like I knew it would, the chunky-knit texture of the sweater lays over the baby bump. I rub it, letting myself sink into the fantasy for a second.

I'd love to see my body swell like this. To know a human being is growing inside me, and I'd be able to love it and protect it. I could take him or her to parks and museums. I'd be there to drop them off on the first day of school, watch them make friends, and see them fall in love with the world in a way I was never allowed.

I'm yanked from the daydream when Preston clears his throat. "You done?"

My eyes snap up to the back of his head. "Yeah."

He turns. His jaw loosens. His gaze turns even more tender as he takes in the pregnancy illusion.

Feeling off-balance from the extra pounds, I shuffle over to him. "All right. Well, since I'm eating for two, I expect breakfast. I'm starving."

Preston laughs. "That I can do."

I'm grateful for the sunglasses Preston insisted I wear, because the shades help to tone down the headache-inducing brightness of the world.

In the thirty-minute drive from the storage garage, I've been both excited beyond belief and a little terrified.

Although I haven't seen the outside in about seven years, I remember it being loud and colorful. But being immersed in it now is a little overwhelming.

I watch the sights fly by as we speed down the street. All the vehicles go so fast. Stores are packed closely together. Signs with bold letters make me want to buy things.

The breeze coming through the cracked window isn't anything like home. I smell exhaust from an old truck that's putting out some gray fumes. Nearby restaurants permeate the air with mouth-watering aromas.

Horns honk, engines rumble, and the man on the radio is talking about a recent sports event as Preston slows and turns into a fast food parking lot.

We stop by a yellow crosswalk near the door and let a family pass in front of us. A mother has three kids in tow—one on her hip, one holding her hand, and the last clinging to her jeans. She's too occupied to give us a glance, but she does wave her thanks before shuffling her kids into the restaurant.

I smile.

My mom would shit her pants if she could see me now.

On the run. With a man I just met.

Life has never been better.

Well, it might get better in a few minutes when we get some food.

Preston inches forward in the drive-thru and leans toward the speaker outside his window. "Two bacon biscuits and two orders of hash browns."

"And pancakes," I whisper, and he adds my request, along with coffee for himself and a Coke for me.

What? A person can drink soda at ten in the morning. My mom would argue otherwise, but her rules don't apply anymore.

The intercom blurts our total at us, and then we're moving up in the line.

I'm about to offer some of the cash from my fanny pack when Preston takes out his wallet. "You ever had fast food before?"

"Once. A long time ago. When I was too young to be left at home alone, my mom would take me to the city sometimes when the grocery delivery person was either fired or they quit."

Preston looks surprised. "She took you out?"

"Just a few times. She was always super weird about it. I mean, she's had problems with paranoia, and it's like she thought I'd vanish into thin air or something. She literally made me wear a leash."

"How long's it been since the last time?"

"I was eleven, I think." A humorless laugh puffs from me when I remember my age discrepancy. "Or I guess I was twelve or thirteen, actually. Too old to be acting up in the store, but that didn't stop me from throwing a fit. It was getting to a point where I felt like I was losing my mind inside that house. I just wanted to talk to people. I wanted to be seen and heard, so I made a scene. Started throwing junk food in the cart. Being loud. I actually sat down in the middle of the aisle and refused to move. My mom had to drag me out." Heat fills my face because it's really embarrassing to admit all that.

"None of that is your fault, you know," Preston tells me as he takes the brown sacks from the person at the window. "The way you acted in that situation is normal."

"Is it?" I ask skeptically.

"Anyone would crack under the circumstances you were in. People aren't meant to be isolated the way you have been."

"What about you?"

"What about me?"

"You seem isolated. I mean, you've been on our property for two months and never had a visitor. You don't talk to us either. It's like you're all alone. Unless you've got people somewhere. Like family or a girlfriend…" I trail off, and my fishing is pathetically obvious.

Thankfully, Preston doesn't call me out on it. He gives me a level stare. "I've been alone for a long time, but I'm not anymore."

Flutters flare in my middle as we hold meaningful eye contact.

I don't know how he does that—make me feel special and normal at the same time. Between the kiss earlier, the way he touches me when he wants me to really hear him, and the way he's looking at me now… I feel crazy in a different way.

Love crazy.

When I'm with Preston, I'm not insane. I'm infatuated.

CHAPTER 11

Preston

"Since our identities have changed," I start, "and they might change again, we should pick a term of endearment for each other instead of saying names. Something that can stay constant."

Rosalie's sitting cross-legged in the passenger seat, surrounded by food. Her Coke is in the cupholder by her knee. Her pancakes are on the dash. A hash brown is on her thigh and her breakfast sandwich is in her hand.

She scoffs around a big bite. "Like honey or sweetie?"

I shrug, keeping one hand on the wheel as I drive while sipping coffee from the other. "Whatever you want."

"Pookie bear." Rosalie giggles between sips of her soda. "Love muffin."

I grimace, and it makes her laugh harder.

I fucking love seeing her like this.

Happy. Free. Kinda-sorta mine, at least for the time being.

She still has the pregnancy suit on, and the belly bounces with her laughter. I'd be lying if I said I didn't like the illusion. It's easy to get carried away and picture her as mine forever.

Slipping that ring on her finger felt right, and I want it to stay there.

"But seriously," she says. "I've always wanted to call someone 'babe.' How about that?"

"Babe is good," I respond.

Better than good, actually. Something I could get used to.

Rosalie suddenly makes an alarmed noise, and when I look over at her, the color has drained from her face. As she takes the sunglasses off, she stares straight ahead through the windshield as if she's looking death in the face.

"Sorry," I say, glancing at the expanse of water in front of us. The lake is just beyond the street we're approaching. "Close your eyes if you have to. We'll get past it soon."

"Where are we?" Rosalie asks, nervously toying with the plastic straw in her drink.

"The southern coast of Lake Michigan."

"We're not going to go over it or anything, right? No more bridges."

"Nope, and we won't be here long. There's just somewhere special I want to see as we drive by it."

Relaxing a little, she nibbles on her hash brown. "Where?"

"There." I take a left and point at the lighthouse in the distance. "I usually stop here when I'm in the area."

"But we're not stopping?"

"Nah. I'll just look this time."

"This place is special to you," Rosalie concludes, and I nod. She curiously tilts her head. "Why?"

I want to tell her about the lighthouse puzzle and my tragic loss of it, but I can't get the words out.

I thought I was over that shit, but for some reason, Rosalie makes me feel exposed and vulnerable. My throat's closing up in a way that's unfamiliar. Like I might fucking cry.

I'm not about to give Rosalie some sob story when I'm supposed to be showing her a good time, so I shrug it off. "I've just got a thing for lighthouses."

"Then you should go there."

"It's on the water," I inform her. "Like right up against it. The ledge drops off on the other side of the building."

"Okay." She swallows audibly. "I can do it for you."

I glance at her eyes and notice they're steely with a mixture bravery and determination, and damn if that doesn't put a crack in my black heart. "You sure?"

"Uh huh."

The tall landmark looms over us as we get closer. It's beautiful, with a white tower, red railings around the platform at the top, and a roof so blue it blends in with the cloudless sky beyond.

By the time we roll up to the parking spot near a gift shop extension of the lighthouse, Rosalie's looking like she might puke her food back up.

"Baby, it's okay." I rub her knee, hoping to soothe her. Much to my surprise, she tangles her hand with mine and squeezes.

She sucks in a breath, then blows it out. "You want to go inside the store?"

"I won't leave you out here by yourself."

"I'll go with you." At my raised eyebrows, she insists, "I—I want to. I mean, what are the chances I'll be here ever again? I need to seize these opportunities. And you've done so much for me already…"

Looking back at the store, I observe the floor-to-ceiling windows that wrap all the way around it. The design is meant to give a panoramic view, so you feel like you're on the water. Not exactly something Rosalie would normally volunteer for.

But she's doing it.

For me, and for herself.

It'd be a risk to take her out, but there aren't many people around.

Two customers are milling about the merchandise. Behind the counter, the clerk seems bored, with his college-aged face buried in his phone. For black Friday, the place is pretty dead. I guess most people are doing their shopping at big department stores.

"All right," I tell Rosalie, earning a wobbly smile from her. "Sunglasses stay on and stay close to me. Don't talk to anyone."

She's so fucking cute when she mimes zipping up her lips.

Once we walk around to the front of the car, Rosalie automatically slips her hand into mine. Her skin is clammy, and she holds on tight, but she doesn't waver in her decision to go ahead with this.

We make our way across the parking lot, and I open the door for her like a husband would for his wife.

Rosalie immediately swivels to the right, purposely keeping her back to the lake view. It puts her in front of a section with rows of T-shirts, other apparel, and lighthouse-themed trinkets.

"Oh," Rosalie breathes out when she sees glass shelves full of snow globes.

Dragging me with her, she flits around, touching everything. She's light on her feet, almost doing a combination of tiptoeing and skipping at the same time as she glides her fingertips over various fabrics and textures.

She stops dead in her tracks by a spinning case of jewelry.

"See anything you like?" I ask, and she glances back at me with a smile, the sparkles reflecting in her aviators.

"All of it."

Directly in front of her face, there's a lighthouse necklace. It's a silver charm with cubic zirconia where the shining light should be. Dangling, it sways, catching glints from the florescent bulbs above us.

I take it off the rack. "I'm buying this for you."

"Really?" Even behind the dark lenses, I can see Rosalie's eyes are wide with genuine surprise.

Before she can object, I grab a couple of T-shirts in our sizes, too. On our way to the counter, I spy a puzzle on a table full of kid stuff. Toys and such. The puzzle is only five hundred pieces, and it's not like the one I had when I was young, but I'm getting it anyway.

Two people are in front of us in the checkout line, and since we're facing the lake while we wait, Rosalie turns and fiddles with some sunglasses on a stand. As if I'm drawn to her, I pivot so I'm standing right behind her.

God, her hair. It's so shiny and silky. Unable to help myself, I softly run my fingers over the braid down her back. So smooth and cool between my fingers. A shiver runs through me, and I almost shudder.

What I wouldn't give to feel it framing my face as Rosalie rides me. Better yet, I can picture her on me reverse cowgirl, with the long strands tickling my stomach.

"Excuse me." A voice comes from my left, but I ignore it because she can't be talking to us. It's not our turn yet. But it comes again. "Excuse me, you two. Sir? Ma'am?"

Realizing she is, in fact, speaking to us, I look over to see an older woman with an arm full of stuff.

Now that she has my attention, she smiles while gazing at Rosalie's belly. "Would you like to go ahead of me? I remember what it was like standing around on swollen feet."

Shit. Rosalie's still got her sunglasses on, but this woman's getting a good look at both of us.

"Yes," I accept quickly, if only to get out of her scrutinizing gaze. "Thank you."

I shuffle Rosalie forward and put our stuff on the counter. The guy working behind it is still completely uninterested in his surroundings, but I can't say the same for the nosy woman.

"When are you due?" she asks Rosalie, who's currently focusing on her own hands until we're done with this transaction and we can get the hell out of here.

"February fifteenth," I toss the random date over my shoulder while dropping some cash to cover our total.

"Oh, it might be a Valentine's Day baby," the woman titters happily, clearly pleased with herself for bringing up the idea.

The guy hands me my change and reaches for a bag to put our purchases in.

"No need," I tell him. "We'll carry it. Thanks."

I gather everything, hook my arm around Rosalie's waist, and hightail it out of here. We're both stiff with tension as we get back into the car. No words are spoken as I start it up and drive away.

Keeping to my original plan, I drive to a motel on the outskirts of town. After ordering Rosalie to stay in the vehicle while I get us a room, I walk up to the office window under a faded red overhang. When the motel manager slides the partition back—also looking incredibly bored—I give him a spiel about how my pregnant wife and I are on a babymoon trip, but she's too car sick to travel, so we might be staying for a few days. I prepay three nights in advance and ask that we're not disturbed.

In reality, we'll probably only stay until tomorrow morning. Best to keep moving once we've gotten some rest.

After we get into a room with one king bed, Rosalie finally pipes up, "Is it bad that someone talked to us in the store? You seem upset about it."

I hate that just a simple interaction is reason for concern. But it is.

Still, I play it off like it's not a big deal. "She was just being polite. She's probably already forgotten about us."

"Do you really think so?"

I hike a shoulder. "Something about people, Rosie... they're usually very self-absorbed. That woman has no reason to remember us."

"What happened to the pet names, *babe*?" she points out playfully, effectively lightening the somber mood.

"You got me. I just really like calling you Rosie."

Satisfaction flares in her eyes, and I can tell she likes it, too. Regardless of her protests earlier, Rosie Doll is who she'll always be to me.

Her lips curl up as she thoughtfully taps her chin. "I'm still considering pumpkin pie. Cookie is a contender, too."

"I think you should stay away from foods," I say. "I'm not that sweet."

"I don't believe that, honey."

Chuckling as I reach for our luggage, I unzip my black duffle bag where I'd stashed our new items we just bought. Unrolling the T-shirts, I find the necklace snugly tucked in the middle of the fabric, and I rip the sticky sales tag off the metal chain.

Rosalie's sitting on the side of the bed, blinking up at me with those dazzling, innocent eyes. I crouch down to her level, and it feels intimate to be kneeling in front of her like this.

I have to get close to secure the chain around her neck, and her legs automatically open to make room for me between her thighs. My stomach bumps into the pregnancy belly. The scent of roses wafts from her hair, and my cock swells.

After the clasp is latched, I let my hands linger. Rosalie's neck is so thin and delicate. So pale and soft.

She's too small. Underfed.

Deprived of life.

And her deprivation just reminds me of my own. The only difference between us is, she didn't choose the life she has, while I did.

I've been punishing myself for years, but Rosalie makes me want to leave my self-imposed prison. She and I are two very lonely people, but I don't feel alone when I'm with her. I think even if it were just us left on the planet, I'd feel whole as long as we're together.

I've been hovering for far too long now, and there's a palpable energy between us. A crackling tension that makes my skin tingle.

To make it seem like I'm not creeping on her, I adjust the chain so the clasp is behind her neck before standing up and taking a step back.

Rosalie's humor has faded away, and I notice her studying my face.

We lock eyes, and I stuff my hands in my pockets so I don't do something stupid. Like push her down and rub my erection on her pussy. "What?"

She cocks her head. "Why were you staring at me like that, sugar?"

A smile tugs at my lips, because she's really overachieving with the nicknames. "Like what, kitten?"

Her face screws up with distaste at my attempt. "I don't know. I'm not very good at reading people. Sometimes you look at me, and I don't know what you're thinking. So I thought I'd just ask."

Damn, she's direct. Suppose I could be the same.

"You're beautiful," I blurt, backing up even more to give her some space. "Everything about you is gorgeous, and seeing you sitting here, laughing about pet names, wearing the necklace I bought you, and the ring... it makes me want things."

"What kind of things?" She toys with the wedding band, twirling it around and around her finger.

"Things I've never had," I answer. "Things I never thought I'd have. Love. Family."

Confused, Rosalie wears a little wrinkle between her eyes. "Why would you think you can't have that? You're a handsome guy. You're smart. You're employed. You can hold an entertaining conversation. Aside from the whole lying-to-me-on-the-internet thing, you seem like a total catch. I don't have to be worldly to know anyone would be lucky to have you."

I can't remember the last time I was genuinely speechless because of someone's praise, but I am. My empty heart soaks up her compliments like a sponge in water.

Earlier today, Rosalie said she wanted answers.

While I don't want to tell her what I know about her past, I can tell her about mine. I can be open about who I've been, who I am now, and what I want.

Sitting on the couch across from her, the words are on the tip of my tongue. Words I've only spoken out loud to two people in my life—Krystal and the government therapist I saw after I got out of the military.

I take a breath and train my eyes to a random spot on the dark-blue carpet.

"I came into this world unwanted. I'm afraid I'll leave it that way, too. Rough childhood is an understatement for how I grew up."

Before I know it, my life is spilling from me like a bursting dam. I talk about being found in a dumpster, the foster homes, and feeling like a nobody. Rosalie listens intently as I recount all the abuse and rejection I've suffered, although I stop before I get to the Krystal era of my teenage years.

"When I was a kid, I actually thought I deserved it. When you're told you're something over and over again—in my case, *bad*—you start to believe it. I believed I was a bad kid."

"I didn't know you then, but I'd bet my life that you weren't." Rosalie doesn't sneeze. She's being completely honest.

Slowly, she rises from the bed. My pulse goes wild when sits next to me. I'm hyperaware of her closeness. The way the cushion dips. Her scent. Her heat.

"Can I show you something?" Before I can answer, she's

unzipping her fanny pack. She hands me a folded piece of paper and sighs, "Go ahead and read it. I'll warn you, though—it's dumb. I never told Jessa about it because it's silly."

When I unfold the paper, different colored ink has been scrawled onto the worn sheet. It's a bucket list. And what's written isn't anything off-the-wall or difficult to achieve.

What Rosalie wants most are average, every-day occurrences that people take for granted.

She just wants a normal life.

I can relate.

Aren't we a pair? Two people who have no idea where we came from but are totally sure of what we need in our future.

"Basic bitch?" Grinning, I raise an eyebrow at the last item on the list.

"That's the dream." Rosalie chuckles, then points at the winging eyeliner goal. "You helped me with the first one. I don't know how you know how to do makeup so well, but you made me realize I shouldn't be pulling and stretching my skin while I do it, because it always ended up being droopy. Oh! And this one can be crossed off now, too."

She leans over to the small dining table, grabs a pen, and draws a line through *Kiss someone*.

"I'm glad I made a difference for you." I give her list back. "There's nothing dumb or silly about this. In fact, I think you've got your priorities straight. I'd consider myself extremely lucky—like win-the-lotto-lucky—if I got to cross even half of those off."

She gives me a surprised look. "So, the mysterious bachelor wants to get married."

Our hands are clasped with the paper between our fingers. I don't know how we ended up holding hands, but I guess we touched and neither of us moved away.

I clear my throat, and my voice comes out a little deeper when I reply, "Yeah. If it's the right person."

"How do you know when it's her?"

The answer is loud in my mind. *When she makes my heart pound just by glancing at me. When her nearness makes me sweat. When one look from her can convince me I'm the right man for her.*

Like the way Rosalie's looking at me right now. Like I hung the moon. Like I'm her hero.

As I think about her list, the part about marriage and motherhood stands out, and call it a hunch, but I understand her reaction earlier with the fake ID and the preggo disguise.

She seemed sad about it.

Now I know why.

She wants it to be real.

I could give her that. I just feel like I'd be taking advantage of her innocence if I rope her into a relationship right away.

After all, I'm all she knows. Maybe she should understand she's got options before she settles for someone like me. Then again, maybe not. The selfish part of me wants her. All of her. Now.

"I'll just know," I rasp out the answer to her question, breaking the mesmerizing eye contact. I can't forget where we are or what we have to do. There are pressing matters at hand, so I change the subject back to our getaway. "I need to get some sleep before I even think about driving again. You tired?"

"Not really."

I hand her the remote. "You can watch TV while I snooze on the couch."

"No, you take the bed," Rosalie insists, wiggling in place as she gets cozy.

I'm not going to argue. I'm too tired for that. Dragging myself over to the bed to pull back the covers, I instruct, "Don't call anyone. Don't answer the door. Don't go outside."

"Yes, sir," she smarts.

"That's my good girl," I say groggily, pulling a happy look from Rosalie.

The TV provides some quiet background noise, and I get settled in, relishing in the soft pillow under my head.

I'm asleep in less than a minute.

Being yanked from deep sleep is always unpleasant. My body and brain protests as my shoulder is shaken violently and a frantic voice speaks quickly next to my ear. "Preston. Preston! Babe. Whatever the fuck I'm supposed to call you. Wake up!"

Awareness kicks in and my eyes snap open to find Rosalie wide-eyed and fearful. "What?"

I shoot up in the bed, fists at the ready. While assessing the room for danger, I shove her behind me to shield her body with mine.

"No." Her arm snakes around my chest. Alternating between patting me and pointing at the TV, she cries, "Look!"

My eyes land on the screen.

Shit.

Motherfucking shit.

It's Loralee Pearson, in the flesh. The big faded pink and purple Victorian house is in the background, and there's a press conference set up on the lawn.

Loralee's behind the podium. Her mostly gray hair is perfectly curled around her shoulders, and she's wearing an expensive-looking powder-blue pantsuit. A string of pearls completes her put-together ensemble, and there are tears swimming in her blue eyes as she stares back at us.

The Maryville mayor is beside her, and several police officers are surrounding the pair.

The headline at the bottom reads 'Mentally-ill Teenager on the Loose.'

Grappling for the remote, I push the volume up.

"… very unwell. Not only is she a danger to herself, she's a danger to others. Last night she broke into my safe and took my money and my gun, so she's armed."

Rosalie gasps. "That's not true. I didn't take any weapons—"

I silence her with a slashing motion of my hand and continue to listen to the bullshit Loralee's spewing.

"As long as she's away from home, she'll be unmedicated, and I don't know what she'll do. She's never run away before. I'm afraid this might be some kind of psychotic break."

"That's not true either," Rosalie growls, lifting a plastic baggie from her fanny pack. "I've been taking half my dose and saving the rest—"

I believe her, so I just pat her hand reassuringly without looking away from the TV.

"If you see my daughter, please don't harm her," Loralee begs. "I just want her back home where she can't hurt herself or anyone else."

"Thank you, Ms. Pearson," the mayor says, smoothing his red tie as he takes her place in front of the microphone to address the camera. "I'd like to assure the people that we're doing everything we can to find Rosalie Pearson and bring her home. We know she might be in the company of a man named Preston Walker, a conman. He was hired by the Pearsons two months ago, and we think the pair might've left together. It's likely he's armed and dangerous as well."

Both of our pictures show up side by side. Rosalie's appears to be a recent Christmas photo, and she's sitting in a fancy wingback chair with a fake smile plastered on her face.

Mine is much less flattering. It's a still-shot taken from the front-door surveillance camera. I'm in the process of chopping wood, and I must've looked up for a second. My facial expression is blank, my eyes are hard, and my hair is in disarray from the wind.

With the unkempt beard, I look like a psycho.

"Please help us bring them in," the mayor says. "Any tip leading to the location of one or both will result in a cash reward."

$50,000 pops up in bold red letters under Rosalie, then another $25,000 under me.

An officer moves to the podium and starts rattling off physical descriptions. Heights, weights, and birthdays for both of us. They even talk about our distinguishing features—Rosalie's naturally light hair and her different colored eyes. The gap between my two front teeth and my premature graying.

Fuck.

I run my tongue over the space in my teeth. I never had braces. Wasn't a luxury a kid in the system got to have.

I can restyle my hair, shave my face, and change my clothes all I want, but teeth always stay the same. It's why dental records are a good way to identify a body.

Or, in this case, a missing person.

I made a classic rookie mistake in underestimating Loralee. When I assumed she wouldn't alert the cops, I exaggerated her sanity in my mind. My hopeful thinking got in the way of reality. The fact is, she's unhinged and desperate. The only person in this world that matters to her is missing, so she literally has nothing to lose. She's willing to risk getting caught if it means a chance at capturing Rosalie.

"She lied about me." Rosalie's voice is rough with emotion. "I'm not dangerous, armed, or unmedicated. But she told those lies, and now people are going to be scared of me."

"Exactly." I spin to grip her trembling shoulders. "Don't take this personally, Rosie. Fear is a strong motivator. People are more concerned if their own well-being is involved. If they're scared *of* you instead of scared *for* you, it's a more effective tactic to get people to cooperate. That, along with the reward money, Loralee's making her best play. You're an adult and you left on your own, so it's not like she can declare you a missing person."

"So many people are going to be searching for us," Rosalie says morosely, looking so young without her makeup on.

While I was asleep, she must've washed up.

Foundation, blush, and eyeliner are scattered on the round dining table, like she was about to get ready for the day.

"Change of plans. There's no time to do your makeup." I quickly scoop everything up and shove it into her waiting hands.

"Are we going to get caught?"

"No, we're fine. We've got our covers, but to be extra safe, we have to keep moving. No more motels or public places until we get farther away."

Good thing I never unpacked my stuff. My keys and wallet are still in my pockets, so I grab my leather jacket and the duffle I brought in.

With a helpless expression, Rosalie glances around the room. "But you need to sleep."

"I did sleep."

She crosses her arms. "For like an hour."

"It's enough." Striding across the room, I do a quick once-over to make sure she's not leaving anything behind.

She follows me, chasing me around like a puppy at my heels. Goddamn cute. "What if the motel guy recognizes us? Or those people in the gift shop?"

Valid concerns.

Every time someone does a double take, anyone that stares too long… I'll be paranoid as fuck.

But I'll carry that concern in silence.

There's a pink toothbrush next to the sink. I hand it to Rosalie along with her backpack. "That's why we're leaving. Problem solved."

"Won't it be a problem everywhere we go?"

"Depends."

"Depends on what?" Rosalie seems sluggish. There are dark circles under her eyes, and her mouth suddenly stretches with a yawn.

That couple hours of sleep she got in the car wasn't enough.

Well, she'll have at least a couple more before we get where we're going.

"Do you trust me yet?"

A couple seconds go by, then she replies, "Getting there."

"Watch this." I whip out one of my burner phones and dial the police station in Maryville. A woman answers. Laying on a thick southern accent, I drawl, "Hiya, darlin'. I just seen that crazy girl from the news. Uh huh. Yeaup. She was with that man, too. The bearded guy. They were gettin' some snacks from the Hartman's General Store off exit forty-five on I-59 up north. I overheard 'em say they were headin' to Canada. You're welcome." Pause. "Hang on a sec, now. Don't you want my information? If you catch 'em, I could use that reward money. Elton Calhoun. Yes, ma'am."

I give her a random phone number before hanging up, and I shoot Rosalie a triumphant look.

She gapes at me. "How do you do that?"

"Just make up a story on the fly?" I pick up her Hello Kitty backpack and head toward the door.

"Yeah. You're an amazing liar. It's actually kind of scary."

"Thanks."

"I'm not sure if that was a compliment. How will I know when you're lying to me?"

Gripping the doorknob, I gaze down at her beautiful, suspicious face. "Simple. I won't lie to you."

"But the whole Jessa thing—"

"That was before. I won't do it again. Promise."

"You could be lying now."

"I'm not." I give her a charming grin.

She tries not to smile back. "I think you missed your calling. You should've been an actor."

I affectionately pinch her chin. "But being your hero is so much more fun."

CHAPTER 12

Rosalie

For the second time today, I wake up in an unfamiliar place. The clock on the dash says it's after three in the afternoon, and we're parked on a street lined with cute little houses. Some have cars in the driveways. Others have sidewalk chalk drawings and tricycles on the pavement.

The stress of the day and all the sudden change is catching up with me. My medicine has officially worn off and instead of feeling rested after the nap I just had, I'm achy. My muscles are sore from the long hike, and my head hurts.

"What's going on?" I ask sleepily, glancing over at Preston.

"We're at a friend's place," he replies, seeming way too energized for having missed an entire night of sleep.

He can't be fueled by caffeine. Aside from the fast-food place this morning, we haven't stopped anywhere else for food or drinks. But his eyes are alert behind his glasses, and his shoulders are squared as he looks at a small blue house outside the passenger window. It has a one-car attached garage, a flowerbed of yellow mums, and a fall leaf wreath hanging on the door.

"I'm hoping we can stay here for the night," he says. "We're switching names again, just in case the guy at the motel suspected anything."

A new ID lands in my lap. It has the same picture as before, but the last name is different and my first name dropped an 'h.'

Sara Clare.

I lean over to look at the plastic Preston's putting in his wallet, and I frown at his new name. "You don't look like a Joseph. Are we still married, or has that changed, too?"

"Still married. And we need to keep up the act in here." He tips his head to the house.

"But don't they know you? They'd know if you got hitched. You said they're your friends."

"Acquaintances," he corrects. "To be honest, I didn't want to come here. This is a last resort because Loralee threw a wrench in my plans."

"Why do you seem so surprised by her report?" I ask, genuinely confused. "You know how nuts she is when it comes to me. I mean, I didn't think she'd make up lies, but I'm not shocked she's doing everything she can to get me back."

Preston looks like he wants to answer, but he hesitates, and I remember his promise not to lie to me again.

There's something he isn't telling me.

Just then, there's motion in the reflection of Preston's glasses, and I turn in the seat to see a red-headed guy standing just outside the open door of the house. He smiles and holds up a hand in greeting.

"He looks friendly enough." I swivel back toward Preston.

Unfortunately, I catch my own reflection in his lenses, and I don't like what I see. I'm an absolute mess. I washed my face at the motel earlier, but no matter how much I scrub, I'm never able to remove all the makeup from my face. Leftovers from yesterday's eyeliner and mascara are raccooned around my eyes, and the rest of my face is ghostly pale.

"I need a mirror," I say, and Preston motions to the sunshade.

Yanking it down, I flip open the little flap and groan when I see how my crazy my hair is. The braid is still in place, but frizzy flyaways are spanning out in all directions.

It's embarrassing enough that Preston is seeing me like this. But meeting new friends? My first friends *ever*?

I need to look nice for such an occasion.

"I should probably do my makeup first." I lean forward and reach down toward my bag, but Preston stops me.

"There's no time. You look fine."

"Fine isn't going to cut it. I want everyone to like me. I need to fit in." I know I sound desperate and pathetic, but I can't help it.

"Hey," Preston says softly, tilting my face up by my chin. "You're beautiful. I mean, unbelievably gorgeous. Stop-people-in-their-tracks gorgeous."

"Even like this?"

"Here." Opening the middle console, Preston pulls out a package of wet wipes. Keeping a grip on my chin, he gently sweeps it over my eyelids, then runs the wipe under my eyes with steady precision.

When I look back at the mirror, the crustiness is gone and what's left looks like intentionally applied eyeliner.

"Better," I admit.

"Lip gloss?" Preston asks, and I retrieve the pink shade from my makeup bag.

Again, this guy handles my face like he's done this a hundred times. After smoothing the applicator over my mouth, he instructs me to rub my lips together. I don't know why, but there's something sexy about a manly man who's willing to submerse himself in beauty products.

"Perfect, see?" Preston smiles, clearly proud of his work. Minimalist isn't really my style when it comes to cosmetics, but I don't look like I just rolled out of bed.

"It'll do."

"Good. Now, keep something in mind—Jay's a nice guy, but as far as I'm concerned, everyone could be the enemy. It's you and me against the world. Hopefully, the news hasn't traveled this far. Try not to say more than you have to, *Sara*." He puts emphasis on my new name as a reminder. "Jay already knows me as Ethan, so it's probably best to keep things simple and let him call me that."

Nodding, I step out of the vehicle and meet Preston in the driveway. Maintaining the appearance of a blissful married couple, he grabs my hand as we walk to the front door. My heart does a happy flip when our fingers lace together.

"Sara, this is Jay," Preston introduces us when we make it to the stoop. "Jay, meet my wife."

Jay's eyes go wide, seeming shocked by the announcement, but he doesn't miss a beat. Barely glancing at my pregnant tummy, he leans against the doorframe wearing an easy-going smile. "Congratulations, man. No wonder you've been impossible to get ahold of. I thought maybe you'd died."

The joke doesn't hit its mark.

When I look at Preston's face, his jaw is all twitchy, and his gaze keeps darting around. It occurs to me that we're out in the open. Totally exposed to anyone seeing us.

As tension radiates from Preston, he asks in a low, impatient tone, "Can we come in?"

Jay tosses a look over his shoulder. "I just got my son down for a nap. So, yeah, but you have to be quiet."

"Sorry for dropping by out of the blue." Preston puts a protective arm around my shoulders as we shuffle inside. "It was a spontaneous decision."

"It's okay." Clearing some sippy cups from the coffee table, Jay waves us toward the couch. "That's kind of your MO, right? Showing up out of nowhere? I'm just glad you weren't lurking behind a dumpster this time."

Jay's teasing finally pulls a smile from Preston and a

questioning quirk of an eyebrow from me. There's a story there, but Preston just shrugs.

When I sit on the couch, something squeaks under my butt. I pull a dragon puppet from between two of the cushions.

"Sorry." Jay grins fondly at the toy before taking it from me and motioning to all the colorful balls and blocks littering the living room. "Kind of a mess in here."

I don't mind at all. In fact, I like it.

I was never allowed to leave my toys out like this. My mom always wanted things clean and organized.

As far as living rooms go, it's a little cramped in here, but the space is open to the dining nook and a kitchen. Down the hall, I'm guessing there are two or three bedrooms.

For some reason, this tiny, cluttered room feels more like home than anything I've ever known. I'm used to spacious rooms, polished wood floors, sparkling chandeliers, and high ceilings decorated with fancy 1920's tiles.

Maybe it's not about the décor or the size.

Maybe it's about family and love. The kid Jay talked about isn't even in sight, but his presence is everywhere. Sloppy finger paintings are framed on the wall. DVDs are haphazardly stacked next to the widescreen TV. Dishes from today's meals are piled high in the sink.

"So what brings you two by?" Jay's question brings me back to the moment.

Looking to Preston, I let him take the lead, and he starts by asking, "Have you seen the news at all today?"

The question makes Jay suspicious. His eyes narrow as he takes a seat in a recliner by the window. "No. Gus wanted to watch Tangled. Twice. Why? Is there something I need to see?"

"How's the PI business working out for you?"

Allowing Preston to change the subject, Jay answers, "Great. It's a nice-ass job." He leans toward me. "Let me tell you a story about this guy. So, back when I was in prison, a private investigator pays me a visit. He wants me to gather information on my cellmate. I do what he asks, then he disappears after saying he owes me a favor. Thought I'd never see him again. Then he shows up out of nowhere in September offering me his entire business, tech equipment and all. Full of mystery, this one." He wags a finger at Preston. "Of course, you probably already know all that, seeing as how you're married to him now."

God, the constant reminder of the fake marriage is like a thorn getting wedged into me deeper and deeper. And no, I didn't know any of that.

Full of mystery, indeed.

"I needed a replacement who was untraceable," Preston explains to both of us, but he's looking at me. "Someone perceptive, observant, and smart. Someone who needed a job, who could seamlessly take over for me." He glances at Jay. "You qualified, and you weren't a client, so I knew there wouldn't be a paper trail leading from you to me."

Jay drums his fingers on his thighs. "In case you needed a favor from me again, right?"

Keeping his eyes on Jay, Preston drapes an arm over my shoulders to pull me closer. "The favor exchange seems to be working out. For two guys who don't know each other well, we make a good team."

"I can't argue that, but why don't we cut the shit, Ethan?" Jay gets to the point. "Why are you here?"

Preston blows out a breath. "We need a place to lay low. Just for a day or two."

"What kind of trouble are you in?"

Laying it all out on the table, Preston admits, "The kind where I'm being hunted by the law. The mafia might be on our tail soon, too."

"Fuck, man. What the hell did you do?"

"It's me," I chime in quietly. "He's… helping me out of a situation."

Jay gives me a sympathetic look, braces his elbows on his knees, and spears Preston with a serious stare. "Listen. With all due respect, I can't have you bringing this shit to my house. I have a fiancée and a son. When you gave me my job, you never said it included putting my family in danger."

"You're right," Preston sighs, holding up his hands. "I get it. How about a few hours? I've got a van stored in the next town over." He hitches a thumb at me. "Can she hang out here while I go switch out my vehicle?"

"You're leaving me?" My head whips toward him. "You can't. I won't stay here without you."

Tender hands frame my worried face. "You have to, baby. It'll only be an hour."

"What if you don't come back? What if they catch you and I never see you again?"

"Not gonna happen."

I wish I could be that confident.

While my thoughts are running through worst-case scenarios, Preston moves into my personal space. Even though he's not wearing leather anymore, he still smells like it. The pleasant scent mixed with citrus and spice surrounds me as his face gets close to mine. He releases my braid from the tie, and loose waves fall down my back as he weaves his fingers through it. Then he tilts my chin up.

He kisses me.

And my worries scatter.

This kiss is different from the one before. Less wild. More patient.

Slow and steady.

A promise.

Maybe we should communicate like this from now on. Lips and tongues are good for more than speaking.

As Preston licks his way into my mouth, my hands go to his chest. My fingers slip inside the suit jacket. His skin is warm through the fabric of his shirt, and underneath the cotton, I can feel the texture of coarse hair on his body.

Before I can fumble with the buttons keeping me from getting skin on skin, Preston turns his head, breaking the kiss.

Panting, he buries his face in my hair. "I'll come back, okay? Remember, nothing could keep me from you."

Dumbly, I just nod.

Maybe his plan was to kiss the sense out of me because, before I know it, he's leaving through the front door. I'm numb as I watch the car speed away from the curb, but as soon as it's out of sight, a feeling of deep loss seeps in.

I'm vaguely aware that Jay has vacated the room—probably because he didn't want to stick around to watch Preston and me get all smoochy.

Without even realizing that I'm doing it, I'm digging under my big belly suit and getting into my fanny pack. The wads of cash almost bust out when I open it, but I don't want the money.

I find the pills and fish out a half a tablet.

Hesitating, I stare at it in my palm. I never take my medicine during the day, and I know I shouldn't now. With the new developments, I have no idea how long it will take to get settled somewhere.

I won't take it.

Putting it back, I decide to suffer through my anxiety as I sit and wait for Preston to return.

∽

I've never had the chance to realize how socially awkward I am until now. And dude, it's bad.

Is this what my mom meant when she said I wasn't fit for society?

I wasn't left alone in the living room for long after Preston left. While Jay checked on his napping son, his fiancée Casey came home from work. When she'd asked me my name, I dutifully replied, "Sara," then promptly sneezed her in face.

So.

That's how my first potential female friendship is going down.

Like a sinking ship.

I'm not sure if I prefer the uncomfortable silence that occurred during the seconds when it was just Jay and me, or the curious questions Casey keeps firing my way.

To make matters worse, Jay's hovering around in the kitchen behind me, which means there's more than one witness to this shitshow.

"How did you and Ethan meet?" Casey chirps from across the dining table. Such an innocent thing to ask.

"Online." That's the simplest honest explanation I can come up with, and I decide to eat more of my food, because if my mouth is full, I can't talk.

Fortunately, my awkwardness hasn't impaired my appetite. I don't know what it is about traveling, but I'm so fucking hungry.

I take another bite of the juicy burger and chase it down with some greasy fries. Luckily for me, Casey works at a diner and gets a hefty discount. The food I'm eating was intended for Jay, but as soon as Casey saw my stomach, she insisted I eat his portion. Like a gentleman, he graciously agreed.

I'd feel worse about taking the guy's dinner if it didn't taste so damn good.

Some mustard drops onto my belly, and I wipe at it with a paper napkin. My mom would have a fit if I was this messy at her table. In our house, we never eat with our hands. Meals are always a rigid affair, with designated utensils, squared shoulders, and straight backs.

"I guess people are getting into internet dating younger and younger these days," Casey responds happily, seeming unaffected by my bad table manners as she gets up to wet a kitchen rag for me.

She hasn't asked how old I am, and I'm glad. Because I'm not even sure how to answer that. Twelve hours ago, I thought I was eighteen. Really, I'm a year older.

Then there's my new identity. How old is Sara Clare supposed to be again? I have no idea how the hell Preston keeps track of all this crap.

Due to my lack of experience with people, I'm not great at estimating age, but Casey doesn't appear to be much older than me. Her dark brown hair is pulled back into a ponytail, and her face is youthful. There's a hint of seriousness in her blue eyes, like she's either an old soul or she's been through the wringer.

Maybe Casey's seen some shit.

I wonder if my eyes look like that. Can people tell I'm carrying a lifelong burden?

"Here you go."

I take the damp towel from her with a mumbled, "Thank you," and start scrubbing at the stain. "It wasn't a dating site," I inform her truthfully, because at least I can tell her that without giving any secrets away. "We started chatting on one of those interactive card games."

"Oh, cool. I've actually never played anything like that because—" Her face lights up as she looks past me. "Because of this guy right here. There's my goobie goo." She opens her arms, and a little boy toddles over before climbing into her lap. "He keeps me busy. No time for games or social media, though I'm thinking about getting a Facebook account."

"I'm not on social media either." At least Casey and I have that in common.

Her son is adorable. He's wearing a blue-striped shirt under a green princess dress, and three of his fingers have shiny rings on them.

Most random outfit ever.

Sticking his thumb in his mouth, he grasps Casey's shirt collar as he looks up at her with sleepy eyes. She kisses his blond head, and a bolt of jealousy strikes me.

Casey and Jay have the life I've dreamed about.

The little house. The love. The family.

All kinds of people get to have this. It's normal.

What have I ever done that makes me unworthy of something so simple?

The kid's still staring at me with wary hazel eyes, and I give an awkward wave. "Hi, uh, goobie goo. I'm Ro—" I rub my burning nose as I correct myself "—a friend."

"His name's actually August, but we usually call him Gus," Casey supplies. "Or goobie goo, bubbie, bud. You know, he'll answer to pretty much any variation of those nicknames."

Oh, great. I addressed Casey's kid as *goobie goo* because I took her literally when she called him that. Of course that isn't his name.

Kill me now.

To mask my embarrassment, I change the subject. "How old is he? Four?"

Casey shakes her head. "A year and a half."

Shit. Again, I'm not great at estimating someone else's age, and I guess that applies to children, too. I've never been around a kid before. Movies and TV shows don't always represent them in the most realistic way, so I'm completely clueless.

Having finished my food, I push the wrappers away, prop

my face on a hand, and give my attention to August as I try to salvage this interaction. "So, what do you like to do for fun?"

He just stares back, and Casey fills in, "He doesn't have a ton of words in his vocabulary yet, but he loves Disney movies and anything shiny."

Feeling silly for trying to start up a conversation with a baby, I muster up a fake grin. "Hey, I like those things, too."

God, when will Preston be back?

This is painful, and I'm officially the worst at making new friends.

Craning my neck, I look to the kitchen and find a clock behind Jay, who's looking very interested in whatever's on his laptop screen.

Preston's been gone for almost an hour.

Shifting nervously in my chair, I sweep my hair over my shoulder and start braiding it, just so I have something to do with my fingers.

Suddenly, August's thumb pops out of his mouth and he points at me. "Rapunzel!" He tugs at his mom's shirt some more, then begins wiggling off her lap. "Rapunzel."

My heart's in my throat the whole time I watch him toddle around the table to me. His eyes are transfixed on my hair, and he starts to reach out once he's close.

"Gus," Casey scolds lightly, getting up to retrieve her son. "You can't just touch people's hair without permission."

His lower lip quivers, and it's so cute I can't stand it.

"It's okay," I say, holding my hair out to him. "You can feel it if you want to."

Face brightening, he doesn't waste any time, almost as if he thinks the offer might be snatched away. Little fingers pet my strands, and he brings some of it up to his face to rub it on his cheek. "Soft."

I smile and take another chunk of hair and rub it on his

other cheek. He giggles, and it's a sound that gives me all kinds of feels.

All shyness gone, he starts to climb onto my lap. I give him a helping hand and he ends up sitting sideways with his head leaning on my shoulder.

I'm stunned and a little bit frozen in place. He's lighter than I thought he'd be, and I like the way he smells.

Gathering a bunch of my hair, he drapes it over his own head as if it's a wig. Seeming content, his thumb goes back into his mouth.

My heart clenches in a good way. "I like your dress, Gus."

"Tan ku." With his mouth full, his thank you is distorted, but I understand it.

"You're welcome. I love the color green."

Momentarily, Gus removes his thumb to point at my left eye. "Green."

"Yeah. Like that."

"You're good with kids," Casey states, observing us.

"I am?"

"Yeah." She nods. "He doesn't warm up to many people like this. Like ever." Tilting her head, she smiles softly as she gazes at my belly. "You'll be a great mom."

It's one of the best compliments I've ever received.

Maybe I'm not so terrible at making friends.

CHAPTER 13

Preston

If Jay didn't think my presence meant danger before, he definitely does now.

I'm not fooling around with my disguise. My new look is about as extreme as I can take it, and there's tension in the air as he stares at my hipster outfit.

I've still got on the glasses, but now I'm wearing a brown beanie on my head, a red plaid flannel shirt, and ripped black skinny jeans. The temporary snake tattoo on my neck and the fake lip ring complete the ensemble.

"You moving in?" Jay eyes the rolling suitcase in my grasp.

"Don't be rude," Casey chastises him with a disbelieving laugh. She stands from the dining table to pick up her son, who's practically climbing Rosalie like a jungle gym.

When I left, she was visibly uncomfortable. Now her smile is genuine as she carefully extracts a handful of her hair from the kid's grasp.

I guess children have a way of breaking the ice.

"It's great to finally meet you, Ethan," Casey says, bouncing her son on her hip. "We're so thankful. I can't tell you how awesome the PI business has been for Jay."

She must assume I'm stopping by to check in on her fiancé and see how he's doing with the workload I dumped on him.

Which means Jay hasn't had time to tell Casey why I'm really here.

Good.

It might buy us some time.

"Would it be okay if Sara uses your shower?" I ask, keeping my gaze directed at Casey. I've barely seen Jay and Casey together, but I can already tell she has the final say in things. If Jay and I were better friends, I might goad him about being whipped. "We're on a road trip, and the last motel we went to didn't work out."

"Of course," she answers before he can stop her. "Bathroom's down the hall. First door on the right."

I nod my thanks, and Rosalie meets me in the hallway. I usher her through the door of a modest bathroom.

When I notice her sniffing her shoulder to see if she smells, I chuckle. "You don't stink." I pat the handle of the rolling suitcase. "I've got the next step to your disguise in here. How do you feel about being a brunette?"

Her hand goes to her hair. "You want me to dye it? Permanently?"

"Have to," I reply regretfully.

I'll still think she's the most beautiful girl I've ever seen no matter what color her hair is, but I'll miss the blond.

I twirl a lock of it around my finger. "We have to cut it, too."

Rosalie's eyes bulge. "Cut it? No. No way. My hair is the one thing my mom let me have control over. I've been growing it out for years."

"Not super short. Maybe just..." I make a sawing motion with my hand a few inches below her shoulder. "Right here."

"That's like ten inches!" she shrieks, backing up against the sink.

A knock comes at the door, and Jay inquires, "Everything okay in there?"

"Yeah," I respond, smirking. "Did I mention it's our honeymoon? It's the first time Sara's seen my—"

Rosalie's hand covers my mouth, and she's practically fuming as she glares up at me.

"Don't finish that sentence," she whispers, her lips twitching with humor she wants to contain.

Chuckling, Jay leaves us alone, and I start to unzip the luggage.

I set a comb, scissors, the box of dye, and a couple old towels down on the counter. "We'll cut some length off first."

Rosalie pouts as she turns to look in the mirror. "Are you sure you know what you're doing?"

"Do you know who you're talking to? It's been a while since I've done this, but yeah."

A sense of calm comes over me as I run a comb through her strands. I part her hair down the middle and feel the cool silkiness slip against my fingers. Unable to help myself, I spear my fingers through her locks and make a fist at the nape of her neck.

Rosalie's eyes appear a bit glazed as she pushes her head back against my hand. "It feels good when you do that."

My dick gets hard.

I've always had a fascination with hair, but I didn't realize it was a fetish until Rosalie. I can't stop thinking about it. Fuck, the way her hair would look wrapped around my hand while I take her from behind.

"On second thought, maybe I won't cut much off." Sinking my fingers deeper, I massage her scalp. "Just like five inches. Once we've colored it, it'll be easier to transform your look. There are a lot of other ways to style your hair."

She lets out a satisfied sigh and asks, "Like what?"

"Ponytails, braids, updos."

She gazes at my reflection in the mirror. "Seriously, how do you know all this stuff? Did you go to cosmetology school?"

The answer is painful. So painful, I haven't talked about it in almost ten years. But Rosalie's being brave for me. I owe it to her to share this.

Plus, I want her to know me. Really know me.

Krystal was a huge defining factor in my life. She made me who I am today.

"I had a sister. A foster sister."

"Had?" Rosalie's question is hesitant. "Meaning, you don't anymore?"

"Correct." I drape the towel around her shoulders to keep her sweater from getting dirty.

"What happened?"

I'm quiet as I section off her hair. Two parts in the front, one in the back. Putting the scissors near the bottom of her shoulder blades, I start cutting straight across.

Snip, snip, snip.

Rosalie patiently waits for my reply, and after I've gotten the line evened up, I say, "Krystal and I got placed in the same foster home about a week apart. We had a lot in common—both fifteen, both rejected by the people who should've loved us most... both born as males."

Rosalie turns her head to glance at me over her shoulder. "Huh?"

"Do you know what it means to be transgender?"

She looks forward again. "Yes. I watched a documentary about it. It's like being born with a body that doesn't match your brain. It's when someone looks one way on the outside, but it isn't who they feel like on the inside."

"Exactly." I'm a bit surprised at how simply she put it, but I have to remember that just because Rosalie's been sheltered doesn't mean she isn't educated or compassionate. "On the inside, Krystal—formerly Christopher—was a girl. When she came out to her parents at thirteen, they—" I stop as I feel the emotion well up. I clear my throat. "—they tried to beat the gay out of her. Her words, not mine."

"That's awful," Rosalie whispers, letting me rotate her so I can get to the front section on her right.

I keep talking while I cut some face-framing layers. "She ended up in the hospital for a week, and her parents went to jail for abuse. After that, she bounced around foster homes for a while. No one wanted to accept her as is. The home she was in before coming to the Marshalls' was pretty strict. They wouldn't let her wear the clothing she wanted, and they refused to use female pronouns. One night when the family was away at a movie, she slit her wrists. They got home just in time to call an ambulance and save her."

"That's really scary. I can't imagine hurting myself in that way. Wait…" Rosalie's staring at me out of the corner of her eye. "Is that why you kind of freaked out on me about the overdose?"

I nod. "Self-harm and suicide are sore subjects for me."

"Yeah, I can understand that now."

"Being at the Marshalls' was a dream come true for both Krystal and me," I continue. "Mr. Marshall was a pastor at a LGBTQ-friendly church, and he and his wife made us feel like we were wanted. For the first time, we were home. We both tried to be on our best behavior, because we didn't want to get moved to a different foster family. That was our worst fear—being separated. At least, it was mine. Krystal was my family. I knew she wrestled with her mental health, but I thought my love was enough to keep her grounded, and I literally fought for her. If anyone said shit about her at school, they regretted it. I got suspended a few times. Almost got expelled all together."

I chuckle a little when I remember how Mr. Marshall used to just pat me on the back and tell me it was all right when I'd get sent home with a bloody lip or a black eye. He never directly said so, but I think he approved of my actions.

"You were being a good brother." Rosalie gives me a soft smile.

"Krystal used to get so pissed at me for causing trouble, but I knew deep down it meant a lot to her that she had someone sticking up for her." With guilt burning in my gut, I forge ahead, getting closer to the worst part of the story. "When I was seventeen, one night I snuck out of the house. There was a party across town, and I wanted to go. Krystal was sick—just a cold or something, but she didn't feel up to going out, so I went alone. I didn't have a car, so I did the stupidest thing ever—I stole our neighbor's truck. They were out of town, and I thought I could borrow it and bring it back the next morning. No one would know, right? Well, the plan might've worked… if I hadn't wrecked it."

Rosalie gasps. "Oh, no."

"It was raining and dark. I didn't see the big patch of water on the country road until it was too late. I hydroplaned and lost control."

"Did you get hurt?"

I'm done with the haircut now, so I unpack the coloring materials from the little box, laying the items on a folded-up towel next to the sink. "Not too bad. A few bumps, bruises, and a mild concussion. Considering I rolled the truck four times, I was pretty damn lucky to walk away from the crash. The crime landed me in juvie for a month." Vigorously shaking the bottle of dye, I brace myself for the next part. There's no way to sugarcoat it. My voice comes out gruff when I say, "While I was locked away, Krystal hanged herself in the closet."

"Oh, Preston." Rosalie turns, her feet shuffling over all the hair on the floor. "I'm so sorry."

"Yeah, me too."

"You know it's not your fault, right?"

"But it is." While I appreciate her immediate defense, she's wrong. I'm to blame. "I'll never forgive myself for not being there. If I hadn't been gone, maybe she'd still be alive. And the part that really kills me is that the Marshalls were planning to adopt us both. We would've been siblings for real, if I hadn't been such a dumbass and she'd just been able to hold on."

Wrapping her arms around my middle, Rosalie presses as close as she can with the big lump on her stomach between us. "Almost fifty percent of transgender people are suicidal at some point in their life. I realize you probably already know that—I'm just regurgitating what I learned in the documentary, but it's a fact you can't deny. You couldn't watch her all the time."

"Well, I'll never know because I fucked up."

Separating from the hug, I slip on the gloves and start applying the dye to Rosalie's hair. I appreciate that she's trying to comfort me. More than she knows. But no one can ever convince me I didn't play a part in Krystal's death. The Marshalls never blamed me, but of course they wouldn't. I was the one kid they had left, and they didn't want to lose me, too.

Only, they did in a way. I changed. I was so shattered by Krystal's death that I suppressed the fun side of myself. The side that fuels humor, lust, and spontaneity. I stopped drinking and using drugs. I quit dating. Figured if Krystal couldn't party, neither should I. If she couldn't fall in love, have sex, have a family, I shouldn't get to either.

I've been living my life like a monk because of it. Always serious. Always business. Just trying to live my life one good deed to the next, but never feeling like it was enough.

Until Rosalie.

She feels like a chance to redeem myself. I couldn't save my sister, but I can rescue her.

Rosalie fidgets with her hands. "I wish I knew what to say to make it better for you. I'm not very good at this. Whenever my mom was in distress, she'd get all distant, pop a pill, and chase it with bourbon, so I don't have much practice at comforting people."

"You're perfect. You're listening, and that's really all you can do." I try to smile.

"What about the good times? What did you and Krystal like to do together?"

My smile becomes real as I keep coating Rosalie's hair with brown goop. "Makeovers. For her, not me. She'd beg me to brush her hair, braid it, do her makeup. I was pretty bad at it in the beginning, but I got better."

"And that's how you know all this stuff."

"Yep. The pictures I sent you when I was pretending to be Jessa… That's Krystal. I put those blue streaks in her hair."

"Well, you have my permission to do my hair anytime you want…" Rosalie frowns thoughtfully and adds, "As long as you don't end up thinking of me as a sister."

I smirk, because she has no idea of all the dirty ways she's starred in my fantasies. "Oh, baby. There's literally zero chance of that happening."

There's a peaceful quiet in the room as I finish spreading the dye around. Once the ends are fully saturated, I twist Rosalie's hair into a bun and place the shower cap on her head.

"Let that sit for twenty minutes, then rinse it out in the shower." I turn to leave the bathroom before I do something reckless. Like get in the shower with her.

"Wait." She grabs my arm. "Can you help me get my sweater off? I don't want to stain it."

She's right. There's dye on her neck near the hairline, and she might rub some off on her shirt if she's not careful. We can't afford to ruin any clothing.

Which is why I convince myself stripping her down is a gallant effort. I'm taking one for the team.

Fuck that. I'm getting turned the fuck on.

The bottom of the sweater is bunched in my hands. Even though that damn pregnancy suit is in the way of me touching her real stomach, it doesn't matter. Just the thought of brushing my fingertips over her smooth skin is enough to give me a hard-on.

My erection strains inside my too-tight jeans as I help Rosalie get her arms out.

Finally, I'm stretching the neck hole and maneuvering it over her head without so much as a speck of damage to the material.

Breathing through the hammering of my heart, I fold the sweater and hang it on the towel rack.

"There you go." My voice is huskier than usual, and I clear my throat.

Holding eye contact with me, Rosalie's fingers go to the fasteners for the pregnancy suit at her shoulders. One side drops, revealing the white sports bra underneath. It falls just enough for me to see her stiff nipple inside the fabric.

Face blanketed with an innocent expression, she holds eye contact, her lips slightly parted and her cheeks pink.

This is just like all the times she stood in front of her window and undressed.

In this moment, I know she did it for me.

I *know*.

And that's why I have to get out of here.

I leave the bathroom so fast I end up slamming the door a little. Wincing at the loud sound, I glance down the hallway. There's no sign of Jay, Casey, or their son, but I'm too tired to seek them out. Plus, I won't leave Rosalie unprotected.

Sitting, I face the bathroom door as I slump against the wall. Everything is calm and quiet, and fatigue finally overpowers the adrenaline coursing through my veins. When the shower starts going, the sound of running water is soothing, and before I realize it, I've dosed off.

Then the floor creaks next to me, and I startle awake.

"Hey." Jay leans down to pat my shoulder. "It's just me, man."

Blowing out a breath, I pinch the bridge of my nose. "Sorry. We'll be gone soon, I swear."

"About that." Jay's looking at me with sympathy, his hands shoved in his pockets. "You can stay tonight."

"Really? You sure?"

"Yeah."

Suddenly suspicious of his quick change of heart, I narrow my eyes. "Why?"

"I did some research." He pauses. "Preston Walker."

Shit. He found the report. Is he planning to keep us here until he can turn us in? That reward money could make the most loyal of friends turn on each other.

My eyes dart to the bathroom door. The water's still running. I might have to drag Rosalie out of here half-naked to make a quick exit.

Standing up, my muscles are tense as I wonder if I walked us into a bad situation. And if I'm going to have to fight my way out.

Jay and I are basically matched in height, but he's bulkier than I am in the shoulders, so I'm guessing he's got better upper body strength. Plus, the dude was in prison for almost two years. You have to be scrappy to survive in there. But then I've got military combat training.

If I had to take him on, I think I could win.

Jay's face darkens when he notices my fists at my sides. "Calm down, man. I'm not the bad guy."

"Why'd you change your mind, then?"

He smirks. "Because Casey won't let me run our guests off, even if they mean trouble."

"I don't want trouble for you—"

Holding up a hand, he cuts me off. "I know. And I'm not gonna say anything, okay? You guys are safe here. I promise."

"Why? Why wouldn't you—?"

"Because I wouldn't trade a friend for cash," he replies seriously. "You saved my ass, Ethan. You made it possible for me to provide for my family. Plus, there's something really off about her mom." He tips his head toward the bathroom. "Like there's some weird shit going on there."

This is why I chose Jay to take over my business for me—he has a special way of reading people and evaluating situations for what they really are. As far as I know, he's never had his IQ tested, but I'd be willing to bet it's way above average. The fact that he had a shitty childhood derailed his potential in school, but his life is back on track, thanks to me.

I feel like an asshole for assuming he'd throw us under the bus, but I'm just not used to relying on other people.

I sigh, relief flowing through me as I let my guard down. "Has the news made it to Illinois, then?"

"Nah, no trace of your story here yet. I ran your old driver's license photo through facial recognition software. It led me to the report in Michigan. Also, it's the weirdest thing." His face screws up. "I can't find much on Rosalie Pearson. I mean, she doesn't even have school records. It's like she's been wiped from the system."

That's because she was never in the system in the first place, but Jay doesn't need to know that.

I should've known he'd do some digging. With my old laptop and all the tech programs on there, he can probably find just about anyone.

"One night," I tell him. "That's all we need."

"All right, well, here are the conditions. No weapons in the house." Jay lifts a finger, ticking off the rules. "No drugs. Put your vehicle in the garage so no one sees it. And after you leave, you were never here."

Grateful, I nod.

Now that I'm not in fight mode, exhaustion hits me with alarming force all over again.

I need to sleep. I've gone longer periods of time awake before, but I'd prefer to be at my sharpest while Rosalie and I are on the road.

Jay claps my back as he passes me to go to the bedroom. "You guys can have our bed, and Casey and I will camp out on the air mattress in Gus's room tonight. I'll get the sheets changed."

Craning my neck, I watch him go through the doorway to a somewhat small room with a giant bed. With the nightstand and the dresser, there's barely any floor space, which means Rosalie and I will probably have to sleep side by side tonight.

Next to each other.

In the same bed.

Fuck.

I'd known our sleeping arrangements were going to get cramped at some point, but that was before we kissed. Before I realized our sexual attraction is off the charts.

I'm not sure Rosalie will be able to keep her hands to herself.

I don't think I want her to.

CHAPTER 14

Rosalie

I barely recognize myself. All I did was go from a blonde to a brunette, but I can't get over how different I look. I'm in a dark-blue T-shirt and plaid pajama pants Casey let me borrow, and the reflection in the mirror isn't me.

This is some other girl. A girl with baggy, casual clothes and a ponytail. A girl who looks like she could be in college.

I like her and all the possibilities at her feet. What lies ahead in the future is a mystery, but anything could happen.

Since Jay cracked our cover, the preggo suit isn't needed while I'm in the house. It's kind of nice not carrying all that weight around. It's also nice that I don't have to lie about who I am.

Dinner with the family went much better than my ravenous face-stuffing earlier with the diner food. While we ate pizza, there was a lightness to our conversations. Jay and Preston swapped investigator stories, and Casey and I discussed hair and makeup. Gus was good for entertainment, always demanding attention in gibberish. The kid really knows how to own a room.

I'm still wearing the wedding ring. Even though that part of our story is blown, I guess I just like the way it feels on my finger. Tilting my head, I hold my left hand up to my chest next to the lighthouse necklace and watch the way the jewelry sparkles as if they're a set.

A knock comes at the door. "You decent?"

"Yeah," I answer, and Preston's in the room a second later.

He shuts us both in, and the space suddenly feels even smaller with him in here.

Fulfilling my bedtime request, he extends a glass my way. "Your water."

I take it from him and set it next to my fanny pack on the dresser, then I dig out my baggie of meds. I go for one of the few full pills I keep for special occasions. After the day I had, I need it.

I have the tablet halfway to my mouth when Preston stops me.

"Whoa." He puts his hand over mine. "What's that?"

Before I have a chance to explain, he's plucking the pill from my fingers and snatching the plastic baggie.

"My medicine." I make a swipe for it, but he spins out of reach.

Inspecting it like the detective he is, he asks, "What is it?"

"Anti-anxiety pills, if you must know." Geez, he's nosy.

"What's the name of the medication?" He puts the pill close to his eye, then licks it.

"Give it back." Impatient, I make a grabby motion. "I don't care if you got your spit on it. I'm still taking it. I have to. I can't sleep without it."

"You don't know what this is." Preston pins me with a stare. It's not a question. Rather, a conclusion.

I let out an exasperated noise. "No. My mom probably told me at one point, but I don't remember what it's called. I mean, how many different anti-anxiety drugs can there be out there?"

As soon as I see Preston's sympathetic face, I realize the answer is a lot.

There are certain things I've blindly trusted my mother with. My mental health was always one of them.

From the skeptical look Preston's giving me, I gather he thinks that was a mistake.

Suddenly, he tosses the pill into his mouth and swallows.

"What are you doing?" I ask, alarmed as I try to get the bag from him again. And fail again.

"We'll find out what it is in a few minutes. If it's an SSRI for depression, I probably won't feel anything immediately. If it's a benzodiazepine, I'll get calm and sleepy."

Anger flares inside me. "You're being very intrusive right now. You're crossing a line, Preston. Why are you doing this? What does it matter what kind of drug it is as long as it works?"

Instead of answering me, he goes back to studying the contents of the bag. "How long have you been taking this?"

"Since I went to the hospital six months ago. After I got home, Dr. Rutherford came to the house and gave me my own prescription. Can I have it back now?"

"No." Preston shoves the baggie deep into his jeans pocket where I know I can't get it unless I knock him out or something.

Which doesn't sound like a terrible idea at the moment.

"Just give it back," I say, low and serious.

"Afraid I can't do that, baby. Not until I know they're not harmful."

I laugh—cackle, actually—and I'm aware I sound slightly insane. "You can't take away a crazy person's medicine. Even if I wanted to get off it—which I don't—I'd have to wean myself. I've tried to go a couple days without it before, and it wasn't fun."

"What did it feel like when you quit cold-turkey?"

Shrugging, I sit on the side of the bed. "I was achy. Tired. Just kind of sick feeling."

"When was the last time you had a dose?"

"Last night before I left my house."

Preston brings the bag back out, and for a second, I think he's going to relent and hand it over. But he doesn't. Instead, he takes one of the whole tablets and pinches it between his thumb and forefinger.

He holds it in front of my face. "What do you see?"

"A white pill?"

"Anything else?"

"Is this a trick question?"

"True prescription pills have markings," he tells me. "Little indents to help identify them. Sometimes numbers or lines. This has none."

"So?"

"So, whatever you think this is, it isn't. It's not from a real pharmacy."

"My mom takes them, too, so they can't be bad," I argue. "She's a total health nut, always making us eat the same boring foods. I mean, she drinks a lot of alcohol, but I've never seen her smoke a cigarette. And—and Dr. Rutherford has come to the house to see me for other things before, like when I had a bad chest cold. He gave me antibiotics…"

My voice fades away as my defense weakens.

Being away from my home, even for a day, has allowed me some perspective. I've met people. People with alert faces and clear speech.

Mom almost always has glassy eyes, a slur to her words, and a wobble in her step. I'm used to seeing her that way. It's just how she is.

But what if it isn't?

What if she's intoxicated? What if her medicine isn't medicine at all?

"Is Dr. Rutherford even a real doctor?" I whisper, more to myself than to Preston.

He answers me anyway. "I highly doubt it." Sitting next to me, he takes my hand in his. "When you accidentally OD'd, do you remember if Loralee's bottle had a label on it?"

"I didn't," I confirm. "That's one of the reasons I got myself into trouble. I didn't know how many to take, but I've seen her pop four or five at a time like it's no big deal."

"That's because she built up a tolerance." Slowly blinking, Preston shakes his head a little as his eyebrows go up. "There it is."

His face relaxes as the drug takes effect. He closes his eyes as his shoulders slump. And I'm jealous because I know he's feeling the bliss I get every time I take a dose.

With my fists tightly balled, I watch his serene expression turn to worry.

And then I start to worry. "What?"

His slightly glazed eyes go to mine. "It's an opioid. I'm almost positive."

"As in, the opioid crisis I watched a documentary about?" I ask, and he nods. "How could you even know that?"

"Because I've done enough drugs to know what a painkiller feels like. This is some potent shit. You take a full one of these?"

"Not all the time." Crossing my arms, I explain that I used to, but I started cutting my dose in half and saving the rest for my getaway.

"Good girl," Preston praises. "That's good. Without meaning to, you've already been weaning yourself off."

"But I don't want to stop taking them." I sound pathetic and whiny, but I feel lost when I think about not having my pills anymore. They've become something I look forward to, something I depend on.

It's ridiculous, but they're the closest thing I have to a friend. Besides Preston, of course.

Draping an arm over my shoulders, Preston's voice is soothingly soft when he says, "You have no idea how dangerous these are. Not only are they highly addictive, these counterfeit pills can be laced with other drugs. Deadly drugs."

"Why would my mom put me in danger like that? She loves me."

"My best guess? Addiction is a common way a captor holds onto their captive. When she realized her hold on you was slipping, she made you physically dependent on her."

Mentally, I feel like someone just whacked me in the head with a baseball bat to knock some sense into me. Because my mom's batshit, but I've never even suspected she'd do what he's suggesting. But would I put it past her? No.

I look at the pills. The pills I thought were helping me. The pills I thought were a necessity to fix my mental illness.

Lies upon lies upon lies. My mother lied about my age. She straight up lied about me to the public. She lied to me about my medicine. What else has she been dishonest about?

"So, this whole time," I start, swallowing hard, "I wasn't being treated for anxiety?"

"No."

"Do I even need to be?" I glance at Preston. "Am I really sick? A crazy person doesn't know they're crazy, right? So maybe I'm not able to be objective about it."

Preston rubs my back with gentle circles. "Rosalie, I've met a lot of people in my life. I've known some who were suffering, medicated and unmedicated. It doesn't make me a professional, but personal opinion? No. Your mind is fine. Your ways of thinking are rational. Your anger is warranted. I do think you're dealing with some trauma, but anyone in your position would be."

Validation. Preston's giving me permission to be who I am, to feel the way I feel.

For the first time in my life, someone's telling me I'm normal.

Unfortunately, my relief is overshadowed by shock and disappointment.

Betrayal.

I've always believed my mom would do what was best for me. That's what moms do. But she put my health at risk for her own selfish reasons.

"Be right back." Preston places a kiss on the top of my head before getting up.

"Where are you going?"

"We can't keep these around." He shakes the baggie. At my questioning expression, he elaborates, "I'm going to flush them down the toilet."

As he leaves the room, I have to force myself not to run after him and beg him not to do it. He's right to get rid of them. In that documentary I watched, I remember judging those addicts. I had thought to myself, *why can't they just stop?*

Because they're one hell of a Band-Aid. That's why. At times, those drugs made my bleak life euphoric. They kept the nightmares at bay. They made everything okay.

By the time Preston comes back, I'm just sitting on the side of the bed, completely despondent.

"What am I going to do now?" I ask after the quiet click of the door latch.

Preston comes over, and the mattress dips when he sits next to me. "Well, I'm going to be honest—you're not going to feel great over the next several days. You'll go through withdrawals. You might experience headaches, muscle aches, and nausea. The good news is, you weren't on the drugs for that long, and you already started cutting down your dose, so maybe it won't be so bad."

"Easy for you to say."

"Once we get settled somewhere, we'll get you a doctor. A real one. And if they think you need to be on something, they'll prescribe it." He sounds so optimistic, but I don't share his attitude.

Because who knows when that will be? In the meantime,

I'm going to have to go back to feeling like I did before. Trapped inside myself.

Although I guess that isn't true anymore. I'm free.

I have so much to be excited about. Reasons to be happy.

Glancing down at the ring on my finger, I get an idea.

"In exchange for my compliance," I begin, sending a sly glance at Preston, "I want something from you in return."

He tucks some hair behind my ear. "Anything."

"Help me cross off the stuff on my list."

"Which ones?"

"All of them." Staring down at my hand, I spin the ring around and around.

Silence stretches between us, and my heart's pounding so loud I swear Preston can hear it. Finally, he asks, "You'd marry me?"

I can't look at him. "Well, as far as proposals go, that one really sucks, but yeah. I'll take it."

Notching his finger under my chin, he forces me to look at him. There's at least a foot of distance between my mouth and his, but I swear my lips react to the thought of kissing him again.

If I'm being honest, other places on my body are affected, too.

Tingly and hot.

Preston does this to me. He always has, ever since the first time I saw him chopping wood, and now that I know him, my infatuation has multiplied.

"Rosalie, this isn't a game," Preston says, more serious than I've ever heard him before. "If you promise to be my wife forever, I'm going to hold you to it."

"Good, I wouldn't expect anything else," I quip. Preston still looks apprehensive instead of overjoyed, and I start to get self-conscious. "That is, unless you don't want to be with me. I mean, if you don't want to be stuck with me, I'd understand."

"Baby, if you knew how I really feel about you… how obsessed I am… you might not be asking me to do this. You might be running for the hills."

My heart leaps with happiness and aches with compassion at the same time.

Preston still thinks he isn't good enough. Deep down, he's still that little boy who got rejected over and over again.

Well, he's more than my best friend. More than my obsession. More than my hero.

He's everything.

And it's time he knows it.

"Rosie, there's so much for you to experience," Preston goes on. "There are literally billions of people out there to meet—"

I cover his mouth with my fingers to shut him up. "I could meet everyone in the world, and I'd still want you. Do you hear me? You're the only one I want."

CHAPTER 15

Preston

One thing I love about Rosalie—yes, *love*—is her honesty. I know when she's telling the truth, and she's being so real and vulnerable right now.

In the past several seconds, she's granted me my greatest wish.

To be chosen.

She's choosing me over everyone and anyone.

I'm her number one.

And she's mine. She's my one.

Slipping her hand away from my mouth, she leans forward and replaces her fingers with her lips.

My body immediately reacts. As our kiss seals the deal, my cock becomes a steel rod in my black sweatpants.

Rosalie licks at my bottom lip before nibbling on it with her teeth, and I grip the back of her neck to hold her head in place while I fuck her mouth with my tongue.

In the span of the few kisses we've shared, she's become good at this. She uses her whole body while letting me lead.

Arched back. Her nipples rub against me.

Pliant limbs. She's submissive.

Wandering hands. Her delicate fingers trail over my abs.

She's so eager to feel all of me.

And as much as I hate to stop kissing her, I don't want to push for too much too soon.

"Rosie." My breathing is ragged as I rest my forehead on hers. "Baby. We gotta slow down."

"Why?" Her desperate kisses start up again on my chin and my jaw.

When her lips make it to my neck, I groan.

"Because I want to fuck you," I say honestly. "I want to fuck you until we both come, and then I want to fuck you again. And even when you're sweaty and tired, I'm going to keep fucking you, and I won't stop until neither of us can move."

A tremor racks her body, and when she sways back to look at me, I don't see fear in her hooded eyes. I see dilated pupils and excitement.

Shit. That warning was supposed to scare her, not turn her on.

She smirks, making her look devious and innocent at the same time. "I like it when you say fuck."

Her tentative hand lightly grazes my chest to my stomach. When she continues her descent, I realize her intention and catch her wrist before she can grab my cock.

"Not tonight."

"Why not? Please, Preston." She pouts the sexiest pout.

I want her so fucking bad.

Ten years ago, if someone had told me I'd refuse sex with a gorgeous girl who was literally begging me for it, I would've laughed.

I'm not laughing now. "We need to be married first."

Rosalie's eyebrows draw together. "Is this a religious thing? I guess we've never talked about that."

"I do believe in a higher power, but it's not about that. We've been in each other's company for less than twenty-four hours."

"But I've known you for a lot longer," she argues, and damn it, she's got a point.

I shake my head. "I want to do this right. Everyone's definition of 'right' is different, and that's okay. But when it comes to you and me…" Cupping her jaw, I bring her face close to mine. "I want the dream. The white picket fence, kids, and a dog. Anniversaries we'll get to celebrate with our great grandchildren at our feet."

"You want to be basic bitches together?" Her smile spreads.

I chuckle. "Damn straight."

She bites her lip. "Okay, then I respect your wish to wait, but in the meantime, could you leave the room for a while?"

"Why?"

Clearing her throat, she averts her eyes to the floor as her cheeks go red. "Because."

"Because why?"

Flustered, she toys with her brown ponytail. The strands are shiny, and the darker color makes her eyes stand out more.

For a brief second, I picture her on top of me naked. I imagine what it would be like to skim my fingers up the smooth skin of her back and let them get tangled in her hair while she rocks over me.

My dick hardens more—if that's even possible—and I resist the urge to squeeze it and get some relief.

"Because if you're not going to touch me, I'll have to do it myself. There's no way I can sleep with my body this worked up. And you took my medicine away, so…" Rosalie shrugs.

Manipulative little thing.

Though, I know there's truth to her claim. She's going to have a hard enough time tonight if she starts withdrawals. Sometimes a good orgasm can help.

Gently, I push her shoulders until she's reclined on the bed.

She goes willingly, lying back on the pillows, her back melding with the mattress.

My fingers go to the bottom of her T-shirt. "If you think for one second I'm going to stand around out in the hallway while you get yourself off, you're mistaken."

"But you said—"

"I said we couldn't have sex. I didn't say anything about messing around."

Pushing up her shirt, I bare her breasts. I've seen them from a distance before, but fuck, they're even better up close. My mouth waters when I think about sucking those rosy nipples into my mouth. Scraping over them with my teeth.

When I drag my thumbs over the tight buds at the same time, Rosalie's back bows and she moans. Her breathing has picked up, and I can see her quick pulse jumping on the side of her neck.

That's the thing about being as pale and thin as she is. Her skin is almost see-through.

I want to lick her veins. Bite her throat. Kiss each rib.

When I curl my fingers into the waistband of her pants, Rosalie starts to push her shirt down.

"Leave it." The command comes out a little harsher than I meant it to, but my cock and my self-control are at war.

My mind feels foggy, and I'm having trouble remembering why we shouldn't fuck. Part of that could be the painkiller I took. Now that I've had time to fully absorb it, I don't think the dose is high enough to fuck me up, but I do feel a bit loopy.

Tugging Rosalie's pants and panties down to her knees, I make a guttural sound when I see the patch of blond hair between her thighs.

She covers herself.

I bat her hands away. "I've already seen you naked."

She gasps a little. "I knew you watched me in my room."

"And I know you were thinking of me when you stripped down." I circle her navel. "When you flaunted these perky tits in the window, did you imagine my hands on you?"

"Always."

Her cheeks grow pink again, and I have a weird moment where it almost feels like this isn't real. Like I'm watching someone else get everything I desire.

The vision before me is almost obscene, the way Rosalie's still got clothes on, but her intimate places are bared to me.

I pull her pants all the way off so I have access to her pussy, but I leave the shirt on. If she's completely nude, I'm not sure I'll be able to refuse her again if she asks for sex.

At least I'm still covered, but my tank top suddenly feels too constricting.

"Ready, baby?"

Rosalie nods quickly.

Placing one hand on her ribs, I brush the underside of her breast with my thumb while I trail the other hand up her inner thigh.

When I make it to her pussy, my finger slides right through her slit, and she moans again.

She's so hot and wet down there, and my lungs feel like they're trapped in cages. No matter how much I breathe, I can't seem to get enough air.

"Spread your legs," I tell her. My voice doesn't even sound like my own. It's rougher. Gravelly.

Rosalie does what I want, raising her knees up and planting her feet wide on the mattress. Her pretty little pussy is pink and glistening, and I can't believe it's mine.

More or less, we're engaged. I don't know how we can get married while we're on the run, but I'm determined to make it happen.

We can have it all, Rosalie and me. We've quickly formed

an unconventional relationship, but I'll get it back on track to something normal.

Average basic bitches. That'll be us. We'll be so mundane and happy, it'll make people sick.

Keeping my eyes connected with hers, I twist my hand, and my middle finger finds her entrance. I slide it in.

She tenses up, and her snug walls squeeze me so hard I can't get past the second knuckle. Damn, she's tight.

"Relax, baby." Nestled in her pussy lips, her swollen clit is there. I press my thumb to it.

Her back arches, and she whimpers.

Shushing her, I scoot up on the bed to lie down while keeping my finger lodged inside her. I kiss her hard, then I rise up enough to gaze down at her beautiful face. "Do you think you can be quiet?"

"I don't know," she whispers, her breathing choppy. She's already flushed, sweaty, and shaking. "I've never felt like this before."

She's not the only one.

She makes me feel like a goddamn sixteen-year-old. I could nut in my pants right now.

I begin to pump in and out of her while drawing circles on her clit.

"You're gonna come soon," I tell her, shifting down a little so my face is right by her breast. "Just breathe through it and grab onto me if you have to."

"'Kay." She grasps the back of my tank top with one hand and grips the forearm I've got between her thighs with the other.

She closes her eyes and starts to move with my hand, undulating her hips.

While she loses herself in the moment, rocking, digging her nails into my arm, and biting her lower lip, I just try to concentrate on not blowing my load.

Every time Rosalie writhes, her hip nudges my cock, sending jolts of pleasure through my body. Her tits thrust up into the air, begging to be sucked.

Speeding up the motions with my hand, I take her nipple into my mouth. Hard. I lave it with my tongue. Flick it.

Her pussy gets wetter.

I can actually hear the squelching sounds.

"Preston," Rosalie hisses out, punching the mattress a couple times before grasping the pillow under her head. "I'm—I'm—Ohh."

Her inner walls clamp around my finger, and she presses her lips together to keep her scream inside. It resounds in her throat, and her entire body bucks as she rides the orgasm.

It's possible Jay and his family will hear us.

Right now, I don't really give a fuck.

To prolong Rosalie's pleasure, I keep massaging her clit until the spasms inside her stop.

After it's over, I slip my finger out of her and rub around the area. An exploratory action, meant more for me than for her.

I want to memorize every inch of her pussy.

When she jolts from oversensitivity, I finally pull away.

Needing to know what she tastes like, I bring my hand up to my mouth and lick my fingers. Slightly tangy and sweet.

Fucking perfect.

Rosalie's breath hitches, and I realize she's watching me. I don't stop what I'm doing, though. Not wanting to miss a drop, I keep sucking her off me.

Her expression is nothing short of scandalized, and it's so adorable I can't help laughing.

"I didn't know I could be so… messy." Her face is red again, and I kiss her burning cheeks, one right after the other.

Whipping my tank top over my head, I sit up and use it

to clean Rosalie. She watches me as I wipe between her legs. Staying completely still and open, she lets me take care of her.

I'm proud of myself. It's the kind of pride you get when you do something selfless.

No, it's not just about the orgasm. It's about giving my woman what she needs.

Her legs are like jelly as she lets me put her pants back on. I gently put her shirt back in place before getting up to turn off the light.

As the room is cloaked in darkness, a streetlamp outside the window provides an orange glow.

"I've never seen you with your shirt off before." Rosalie's eyes ping from my shoulders to my chest to my abs. Then her gaze lowers to where I'm tenting my pants.

I smirk. "Like what you see?"

Nodding, she confirms, "Very much."

When I get back to the bed, I nudge her over so I'm on the side of the bed facing the door. If any danger comes, I'll be blocking her. Hooking my arm around her waist, I curl my body around hers.

"Goodnight, Rosie Doll," I tell her, but it's not what I really want to say.

Because the words bouncing around in my head are clearly *I love you.*

CHAPTER 16

Rosalie

As Preston lies behind me, I can feel the fast beating of his heart. And the erection poking my butt.

"What about you?" I ask, still buzzing all over. "I didn't get to touch you."

He chuckles. "So impatient. You don't have to do everything right away. We have time."

I wiggle until I'm facing him. "But I want to do it right now."

"Aren't you tired?"

"Not yet."

"Well." He flops onto his back. "I'm not going to stop you if you want to touch my dick, baby."

For some reason, I almost expected him to say no. He's being so careful with me. It's annoying. I've always been treated as if I'm about to break, and I'm done with that shit.

But.

I can admit to myself that I have no idea what to do with a man's cock. Aside from the flaccid dick pic I got in that message last night, I've never seen one. At home, I was too paranoid to look up porn on my computer.

"Can you… show me what to do?" I ask shyly.

"Yeah," Preston responds huskily, pushing his sweatpants down to mid-thigh.

His erection is a massive shadow against his lower stomach.

It's almost comically large. Of course, I know better than to laugh at a time like this, but I feel giddy, almost like I'm riding the high my medicine gives me.

Covering my twitching lips, I just stare, studying Preston's length. As my eyes go lower, I realize the rounded shape at the bottom of his cock is his ball sac.

"The first thing you'll want to do," Preston drawls, startling me from my ogling, "is touch it. There isn't really much you can do wrong. It's all about friction and pressure. Lots of rubbing."

I reach out. Slowly.

Starting with the tip, I pet his silky skin with my fingertips. His dick immediately reacts, jerking under my hand.

When I wrap my fingers around it, I realize I can feel his pulse here, and I wonder if he aches the way I did before I got off. I want him to come, but not yet.

I'm not done playing.

Staying silent, Preston lets me explore.

Carefully and softly, I become familiar with the texture and shape of his cock. I didn't realize it would be so warm and smooth, and I'm fascinated by the veins under his delicate skin.

I trace the round head. I caress the slit at the top. I travel down to his balls.

Cupping him there, I notice how the skin texture changes.

Preston groans, and his ab muscles clench.

I remove my hand. "Did I hurt you?"

"Just the opposite."

He likes what I'm doing? "But I haven't done much."

"I know." He grunts out a laugh. "It won't take long. I'm pretty wound up from finger fucking you."

Flames lick up my face again, and I'm glad it's probably too dark for him to see it. I've never blushed this much, but I can't help it when he talks about sex so bluntly like that. Like it's fun and dirty. And something I definitely want to do.

Grabbing my hand, Preston fists my fingers around his cock. "Like this."

His grip covers mine as he starts moving up and down, and I like the way the satiny skin covering his shaft is loose enough to glide over the hardness underneath.

Preston guides me from the base to the tip a few more times, then he lets go. I keep pumping up and down, and the guttural sounds coming from his throat are the encouragement I need to know I'm doing it right.

"Tighter," he rasps, and I do what he asks. He nods. "Good, baby. That's real good. Now faster."

As I follow his instructions, his entire body tenses and his breathing becomes erratic. He reaches down to his balls. "Touch me here, too. Tug a little, like this."

My hand replaces his, and I notice the sac has gotten firmer. Tighter. My motions falter a little because I'm trying to do two things at once, but I quickly find a good rhythm again.

Just a second later, Preston's hips thrust up, and a stream of something thick shoots from his cock. It spurts a few times, making a mess of his chest and stomach.

I keep pumping until only a couple drips are coming out.

Realizing I did it—I actually got him off—I slow to a stop and look at Preston's face. He's gazing back at me with awe, his lips parted as he catches his breath.

Sending me a heart-melting smirk, he rakes a hand through his hair. "You have no idea how much I needed that."

I smile. That was fun, and I already want to do it again. Remembering how he tasted me, I wonder what he tastes like, too. Before I can think too much about what I'm doing, I lean forward and lick his tip.

He's salty and a little sweet.

Opening my mouth, I engulf the head and suck on it like a lollypop.

"Oh, fuck." Preston thrusts as he comes a little more on my tongue.

He grabs the base of my ponytail, like he doesn't know if he should push me down or pull me off. After a couple seconds, he goes with the latter.

Tenderly stroking a finger down my cheek, he lightly pinches my chin. "You're perfect, you know that?"

His praise, combined with the way he looks at me like I'm important, affects me in a physical way. My heart thumps and my stomach drops.

Is this what love feels like?

I have no life experiences to compare it to, but I think so.

After Preston retrieves the shirt he used to clean me up, he does the same to himself. Once he's wiped his torso off, he pulls his pants back in place and opens his arms to invite me in.

I snuggle against his side, resting my head between his shoulder muscles and his pec, and he brings the covers up over us.

I'm experiencing a lot of firsts tonight. Including cuddling. This is the first time I've ever been held by a man in bed. It's incredibly relaxing to feel his warmth and smell his manly scent.

While Preston idly strokes my hair, my eyes get heavy. Usually, sleep doesn't come easily unless I'm drugged up. But right now, I can't stop myself from drifting off.

I'm so cold. I can't breathe, and I have no control over my body. A force is pushing me one way and pulling me another. My arms are flailing helplessly, and no matter how much I kick, I can't find anything solid to put my feet on. There's no difference between up and down. I'm tumbling through an endless abyss.

I try to scream, but water rushes into my mouth. It's filling my nose, burning my throat.

It hurts.

I'm dying.

Help!

"Rosalie!"

I wake with a start, and I realize my lungs aren't full of water. In fact, my breathing is fast, and the reason I'm cold is because I'm covered in sweat.

Preston's hovering over me, looking more than concerned as he grips my shoulders. "Baby."

"Yeah?"

"You good?" he asks.

Reluctantly, I nod. "What was I doing?"

"Jerking all over the place. I was afraid you were having a seizure. I couldn't wake you up."

I've never seen Preston scared before, but he is now. His eyes are wild, his breathing is quick, and he's trembling as he helps me sit up.

"Sorry," I sigh. "This happens a lot."

He hands me the glass of water from the nightstand, and I take a small sip, but just the sensation of water running down my throat makes me panic. I end up swallowing too fast and coughing.

"It's okay." Preston pats my back. "You're okay. Want to talk about it?"

"It's always the same." Shrugging, I explain my recurring nightmare to him. "After I wake up, I realize it's a dream, but in the beginning, it's so real and I'm confused about what's happening. This is why I need those pills. You shouldn't have thrown them away. I might be like this every night. You'll never get good sleep again if you're in bed with me."

"I don't care about that," he grunts. "Just care about you. I want you to be okay. Sometimes drugs can mask an underlying issue, but they don't fix it."

My eyebrows draw together. "What underlying issue? Have you finally realized I'm crazy?"

"Not at all." As Preston lies back down, he pulls me with him. "Think you can go back to sleep?"

"I can try. But first, tell me something real."

Preston gives me a squeeze. "No matter what you dream, I'll be here when you wake up."

The reassurance is enough to calm me.

Even though it takes me longer to doze off this time, Preston keeps running his hand through my hair. A couple times when I jolt awake, he's still soothing me, just like he promised.

I feel a little bad that he's losing more sleep, but it's just so nice to know he's here for me, I won't tell him to stop.

I hope he never stops.

CHAPTER 17

Preston

Post Traumatic Stress Disorder. It's clear Rosalie has it. Anyone with a military or psychiatric background can recognize it. I suspected it with her reaction to the creek and pretty much any time we talk about water, but now I know for sure. And I'm pissed as hell that Loralee's solution was to get Rosalie addicted to painkillers instead of getting her the help she needs.

But today isn't the day to let that be a shadow over us.

Because today, we're getting married.

Over coffee this morning, I opened up to Jay. Told him I wasn't sure how Rosalie and I could be married for real while we're in hiding.

And what did that crazy bastard do? He got on his laptop and got ordained.

And that's how an impromptu backyard ceremony got set in motion. Both neighbors on either side of Jay's house have privacy fences up, so we don't have to be worried about being seen, and it feels like we're in our own perfect world.

I'm in my suit, standing in the late morning chilly air of November next to a meadow. All the flowers have dried up and died for the season, but it's still a beautiful backdrop.

Rosalie's inside borrowing a dress from Casey. Gus will be the ring bearer, and I'm vaguely aware of Jay repeating the instructions carefully to his son. The little boy is in his outfit of choice—a pink princess dress. Every time Jay tells him he'll have to give up the wedding rings, Gus balls his little fists around his new temporary possessions.

"My rings."

Jay shakes his head. "Sorry, dude. You can hang onto them for now, but you'll have to give them back soon."

"No." Gus starts to cry, and I have a feeling he might put up a fight when the time comes.

Okay, so this isn't the wedding most people dream about. I'm a little insecure about that, and I tell myself that's why I'm so nervous.

It's better than worrying Rosalie will come to her senses and change her mind about marrying me.

I won't blame her if she does.

She's impulsive as fuck and so eager to experience everything life has to offer. Ever since she climbed out of that window, we've been in a whirlwind of recklessness.

We're living a reality I never saw coming. It doesn't matter how much planning I did to ensure our getaway—I couldn't have anticipated this. Yeah, I hoped Rosalie would return my affections. That eventually, she'd fall for me like I've fallen for her.

I just didn't think she'd do it so whole-heartedly. Or so fast.

Too good to be true. That's what people say about times like these, and I can't help wondering if I'm taking advantage of her naivety, but then I remember the words she said to me last night.

I could meet everyone in the world, and I'd still want you.

All my concerns scatter when the screen door opens with a whiny creak.

I straighten my spine as Casey comes out first, wearing a slinky purple gown. Rosalie's next in a black dress that fits her body like a glove. It's not the traditional white, but who the hell cares when she looks this good?

Her hair—done by me after breakfast—is in a loose updo. Four braids are woven together in the back, and little yellow flowers are tucked into the twisted strands. A couple tendrils frame her face.

There's a bouquet of yellow mums in her hand, and when she steps down onto the concrete patio, her mismatched eyes meet mine.

She smiles.

It's a confident kind of smile, totally absent of doubt.

I don't know what I did to deserve her, but I grin back, making sure she knows I'm not having second thoughts either.

Unfamiliar possessiveness flares inside me as she walks through the yard, closing the gap between us.

Aside from my cars and my business, I've never had anything that was mine.

Truly mine.

Something constant and stable I could count on.

From this day forward, I'll always have a partner. 'Til death do us part.

When Rosalie gets to me, she passes her bouquet to Casey. A shiver racks her body, and although she looks amazing, it's too cold out here. I slip off my jacket and drape it over her, hoping she'll accept it.

She does, sighing with contentment as she slides her arms in. Then she joins her hands with mine. I squeeze her fingers extra tight, and she winces.

I loosen my hold. "Sorry."

I'm just so damn afraid you're going to disappear.

I don't say it, but she seems to understand. Lacing her fingers with mine, she makes sure we're locked together as Jay unfolds a piece of paper he printed out from the marriage ceremony site.

"I'm happy to be here today with Ethan Smith and Rosalie

Pearson..." he says our names in a hushed whisper before droning on with a formal bit about love and commitment.

I barely listen. I'm too busy studying my soon-to-be wife. I can tell she did her own makeup, because it's layered on a little thick. Shimmery cream eyeshadow coats her lids, and her winged eyeliner is extra dramatic. Her lips are pouty and red from her lipstick, and blush highlights the apples of her cheeks.

She couldn't be more beautiful.

"It's time for your vows," Jay tells us, and my mind blanks.

Fuck.

I didn't write any vows. I figured there were some traditional ones already written out for us.

Thankfully, Rosalie's got it covered, and she whispers, "Just tell me something real."

I grin as the easiest truth comes to me. "I want you to be my wife."

She smiles back at me with wetness shining in her eyes. "And I want you to be my husband."

"Good enough," Jay says, motioning at Gus because it's time for the rings.

An adorable argument ensues between Casey and her son. Whatever toddler gibberish he's spewing, it's clear he does not want to relinquish the jewelry. After Casey whispers a promise to get him his own new rings next time they go to the store, he finally gives them up.

Rosalie watches the exchange like it's the most interesting thing she's ever seen. Her head is tilted and there's a longing in her stare.

I know what's next on her list—children.

It's probably not the smartest idea to put a baby in her just yet, but I have to admit the idea's tempting.

After the rings are back on our fingers, 'I do's' are exchanged. And then it's done.

Jay spreads his arms as if he holds all the power in the universe. "I now pronounce you husband and wife. You may kiss the bride."

I feel like I can finally breathe.

Gripping Rosalie's waist, I pull her close and lower my mouth to hers. She's smiling as she throws her arms around my neck. Her kisses are eager and frantic, coming one after the other. Like she needs to seal the deal a bunch of times to make it real.

Oh, it's real, all right.

Our union might not be recognized in the eyes of the law until we file the necessary paperwork—and that might be a long time from now—but we're lawless anyway at this point.

The sound of clapping breaks the PDA up, and Rosalie giggles as she wipes her lipstick off my mouth.

"Let's go inside," I suggest, still not completely comfortable with how exposed we are out here.

"Good idea," Jay agrees. "Plus, we have a surprise for you two."

Practically vibrating with excitement, Rosalie tugs me toward the house and we all shuffle inside. Casey goes over to the fridge and produces a small, plain, round white cake from a bakery and a bottle of non-alcoholic sparkling grape juice.

"It's not a wedding without cake and a toast." She opens a cabinet and rises on her tiptoes to get four champagne glasses and a sippy cup.

Once the juice is poured and everyone has a glass, Jay lifts his. "To the happy couple."

I watch Rosalie as she takes a sip. It must be the first time she's had this stuff, because her eyes widen when the bubbles hit her tongue. Snuggling up to my side, she downs half her drink in one gulp. Even with her lips occupied, she can't stop smiling.

I've never seen her this happy before. During the time I've

known her, she's been sullen, snarky, and sarcastic. She's been sexy, funny, and inquisitive.

Now she's glowing with elation.

I did this.

I made her happy, and damn if that doesn't make me feel like I'm on top of the world.

"You know, we were thinking," Jay starts, leaning against the sink. "Why don't you stay another night?"

"We don't want you out on the road," Casey adds. With Gus on her hip, she moves around the kitchen, collecting plates, forks, and a knife to cut the cake. "Driving straight through your wedding night sounds pretty miserable."

Considering it, I look to Rosalie. She shrugs, tossing the decision back to me.

Before I accept their invitation, I need to know the latest updates on our situation. Do the authorities have any leads? Did anyone recognize us? Should we stay put or keep moving?

"That's very generous of you," I tell them. "We'll think about it. Jay, would it be all right if I use your laptop for a minute?"

"Sure," he responds, going over to the couch to open the laptop sitting on the coffee table. "After all, it used to be yours."

After typing in his password, he motions for me to have his seat. I nod my thanks and get to work. I check all the local news sites first. Nothing on our story has trickled down to Illinois yet, but it's still hot in Indiana and Michigan.

Next, I check my email. It's mostly junk... except for one from Ivan yesterday afternoon and one from Jen Harding this morning.

Jen's subject is blank. She's emailed me before when she's wanted to consult about cases, but it's not a good sign when your FBI contact reaches out to you while you're a wanted man.

Maybe she just wants to thank me for alerting her to Jimbo6969's perverted ways.

A man can hope.

I decide to check hers first.

Mr. Smith,

I need you to call me right away. The large reward on you and Ms. Pearson made me take notice. And do you know what I noticed? First, you going by a different name. Second, Rosalie Pearson has a striking resemblance to an age progression photo of a missing child case I worked fifteen years ago. I'd like to bring her in for questioning and some tests.

I haven't told anyone I recognized you, because I want to give you a chance to come forward. Let's work something out, and I'll make sure you're both safe. Do you still have my card? If not, my information is at the bottom of this email. Do the right thing, Ethan.

The right thing. So objective. If I turn us in, Rosalie certainly wouldn't see it that way. She wants anonymity, and if we're caught and the world figures out who she is, she certainly wouldn't have that ever again.

Plus, she doesn't even know who she is. When she finds out, it's going to change her. It'll rock her to her core. She deserves to process it quietly and privately. Hopefully in the tropical peace of Costa Rica.

I can admit to myself that I'm selfish, too. I don't want to let her go. We're bound together, her and I. From now until eternity.

But with Jen on our tail, we've got problems. It took Jay less than a couple of hours to figure out our game. Facial recognition software is child's play compared to what the FBI can do, and Jen's like a dog after a bone. Now that she suspects Rosalie is a case that slipped through her fingers, she won't stop.

I guess Jen's not a bad alternative if shit really hits the fan. I do still have her card. If Rosalie and I end up in serious danger, she'll be the one I'll call.

Then there's Ivan. His message was sent right after Loralee had her press conference. That woman. Always fucking shit up.

Ethan, I thought you were smarter than this. I'm going to give you some time to come to your senses. A grace period. If I haven't heard from you by tomorrow, you're going to regret it.

I can practically hear his cold, accented voice delivering the ultimatum. Ivan always follows through with his threats, and I think about his previous detective. Killed execution style. Left in the dirt to get eaten by birds and other wild animals.

"We can't stay," I announce to the room, causing the feminine chatter between Rosalie and Casey to die down. "In fact, we need to go right now."

CHAPTER 18

Rosalie

I sip at the Gatorade Preston's been forcing down my throat. He says staying hydrated is important while I'm detoxing. I actually don't feel all that bad yet, but he wants me to stay ahead of it.

I think he's just focusing on me so he doesn't have to talk about what's really bothering him.

Despite the distance we've put between us and Jay's house, he hasn't gotten less tense. His jaw is clenched, and his knuckles are white from strangling the steering wheel of our newest ride—a dark blue minivan.

Whatever he saw on his laptop, it scared him.

When I've tried asking him about it, he just gives one-word answers or says something about how it's smart to keep moving.

We've been on the road for hours. I fell asleep for part of our trip, and that's a good thing. Because apparently, we went over the Mississippi River when we crossed into Missouri. If I'd been awake, I'm not sure how that would've gone.

Still sleepy, I rub my eyes as I look out at the rocky walls on either side of the highway. It's like we've traveled to an entirely different world of hills and trees. I've never seen such scenery up close.

The radio station we've been on for the past thirty minutes starts to lose reception, and the music goes fuzzy.

I turn the dial until I find something with some upbeat 90's tunes, but I can't drown out the ominous silence with music. I need conversation.

Fed up with the lack of communication between us, I turn the radio down to a soft hum and swivel so I'm facing Preston. "You said you wouldn't lie to me."

His eyes dart to me for a second. "I haven't."

"But you're not telling me the truth either. You're saying nothing, which is worse."

He sends me the side-eye again. "How is saying nothing worse than lying?"

"Because you're basically giving me the silent treatment. You're obviously upset, but you won't say why, and it makes me feel like you're mad at me, or like I've done something wrong. That was a mind game my mother liked to play. Whenever she'd get quiet, I didn't know if her mood was directed at me or if it was just a mood she couldn't control. And she seemed to enjoy riling me up that way, because I'd get desperate to please her, to make things right."

Preston's face softens and he reaches over to take my hand. "I'm not mad at you. Not even a little. I'm just worried, okay? And I haven't told you why because I don't want you to worry, too."

"Well, you might as well just spill it, because if you don't, my imagination is going to make whatever it is way worse than reality."

He sighs. "Back when I had my business, I had an informant-type relationship with an FBI agent. Jen and I did each other favors, all off the books. Sometimes I'd help her with cases if I could find information she needed. In exchange, she'd do the same for me." Preston gives me a look full of concern. "She recognized me from the news. She knows who I really am—my real name, my past."

"Babe, I'm not worried about being recognized, and you shouldn't be either," I say, sounding optimistic. "Our disguises are awesome."

Because seriously, we look totally different from our pictures on the television.

Preston's back to wearing his beanie, his lip ring, and sunglasses. That snake tattoo is still on his neck. My brown hair is in my updo from the wedding, and I've got the pregnancy suit filling me out under a purple tunic Casey let me borrow.

"Plus, we have new IDs," I point out. "You're using a burner phone and a vehicle registered under a name this Jen person doesn't know. As long as we stay away from people, we'll be fine, right?"

Tilting his head from side to side, Preston does a noncommittal nod. "In theory."

"Then stop being so freaked out." I playfully poke his shoulder, making him smile a little.

"At least we're almost to our next location." He sounds a little more relaxed. "I've got a great place for us to hide out in seclusion."

"Really?" I look at the camping gear he's got piled in the back seat. "Does it include sleeping in a tent?"

"Nope. I have a safe house."

"A safe house?" This is news to me.

"Well, it's not actually mine. It's an old hunting cabin that belongs to the Marshalls. Let's just hope they're not there right now." Looking out the windshield at the gray sky, he seems satisfied with the fact that a storm might be headed this way. "Forecast says we'll get snow, and it's a little late in the year for them to be roughing it."

"What would they do if they see you on the news? Would they think you'd go to this cabin? What if they tell someone about it? Would Jen question them?" My rapid-fire questions come out one after the other.

Maybe Preston's anxiety is contagious because I'm starting to understand where his head is at. If I were thinking with a true-crime-documentary state of mind, there are always breadcrumbs if someone looks hard enough.

There's a heavy pause, then Preston says, "No. Since the adoption was never finalized, there's no familial connection on paper. Even if Josiah and Cordelia suspect where I am, they wouldn't tell anyone. They wouldn't betray me like that."

It's the first time Preston's talked about the Marshalls using their first names, and there's a hint of affection in his voice.

"Why didn't the adoption happen?" I ask bluntly, glad for a different topic to talk about.

"After Krystal, I just couldn't..." He trails off, and he doesn't have to finish the explanation. The guilt he still carries says it all.

"Do you see them often?"

He nods. "At Christmas, if I'm in the area. Five summers ago, they had a family reunion at the cabin, and I made an appearance."

"Do they love you?"

He shrugs. "I don't know. After I enlisted in the Marines, I didn't see them much. All my calls and letters went to them, but I guess I haven't given them much of a chance to get close. I'm not easy to love, Rosie."

"Is that a warning?"

"Just a fact. A psychiatrist would probably say I push people away because I'm afraid of being rejected. And they'd probably be right."

"You haven't pushed me away."

"What did I promise you?" Preston's eyes are serious when his gaze locks with mine. "Nothing could keep me from you."

He has a way of calming me. He knows how to make me feel secure. I'm so glad he's mine.

"And you know what? I'll always follow you," I tell him, letting out a dreamy sigh as I rub the back of his hand with my thumb. "That's my promise. Wherever you go, that's where I want to go, too. Like you said, it's just you and me against the world."

"That's right, Rosie Doll."

Satisfied with his answers, I kiss his knuckles and turn the radio back up.

By the time two more songs have played, we're getting off the highway. Only a few minutes pass before we turn onto a country road with a gravel lane surrounded by dense forest on either side.

Miles go by with nothing else but trees in sight. There are no powerlines. No other cars. No signs of civilization.

Preston did say our new location is secluded, but this is something else.

Finally, we take a fork in the road. After a couple minutes, the trees start to thin out.

Then I see it. It's a tiny log cabin with a crooked front porch. Old, rustic, and charming. On the side of the house, there's an overhang with chopped wood piled underneath it. There's a detached shed with faded red paint peeling from the wooden planks that are barely holding onto the structure.

Preston glances over at me and warns, "There's no running water or electricity. We'll be living on the peanut butter sandwiches Casey packed for us and whatever canned food the Marshalls left in the pantry."

"That's fine."

The threat of crappy food does nothing to hinder my good mood. I'm just so excited to be here alone with Preston.

As I step out of the vehicle, I hear nothing but the cold wind.

It makes my cheeks and nose go numb, whipping through my hair and ruffling my updo. Turning in a full circle, I see tall trees surrounding us like we're in our own bubble.

Our world.

Whatever we want.

However we want it.

"It's magical," I whisper.

Preston's smile is relieved as he slides the back door open and hoists up our bags. "Glad you think so. I hope you still feel that way when I'm heating up pots of water for you to wash with."

"As long as you're the one washing me," I tack on not-so-innocently, getting the reaction I'd hoped for.

Preston's cheeks heat, and I can't tell if it's from being turned on or being bashful. There's something sexy about a man who blushes.

I wonder if I can make him do it again before the day is through.

He wasn't so shy last night when he was saying all those dirty things to me, and as we trek to the front door, I think about the fact that it's our wedding night.

I'm going to have sex. With Preston. I'm excited and nervous all at once.

Dropping our luggage on the porch, my new husband goes to one of the lanterns hanging by the door. He detaches the bottom, and inside there's a key.

He holds it up triumphantly. "They haven't changed the hiding spot for the spare."

Once he opens the door, I walk inside. It smells a little musty. There's a fine layer of dust covering the surfaces, but it's not cluttered, and the kitchen area is clean. The sink is just a basin with a drain. No faucet. There's a bed in the corner, covered with a colorful patchwork quilt. Four chairs surround a dining table in the middle of the big room, and there's a loveseat by the front window.

Cozy.

I walk over to a white plastic curtain next to some cabinets. When I pull it back, I see a makeshift toilet and a clawfoot tub behind it.

Immediately, Preston starts loading the wood burning stove with logs, and soon, the chill in the air is being replaced by heat.

"We have board games and cards in there," he says, pointing to a closet before pulling two large buckets from underneath the sink.

I go over to check it out.

It's dark in the small closet, but there's a flashlight on a hook to my right. After I pick it up and click it on, I point it at the top shelf. I'm just tall enough to reach it. Dust rains around me when I bring a few faded boxes down.

Grinning like I won a prize, I set the stack on the table and look over the games we'll get to play. Chutes and Ladders. Crazy Eights.

A puzzle.

"Hey, look." As I lift the box, the 1000 pieces inside clatter as they slide around. "You said you lost your lighthouse puzzle."

"Yeah." Preston smiles fondly. "I told Krystal about that, then she told the Marshalls. They got that for me on my sixteenth birthday."

See? Josiah and Cordelia do love him. He's just never let himself receive that love.

Right now, I make a promise to myself—someday, when we're out of this mess, I'll insist on meeting the Marshalls. And somehow, I'll get Preston to open his heart up to his family.

That's what they are. His family. There's evidence of it everywhere.

In addition to the precious item I'm holding, I see other little touches of Preston around the cabin as I snoop.

A fishing pole with *Ethan* scrawled on the handle is hanging on the back of the closet door. On the same hook, there's a blue ballcap. I pick it up. Flipping it over, I look at the bottom of the brim. *Edmond* was written there at one point, but it's crossed out and *Ethan* is next to it.

"Who's Edmond?" I ask curiously.

Preston glances up from the bucket he's emptying. A sponge, a bar of soap, and some other cleaning products are spread out on the counter. "That's the name the state gave me as a baby. I always hated it."

"Gotcha." Something I admire about Preston is his refusal to accept circumstances as they are. If he doesn't like a situation, he takes control and changes it.

I continue my exploration of the cabin.

There are a couple pictures of Preston on a shelf; one is a portrait of him in his military uniform. The other is a younger version of him proudly holding up a big fish. He's probably sixteen or so, because there's hardly any gray in his hair.

He was handsome even then.

"There's a creek not far from here," Preston tells me when he notices I'm eyeing the picture. "But I'm guessing fishing is out of the question for you."

"Hard pass," I confirm with a nod.

He goes outside with the empty buckets. I watch him from the window as he fills them up at a water pump. His muscles ripple with each movement, and I'm reminded of all the times I spied on him from my room.

Only then, it felt like we were separated by an impenetrable wall.

That's not the case anymore.

Now, he's mine, and I'm his.

After tossing Preston's leather jacket to the loveseat, I pull my shirt over my head and let it drop to the floor. Next, the pregnancy suit goes. By the time I've gotten down to nothing but my panties, Preston's lugging the water back inside.

The air coming through the open door is chilly, and when it caresses my bare breasts, it makes my nipples tighten.

As soon as Preston sees me, the full buckets drop from his hands. They hit the floor with a loud thud, and although they don't tip over, water splashes out, wetting the wooden planks.

"Wha—what—wha—" he stammers as his eyes roam every inch of me, and it's cute that he's speechless.

"I don't want to play board games or cards right now," I intone quietly, shivering when a breeze picks up.

Preston kicks the door shut. He does it so hard, the whole house rattles. "Are you sure about this? I can wait."

"Well, I can't. I won't. Do you want me or not?"

"More than anything."

"Then have me already."

He pulls the fake lip ring off and sets it on the table. With quick fingers, he unbuttons his flannel shirt. After he's bare from the waist up, his hands go to his belt. There's jingling and the sound of leather sliding against leather.

The anticipation is unbearable.

Wiggling my toes against the wood floor, I try to stay in place while Preston undresses.

Once his pants are gone, I see a distinct bulge straining underneath the dark fabric of his black boxer briefs.

Like a predator on the prowl, Preston stalks toward me. I back up. He keeps coming, leading me to where he wants me.

The back of my thighs meet the mattress, but I stand my ground. I want Preston to unleash his self-control. At some point, he's going to have to stop treating me like a delicate little flower.

I'll push him until he can't stand it anymore.

Slow and gentle, he reaches up to my hair. Removing the bobby pins one at a time, he lets my braided hair loose. His fingers shake when he takes out the rubber ties, and a quaking breath leaves his lungs as he finger-combs my wavy hair.

He's still holding back, his spine straight and rigid, his shoulders squared.

I run a fingertip over his length on the outside of his briefs. He's so big, the head of his dick is peeking out of one of the leg holes.

When I graze the slit, it's wet and slippery. I hold my finger up. "What's this?"

"Precum. It happens when men are really aroused."

With a naughty smile on my face, I bring my fingertip to my tongue and taste him.

Preston's eyes flare with heat. Cupping my shoulders, he tries to urge me backward.

I resist.

"Get on the bed," he demands, his voice a low growl.

"Make me," I whisper back.

Before I know what's happening, Preston's arms are scooping me up and setting me down. The springs beneath me squeak when I bounce a little.

His body descends on mine, and he presses a hard kiss to my mouth. The kiss changes when he pushes his tongue past my lips, going from desperate and clumsy to slow and calculated.

Kissing along my jaw, he brings his mouth to a place on my neck that makes tingles spread over my entire body.

Preston's breathing is ragged by my ear when he says, "You've been teasing me for months, baby. You like driving me crazy?"

All I can do is nod and swallow.

My legs fall open, and I gasp when his body fits against mine. I can feel his hardness between my thighs.

I'm pulsing there.

Throbbing.

Needing relief, I start rocking my hips to get some pressure and friction. I make a desperate sound because it feels so good, yet it's not enough.

Braced on his elbows, Preston lifts his head to gaze down at me. There's a war of tenderness and needy lust in his gaze.

And something else.

Love?

I don't have time to analyze it further, because he shoves his boxers down and his cock springs out. It bobs up and down between us, the head purple and swollen.

Again, I'm a bit shocked by how large it is. I've already seen it and held it in my hand, but it looks bigger in daylight. And soon, it's going to be inside me.

"It's gonna hurt," Preston warns me.

I gulp. "Hurt bad?"

"I'll try my best to make it easy on you." After he's as naked as I am, he glances back at his pile of clothes on the floor in the middle of the room. "I need to get something from my pants."

"What?"

"Condom. I got it from Jay."

I shake my head. "I don't want it."

Preston looks at me like I'm a mischievous kid. "You could get pregnant."

"So?" I defiantly lift my chin to hide that fact that I'll be hurt if denies me this. "You don't want a baby with me?"

His expression holds so much affection when he replies, "Of course I do. If I've seemed hesitant about anything with you, it's because I'm looking out for your best interests. I'm older than you. I've got an entire life of mistakes under my belt—mistakes that were learning experiences. You haven't had that, and..." He glances away. "I don't want you to look back on this in a couple years and feel like I was one of your mistakes."

"Preston, Ethan, or whoever you are—I won't ever regret you. I..." My voice dies away as I gather some courage. "I love you."

Blinking, his eyes are full of shock as he stares at me. From the turmoil of confusion and surprise on his face, I'm guessing no one's ever said that to him before.

Suddenly, Preston's kissing me, with the full weight of his body bearing down on me. Yet I don't feel smothered. I feel safe.

"Say it again." His request is rough with emotion as his warm breath caresses my chin.

"I love you." I gently kiss his lips. "I love you. I love you. I lov—"

He cuts me off with another deep kiss.

It's the best kiss we've had yet. Because although he isn't saying the words, there's love entwined with every stroke of his tongue, every nip of his teeth on my lips.

My heart is so full.

Preston's chest brushes against mine while he situates himself between my legs. His smooth, hard cock nudges my clit. Taking his length in hand, he rubs the head up and down. Collecting some wetness at my entrance, he spreads it around. To get me wetter.

Just the thought of him pushing inside me does the trick. I feel a small gush, and I'm sure I'm dripping all over his dick.

"Look at that," Preston groans softly as he gazes down between us. "See how you're wetting my cock? You're ready for me." Positioning himself, he prods my tight hole. "Okay, baby. Just relax."

At first, it's just a stretch. Then there's a sting and a burn as he pushes farther in. I try not to let my discomfort show, but I can't help the whimper that escapes me.

Preston kisses me and whispers, "You're so beautiful. I love how impulsive you are. I love how excited you are about life. I love that you sneeze when you lie. And I love *you*, Rosie. I love you."

His declaration of love distracts me from the pain. I don't even realize he's worked himself all the way in until our pelvises touch.

Buried to the hilt, Preston stays still for a minute, kissing my face and stroking my hair.

Worshiping me.

"You feel so good," he rasps. "Fuck, baby, fuck. I've waited my whole life for you."

Soon, the burn turns into a pleasant heat, and there's an urgency behind the pressure inside me.

I wiggle, needing him to move.

When he withdraws a little and drives back in, I choke out a gasp at the sensation of him hitting some spot deep in my body. A spot I didn't know existed until now. He does it again and again, and the rhythm he sets makes the mattress start squeaking again.

I don't mind it, though.

For some reason, the sound to go along with his motions makes it sexier.

Thrust, thrust, thrust.

Squeak, squeak, squeak.

Nose to nose, we hold eye contact. And as I stare into his baby blues, I know I found my person. Somehow, in the most unlikely of scenarios, I met the one man in this world who understands me and appreciates me for who I am.

An intense euphoria descends on me. It's better than when I'm on my meds, better than any experience I've ever had.

My head is light and my chest is heavy as I look down to where Preston's entering me. Every time he rolls his hips, I get a peek of his cock before it disappears into my body.

"You okay?" Preston grunts out, and I can tell he's restraining himself.

"I want more," I pant.

Smirking, he laces his fingers with mine and pins my hand above my head. "You call the shots."

A bead of sweat rolls down his forehead as he hikes my thigh up a little higher with his other arm.

The action spreads me wider, opens me up for him to go deeper.

And he does.

I realize he was going easy on me before as he begins to pound his cock into me.

Throwing my head back, I let out a surprised moan, and Preston takes the opportunity to kiss my neck. Fusing his lips around my skin, he sucks and sucks. Tingles spread from the spot, sending chills down my arms and making my nipples pucker.

I moan more. Louder. Repeatedly. No one can hear us out here anyway.

The bed is still squeaking away as Preston kisses me everywhere he can. He sucks my lower lip into his mouth. He nips at my chin. He flicks his tongue against mine.

His rocking motions get faster.

Just like last night when we were messing around, a pressure is building inside me. I'm on the cusp of orgasm, but I can't quite get there.

Shifting my hips, I try to move with Preston, and when my clit grazes his pelvic bone, a jolt of pleasure shoots through me. I gasp as my whole body jerks.

Realizing what I need, Preston changes the motion of his thrusts, bearing down on me to make sure he's rubbing me right.

My inner muscles flutter.

I cry out, both from feeling good and being overwhelmed.

"You gonna come, baby?" Preston asks, and just the sound of his husky voice asking me that question pushes me closer to the edge.

I nod, and my lips brush against his.

Letting my thighs fall apart as far as they can, I open myself up as much as possible. Preston continues pumping into me, speeding up as we both chase our climaxes.

Rock, rock, rock.

Squeak, squeak, squeak.

His hand leaves mine to cover my breast. He tweaks and squeezes the mound before circling my nipple with his thumb.

Kissing down my jaw, Preston goes to the same place on my neck as before. He sucks hard, and that's all it takes.

A white-hot explosion happens.

I'm already sore from losing my virginity, and the sensation of my tender insides clenching around his hard cock is painful. It hurts, but it's also extremely satisfying.

I don't even realize I'm screaming until I stop. Breathing hard, I go limp as Preston keeps fucking me. My throat feels raw, and my ears are ringing.

"Should I pull out?" Preston grunts. "Last chance to be responsible about this."

I hook my ankles behind his ass to keep him where he is. "Don't you dare."

Growling, he speeds up. He gives three more thrusts before shoving himself so far inside me I lose my breath for a second.

He groans loudly by my ear, and his cock jerks several times as I'm filled with a wet heat. His cum. It's part of me now. There's something exciting and kind of forbidden about the thought of getting pregnant. It's the most reckless thing I've ever done, but I want it.

Keeping his dick right where it is, Preston doesn't bother to leave my body just yet. With his heavy weight on top of me, he stares down at me with the most loving expression. He strokes my face. Kisses my lips, chin, and nose.

And then he smiles with that adorable little gap front and center.

I think I've found heaven on Earth. Just Preston, me, and this noisy mattress.

Who knew a cabin in the middle of nowhere could feel like home?

CHAPTER 19

Preston

After we finished fucking, I cleaned Rosalie up with my shirt again. At this rate, I'm going to run out of clean clothes, but I don't care. Having Rosalie's virgin blood mixed with my cum smeared all over my T-shirt is the best sight I've ever seen.

Except for Rosalie's face, of course. I don't think she's stopped smiling and laughing for the past two hours. The sun has set, and a few lanterns are lit around the kitchen as a can of soup heats on the wood-burning stove.

While we wait for dinner to be ready, we're hanging out on the bed. Rosalie's sprawled across my lap, and she's doodling a 'tattoo' on my inner ankle with a Sharpie pen. I've got her hair in my hands, weaving a Dutch braid over her scalp.

The battery-operated radio is on the counter, playing the only station it can pick up out here. Cell service is complete shit, too.

We're officially off the grid.

And I'm officially in love. After introducing sex to our dynamic, I'm especially possessive and almost a little paranoid that something's going to come between us.

Maybe we should stay here for a while. How long? I'm not sure. Enough time for our story to get stale. After a couple weeks, people will move on to the next big thing.

"I like the name Preston," Rosalie spouts happily as she continues drawing on my ankle. "Will you have to change it once we get to where we're going?"

"I don't know."

"I hope you keep it. Would it be enough to just change our last name?"

Probably not, but I don't want to shoot her wishes down just yet. "I'll think about it."

"I really don't care if I'm a Rosalie or a Sarah. I could be an Odette. Or a Francine." Snickering, she glances at me over her shoulder. "What do I look like to you?"

Before I can stop myself, I'm whispering, "Melody."

Her smile drops. "What did you say? Melody?"

I shouldn't have done that. If she still has memories from her life before being taken, I could trigger something in her mind. And I'm not ready to get into that shit. Not on her wedding day. A day that shouldn't be shadowed by past tragedies.

Thankfully, I don't have to answer.

Scrunching up her nose, Rosalie shakes her head. "I don't know about that. I'm not musically talented. Luckily, I don't have dreams of being a pop star. Have you ever heard me sing?"

"In fact, I have." I tie off her braid, relieved as hell that we're moving onto talking about something else. "You weren't quiet about it in your house. Sometimes hearing you was the best part of my day."

As she finishes the heart she's drawing, I keep touching her hair. Stroking it. Petting it. Winding the big braid around my hand.

It's not until a tremor runs through Rosalie I stop.

"Shit," she curses. "I messed up."

I look down and see a squiggly line where a straight arrow should be through the heart.

She sits up while rubbing her forehead. There's a sheen of

sweat there, and now that she's not smiling, I'm aware of how haggard she looks. Her face is paler than usual, and there are dark circles under her eyes.

My black T-shirt is oversized on her small frame. It's askew, and one of her shoulders is sticking out of the neckline.

I lay my palm on her neck, then her cheeks, then her forehead. No fever. In fact, she's a little cold and clammy. "How are you feeling?"

She shrugs. "I kind of hurt all over, but that's probably normal after sex, right?"

I press my lips together. "I think the withdrawal symptoms are hitting."

And she hasn't complained once. Hasn't resented me for flushing her drugs down the toilet. Hasn't begged for me to get her more.

Although, we're only a couple days out. The worst is yet to come, so maybe I shouldn't be so optimistic.

Rosalie hiccups, which turns into a burp and a grimace.

I frown. "Are you nauseated?"

"A little. I think I'm just hungry, though."

"Here." Getting up and going over to the tall cabinet that acts as a pantry, I grab a bottle of water for her. "I should be making you drink more. Sip this. Slowly."

After spooning our soup into bowls and opening a sleeve of crackers, we sit down at the table and eat. I scrutinize Rosalie closely, watching for any sign that she won't be able to keep her dinner down.

I know a little something about withdrawals because I've been through it myself. Prescription drugs were my recreation of choice when I was a teenager. Vicodin, Oxy, Adderall. Fucking loved that stuff.

But when Krystal died, I stopped, cold turkey. I remember the body aches, the shakes, and the vomiting. Until I quit,

I hadn't even realized I was addicted. I just thought I was having fun.

"The more I think about it, the better it seems that we stay here for a week or two," I say. "We can just lay low, spend time together."

More like, give Rosalie time to work through her shit. Detox is a bitch.

She perks up. "I'd love that."

"It's not going to make you feel isolated? I'll do my best to keep you entertained."

A smile spreads over her lips. "Oh, I'm sure you and I won't have any trouble staying busy."

By the way she says *staying busy*, it's clear she means fucking.

And fuck if I don't want that. My dick wants it, too. Even though we already went at it once today, I stiffen in my pants.

I discreetly adjust my hardening cock. "Then it's settled. We'll stay."

Digging into the sleeve of crackers, I convince myself it's the right decision. We can explore the woods, play games, talk, and fuck while Rosalie recovers.

No one knows where we are. We have no reason to worry.

I just can't help the nagging feeling that danger is coming.

∼

It's almost bedtime, and the past couple hours have been the most normal hours Rosalie and I have experienced together. After we ate dinner, we started assembling the new puzzle we got at the lighthouse gift shop. So far, we've only completed the edges, but I'm sure we'll be back at it tomorrow.

Now it's time to get clean.

Next to the shower, I get up onto the stepladder and pour some heated water into the two-gallon metal container rigged above the tub. Rosalie's standing below it, naked and shivering.

"Are you sure you don't want to take a bath instead?" I ask. "It'd be warmer."

She shakes her head. "This is fine."

I hope to help her get rid of her fear soon. At least when it comes to a simple bath.

"Okay, so when you want the water to come out, pull this chain," I tell her. "It'll open up the spigot. Only use enough to get wet, then let go so it closes. Lather up and rinse. You'd be surprised how quickly you use the water up, but if you run out, I've got more in the bucket."

As I step down to the floor, I hear the metal squeak as Rosalie tugs on the chain. A sigh of satisfaction follows as the heated water runs over her chilled body. There's a lantern back there with her, and I can see the outline of her silhouette through the thin plastic curtain.

The tips of her breasts as she arches her back. The curve of her ass…

"Preston?"

I adjust my throbbing cock inside my sweatpants. "Yeah?"

"It's not closing."

"Huh?"

"I let the chain go, but it's like the plug is stuck or something."

I quickly pull back the curtain and see what she means. The little latch is rusted. Probably needs to be greased. While I try to push it back to where it belongs, the water flows out, soaking my clothes and emptying what's left of Rosalie's shower.

"Shit." I look at Rosalie, and the fact that she's wet only makes my cock harder. Her nipples are beaded up, and shiny drops trickle down her chest. To her stomach. To the blond patch of hair between her thighs. "I can fix this, but it'll have to be tomorrow when I have daylight to work with."

She blows out a huff. "All right, I'll take a bath."

My eyebrows go up. "Really?"

"As long as you take one with me. Maybe I won't be scared if I'm not alone."

Now there's a point I could never argue. Maybe if I can make her associate water with good things—sexy things—she'll be okay with sitting in a few inches of water.

Covering Rosalie with a towel, I go to heat up some more water. Once I've got enough, I pour it in the tub, strip down, get in, and motion for her to join me. She lowers herself in front of me, her legs trembling.

She whimpers when she's seated, and she's so stiff and tense, curled up into a ball as she hugs her knees to her chest.

"It's okay." I run the bar of soap over her shoulders. "I'm going to pour some water on you now."

"'Kay. But talk to me while you do it," she requests, desperation in her plea. "Tell me something real, babe. Something I don't know about you yet."

"I could tell you about my job, what I did before all this." I take a red pitcher I got from the kitchen and let the water trickle over her shoulders, wetting some of her hair. "It's a tricky business—connecting people who haven't seen each other in decades, people who might've just found out about each other. It's not all sunshine and rainbows. Sometimes it's messy."

"I could see that."

"It wasn't just about making a dollar for me. Before I accepted a case, I'd research my clients first. I'd always made sure they were good people because I didn't want to enable toxic relationships. Remember what Jay told you about how we met? Well, his cellmate wanted to find his son, but I refused to do it until I knew the guy was safe to be around. I needed to know if he was violent or dangerous."

"That's smart. How did it turn out?"

"The guy passed my standards. Jay watched him for a couple

weeks and gave me some good info." Rosalie's hair is completely soaked now, but I pour some more of the water over her to keep her warm.

"According to you, my father's dangerous," she says. "He doesn't fit the safe criteria, but you took the job anyway. Why was Ivan the exception to your rule?"

"*He* wasn't. You were."

"Oh." Rosalie sounds flattered. "Where did you live before?"

My talking has distracted her enough that her body is unfolding. Her arms are loosening up as she relaxes a little. Extending her legs, she pushes her feet against the end of the tub, pressing her ass against my raging hard-on.

I hold in a groan and try to stay focused on our conversation. "I had an apartment in Detroit, but I was rarely home because I used to travel a lot for work. That's why it wasn't too hard to give up my lease when Ivan hired me."

"So when you were pretending to be Jessa, and you said you'd been a lot of places—"

"I wasn't lying," I fill in. "Some cases took me all over the Midwest. Sometimes farther. I really did camp out at the Grand Canyon once. And I saw the red rocks in Colorado. Niagara Falls, too, though I'm pretty sure that would be your nightmare vacation."

Rosalie lets out a nervous chuckle. "You got that right. What's the best case you've solved?"

It's not hard for me to think of the most rewarding case I've had during my career—besides the current one, of course. "A woman came to me because she'd given up four children for adoption."

"Four?"

"Yep. From the age of fourteen to twenty-one, this girl had four kids. I dug a little into her background, and her childhood was bad. I don't want to get into the grisly details, but I'll just say she was abused. She ended up as a sex worker in her later teen years, and she just couldn't raise a baby. There were serious complications with her last delivery, and she ended up needing a hysterectomy. She was devastated that she'd never give birth again. By the time she contacted me, her youngest child was twenty, and she'd straightened out her life. She just wanted to know if her kids were okay and if they had kids of their own. It was difficult, because all of them had closed adoptions to different parents. It took me six months to find them, but I did it. They were reunited, and that woman got the family she longed for. She still reaches out to me every year to say thank you."

Resting her head against my chest, Rosalie turns her face to gaze up at me. "It's really amazing what you do, you know that?"

"I enjoy my job," I say humbly. "Or I did."

"You'll get to do it again someday. You don't have to give up your entire life for me." Reaching up, she lightly touches my face.

It's a loving gesture. One I'm not familiar with. A caress that causes a feeling of fullness in my chest.

How does she know how to love me so well? With the life she's had, the isolation she's suffered... I wouldn't expect her to be so in tune with me. To be able to give me what I need all the time.

But she does.

Maybe Rosalie was born with the ability to love. Maybe I was born with it, too. Maybe everyone is. But while Rosalie was able to let hers build over the years, mine was sucked out of me.

And that might be one of the reasons I'm drawn to her. Her heart calls to mine. Like a lighthouse, her abundance of love overflows and shines out, beaconing me to come take some for myself.

It makes me want to give her everything I have in return, including early retirement. I'd gladly give up the PI business forever for her. We could live off my savings for a while. It wouldn't be a glamorous life, but we'd have enough. We'd have each other.

I can envision our future being just like this. With no place to be. No time constraints. Just unplanned days and endless possibilities.

"Let me wash your hair," I say, and she nods while leaning forward.

As I dump bigger amounts of water over her, I watch for signs of any impending freak outs. She keeps her hand on my thigh. Probably to remind herself that I'm still here with her.

After her hair is drenched, I take some shampoo in my hands and get a good lather going. I work the suds into her ends. I massage her scalp with my fingertips.

Tipping her neck back, she pushes against my hands, silently demanding more.

And I give it to her.

I wash behind her ears. I go down to the nape of her neck. With the suds, my hands glide against her skin as I go lower. I soap up her tits.

By the time I'm done shampooing her, she's thoroughly clean, and we're both panting from being turned on.

The conditioning process is much the same, only adding fuel to the fire between us.

Once Rosalie's all rinsed, she turns and straddles me, her pussy just a couple inches away from my throbbing cock. "Are you always like this?"

"Like what?"

"Horny." She smirks.

"With you around, yeah," I reply honestly, because no one has ever affected me like she does. "You sore, baby?"

She nods as I smooth some wet strands away from her face. "Kinda."

"Then we shouldn't fuck tonight."

She pouts. "But I want to."

"Here." Gripping her hips, I pull her closer until her pussy is flat against the front of my shaft. "Rub on me."

Wiggling, she gets a feel for what I'm telling her to do. The second her clit drags against my cock, her eyes roll back, and she does it again. The movement causes the best friction on my dick. With the way my sensitive skin is smashed between my stomach and her pussy lips, I might be able to get off like this.

Rosalie gets a steady rhythm going, undulating her pelvis while bracing her hand on my shoulder for support. "Feels good."

"Yeah," I whisper roughly.

"You need your hair washed, too," she says, reaching for the pitcher as she keeps humping my cock.

A second later, warm water cascades over my scalp, my shoulders, and down between us. Goose bumps of pleasure break out on my entire body when she begins scrubbing my hair.

Now I know why she reacted the way she did when I was doing this to her.

It feels fucking fantastic.

Getting my scalp massaged by her would be enough by itself, but with the way she's still rubbing her pussy on my cock, I've got two tantalizing sensations happening on different parts of my body at the same time.

Spearing her fingers through my hair, Rosalie grips the back of my head and presses her mouth to mine. It's a hungry kiss. Needy. Passionate.

She's forgotten about the suds on my head. Bouncing on my lap, she makes the water slosh up the sides of the tub. Little whimpers and whines resound in her throat as she keeps kissing me and using my body.

Her breathing gets quicker. She speeds up.

My balls tingle.

I cup her tits, squeezing the handfuls while tweaking her nipples.

Letting out a raspy shout, Rosalie hugs me around the shoulders as her motions become jerky.

Water's splashing all around us now, and the waves finally calm once Rosalie goes limp with satisfaction.

Knowing she came, I want to let my release go. Grabbing her by the hips, I move her up and down a couple more times.

My orgasm hits me fast and strong.

Cum shoots up between us like a fountain, coating Rosalie's chest and mine. I growl as the last jets taper off, breathing like I just ran a marathon.

"Best. Bath. Ever," I pant, resting my chin on Rosalie's wet shoulder.

She hums out an agreement, but the blissful moment doesn't last long.

Her body becomes stiff as she clings to me.

"Don't be scared." I run my fingers through her hair. "I'm here, and the bath is over."

"It's not that. I just... I want this," she says with fervor and a hint of fear. "I've never been afraid of losing someone before. Now that I have you, I don't think I could live without you. I want us to be like this always."

Apparently I haven't done a good job of shielding her from the danger we're facing. Because she feels it. It's looming over both of us now.

"What'd I tell you, Rosie?"

"Nothing could keep you from me?" she whispers by my ear.

"And you'll always follow me." I smile while reminding her of the promises we've made to each other.

I just hope like hell we can keep them.

CHAPTER 20

Rosalie

Preston drives into me from behind, and I brace my hands on the counter as I bite my lip to stifle my moans.

"Don't do that, baby," Preston huffs, out of breath from fucking me. "Don't be quiet."

Sinking his fingers into my hip with one hand, he grabs my braid with the other and tugs my head back as he thrusts. Hard.

I have no choice but to moan. And groan. And whimper because he shows no mercy.

The hand that's on my hip slides around to my front. Since Preston knows my body now, all he has to do is expertly rub my clit a few times before I'm coming on his cock. He pumps through my orgasm, and when my knees get weak, he holds me up while his body goes stiff.

Groaning, he shoves his cock deep as he fills me with his cum. I like it when he does that—roots himself inside me, his ragged breathing hot by my ear.

He stays still for a moment, petting my hair and kissing the back of my neck.

Slowly, he pulls out, and I can feel his warm cum dripping from me. It rolls down my inner thighs, making me all sticky.

Since we're both fully clothed, all I have to do is tug my sweatpants up while Preston tucks himself back into his boxer briefs and zips his jeans.

We hadn't planned on having sex this morning, but a quickie in the kitchen sounded like a good idea, and I wasn't going to turn it down.

Turns out, I love sex. A lot.

Anytime, anywhere.

Honestly, I'm partial to the mattress because of the squeaky sounds. Even that bathtub was fun with the splashing and sloshing of the water.

However, the old creaky floorboards beneath our feet provide a nice soundtrack, too.

This noisy cabin is the best.

I want every day to be like it has been for the past thirty-six hours. We've only been here for a day and a half, but I've become attached to Preston's constant presence.

For most of yesterday, the weather alternated between sleet and snow, so we were stuck inside with our little radio and the squeaky mattress.

It was the best day of my life.

Well, except for the whole me-feeling-like-shit thing. Withdrawals are no joke. I've been queasy, and I'm not sleeping well either. My bones hurt. I almost feel itchy, inside and out. It's probably a good thing Preston got rid of the pills. Because if they were anywhere near me, I'd take one just to make this aching go away.

Preston says I should be better by next week. Just have to get through it. And it helps that he's always around to take care of me—pushing me to drink water, keeping a cool rag on my forehead, and making love to me when I need a distraction.

But today, he's embracing being a man of the wilderness. Since the storm has passed and the sun is back out, Preston wants to get our food the old-fashioned way.

"Do you really have to go fishing?" I ask, knowing I'm going to miss him like crazy, even if it is only a few hours.

He cups my face, pinches my chin, and places a kiss on my lips. "If you want something other than soup and crackers, I'll have to catch our lunch."

"Canned stuff is fine. I don't mind." I go over to the pantry and pick up a can of green beans. "Look, I'll eat my vegetables."

"You need protein." Preston grabs his fishing pole on the way to the back door. "Are you sure you don't want to come with me? You could sit back a ways from the creek."

Tempting. He looks cute in his flannel, his beanie, and the tall black rubber boots he found in a closet. Fishing boots. The kind of boots you wear when you're going to be wading in rushing water.

Sighing, I shake my head. "I'll just stay here and try to take a nap. If you're still not back when I wake up, I'll wash our clothes or something."

"Let's hope the fish are biting, and I'll be back soon. Don't leave and get lost."

"I won't go past the clothesline," I promise.

This morning after breakfast, we went for a brief hike, and something I learned about myself?

I have no sense of direction. Once the house is out of sight, it's just trees in every direction, and there's no way for me to tell how to get back.

I walk over to Preston for one more kiss.

Scooping an arm around me, he pulls me in, and smashes his mouth to mine like we're going to be apart for weeks, not hours. I love it. I love him.

With dread in my stomach, I watch him walk out the back door, down the steps of the deck, and into the trees.

"He'll be back before you know it," I whisper to myself, reverting back to my old habit of conversing with myself. "Nothing can keep him away. Nothing."

Flexing my aching fingers and ignoring the pain in my body, I go over to the pantry to get another bottle of water.

After gulping until my stomach protests and threatens to spew it back up, I shuffle over to the bed and lie down. The mattress squeaks when my weight makes it dip, and I miss Preston even more. Curling up on my side, I wrap the blanket around me and pretend it's him.

It's probably not healthy to be this attached to someone so fast.

I don't have to be a psychologist to figure that out.

But I don't want to fight it. I want to embrace what we have. I just want to be thankful for it. Enjoy it.

That's my last thought before I drift off.

My dream starts off good for once. Preston and I are outside, somewhere in the woods surrounding the cabin. He's smiling and my heart is full.

Our peace is short-lived.

All of the sudden, the ground falls away under his feet. His face is terror-stricken as he plummets below the ground. Screaming, I run forward. When I look over the drop, I see a river below. Preston's submerged in it, and he's desperately trying to keep his head above water as he holds onto a branch stuck in the mud.

Do I go in after him?

Horrifying thoughts rapidly come to me. I could stay up here, safe. I'll survive, but he won't. Or I can jump—be with him while risking my own death.

It isn't much of a choice.

I promised I'd follow him anywhere.

Before I can stop myself, I'm crawling forward. Grass, dirt, and twigs scrape at me as I tip over the ledge.

Then I fall.

My eyes snap open. I'm breathing hard and soaked in sweat,

but I'm safe. I'm not falling or drowning, and Preston is probably having a great time fishing.

Sitting up, I let the blanket fall away from my shoulders and glance at the clock.

It's only been forty-five minutes since Preston left.

Not much of a nap.

Oh, well. Now I've got time to do my makeup before Preston gets back, and there really is a lot of laundry to do.

Feeling even more tired now than when I went to sleep, I chuck another log into the stove to keep the fire going.

I grab my makeup bag, and on the way to the table, I turn the radio on. No matter what I do with the antenna, the reception is crappy, and the songs are scratchy at times. I don't care. I still sing along, humming softly as I push a mound of puzzle pieces out of the way to make room for my beauty products.

Wishing I had a YouTube tutorial to follow, I hold up the compact mirror. My hand trembles, but I ignore how wobbly my reflection is because I'm too worried about my face.

I'm so pale. I mean, I look sick. Really sick. More than usual. Preston did say the third and fourth days of detox might be the peak, and I'm feeling it. At least I haven't thrown up yet.

As I try to channel my inner Harlee Verona, I swipe some shimmery pink shadow on my eyelids, along with some thick black liner. After I'm satisfied with my eyes, I carefully apply my foundation. With a little extra concealer and blush, I achieve an okay-ish look.

Next, I go over to the sink basin. It's already been filled with clean water and there's a bar of laundry soap on the counter. I put on some rubber gloves and get to work.

Even though it hurts just to move, I find the task soothing in a way. I focus on one article of clothing at a time. Shirt—scrub, then rinse in the bucket of clean water. Sports bra—repeat. Pants—repeat.

By the time I finish with the pile, the laundry basket is full of wet, clean clothes, and another hour has gone by.

I sluggishly tie my shoes and slide into Preston's leather jacket, but my mood is a little lighter as I lug everything out the back door. Because Preston should be back for lunch soon.

Wincing at the bright sunlight and the pain shooting through my skull, I set the basket down by the clothesline and decide to go back inside to get Preston's old baseball cap to shade my face.

Just as I've stepped into the house, I see movement out the front window. Curious, I creep forward.

There's a flash of black among the trees on the outskirts of the property.

A bear?

The figure becomes clearer, then it breaks into two.

I gasp when I realize a couple of men in dark clothing are emerging from the woods near the lane. They've almost made it to the yard, and they're moving stealthily as they stay partially hidden in the bushes.

My true-crime-documentary mind assesses them quickly.

Preston said the closest residence is a few miles away and sometimes hunters wander this way.

These guys can't be hunters, though. If they were, they'd be wearing camouflage. With their black pants and shirts, they stick out like sore thumbs. Plus, they're not carrying rifles.

Sunlight glints near one of their gloved hands, and I realize one of them has a sleek handgun.

"Oh my God," I breathe out, my heart beating fast.

I duck down and crawl toward the back door. Once I make it out onto the splintery wooden deck, I reach up, grab the knob, and slowly pull the door shut.

After silently sliding off the deck, I sprint past the clothesline. I'm breaking my promise to Preston, but I think he'd approve right now.

I'm probably too noisy as I brush past some overgrown branches, snapping twigs and rustling leaves as I go. A big fallen tree is about thirty feet into the woods, and I dive behind to kneel down. Peeking over the top of it, I watch the house.

In the back windows, shadows move around.

They're inside.

If they're looking for us, they're going to know we were just there. The fire's still burning. The radio is on. The bed isn't made, the puzzle is all over the table, and our clothes are dripping wet.

Which means they can assume we aren't far.

I have to find Preston—there's no other choice, bad sense of direction be damned.

Fueled by determination, I crawl deeper into the woods, staying low on my hands and knees. The ground is still wet from yesterday's storm. Leaves and mud coat my palms and soak into my sweatpants, but I make sure I'm a good distance in before I stand and start running.

I'm not sure where I'm going. I remember Preston telling me the creek is less than a quarter mile away behind the house. In theory, if I go straight, I should get to him eventually.

At least five minutes go by as I stumble over logs and sticks. I'm reminded of the night I made my escape. I'd been so sure I could do it on my own. I was a fool. I couldn't have gotten away without Preston's help.

I didn't trust him then.

I do now.

"Preston!" I whisper-yell. If I'm too loud, the men might hear me. "Preston!"

Confused about where I am, I turn in a circle.

Mistake.

Everything looks the same in every direction, and now I don't know which way I came from or which way to go.

"Preston," I whimper, a little louder now.

Paralyzed with fear, I sink down and sit with my back against a tree.

Even though I have Preston's coat on, cold seeps into me. I'm shaking, and my stomach is lurching. Blood is rushing through my head, creating a quiet roar inside my mind.

I'd give anything for my pills right now. Just a half. A full would be better. Either would give me some kind of numbing peace.

The snap of a twig and the distinct sound of footsteps on crunchy leaves has me holding my breath.

Shit.

The men are coming after me.

In my dream earlier, I was brave. I made the choice to jump when it would've been easier to stay put.

I stay put now.

Dream-me has courage.

Real-me is a wimp.

Covering my ears, I lean my forehead against my knees and try to be as small as possible. Maybe the guys won't see me.

When a hand clamps down on my shoulder, I shriek and jerk so hard I fall over onto my side.

"Rosalie." The person's still jostling my arm, but that person sounds a lot like Preston.

Opening my eyes, I gaze up at the best face in the world. "You're here. You found me."

His lips turn down. "I thought I heard you say my name. The creek's right over there." He points. "Past the tree with the split in the trunk."

I'm closer than I thought.

That's when I realize if I'd been listening better, if I hadn't been so afraid, I would've heard the rushing water. A sound that would normally freak me out doesn't, because there are more pressing matters at hand.

"People are in the house. Two men," I blubber, and Preston's eyes shoot up in that direction with a hardness I've never seen before. "I don't think they saw me run away, but who knows? They could be chasing after us right now."

"What did they look like?" Helping me to my feet, Preston starts picking leaves and other debris from my hair. "Was there a vehicle?"

"Just average-looking white dudes, wearing all black. I didn't see a car or anything. It was just them. One of them has a gun." I'm hyperventilating now, and Preston calmly shushes me while telling me what a good girl I am. How I did the right thing by coming to him and he's proud of me.

"All right." Looking stressed, Preston huffs. "Here's what we're going to do. We'll go around the house while staying in the trees. Once we get to the lane, we can look for their car. They have to be driving something. If it's a government vehicle, they're probably from the FBI. That would be preferable to the alternative."

"You think they were sent by my mom?"

"Possibly." He begins shedding his rubber boots. "Maybe they're just people who lost their way. Could be squatters."

As much as I appreciate Preston's optimism, I highly doubt the men are random. "I don't like this."

"Neither do I, Rosie." Preston slips his hand into mine and we start our trek. "The way I see it, we've got two options."

"I'm listening."

"Well, we could hide in the woods and try to wait them out. See if they eventually leave. But we don't know how long that could be, and it's too cold for you to be outside all day."

"Yeah," I agree. "What's the second option?"

"I have my keys with me." Preston pats his pocket. "Once

we assess the situation, we can make a run for it to the van and get out of here."

"But we'd be leaving our stuff behind. The pregnancy suit, all our clothes."

"Those are just things. We can get more disguises."

An unnerving silence accompanies us as we walk the rest of the way. All I hear are the sounds of nature, our footsteps, and my choppy breathing.

Soon, we're near the side of the cabin.

Staying about fifty feet back in the forest, we crouch down and watch the house. One of the men is standing on the front porch smoking. Dark sunglasses cover his eyes. He has a brown beard, but his pale head is bald.

I shouldn't be judging anyone on their appearance, but he looks mean. He keeps flicking his cigarette aggressively, like he's mad or impatient.

"Let's go." Preston nudges me, and we make our way toward the lane to scope out their ride.

About a hundred yards away, we find a huge RV parked smackdab in the middle of the road to our only exit.

I make a sound of distress and whisper, "Even if we do get the van, they're blocking the way."

With his eyebrows pinched together and his jaw clenching repeatedly, it's safe to say Preston is just as troubled as I am. And that's not reassuring.

"I can squeeze by on one side," he says, injecting confidence into the quiet claim. "I'll probably lose a mirror, but oh well."

"What's your take on these guys?"

"I didn't see any badges, and they're driving a fucking RV, so they're not FBI. With the way they're dressed, I'd say we can rule out campers, too."

"That leaves my mom's reward hunters?"

Preston hesitates, like he hates to speak the next possibility out loud. "Or your father's men."

"The mafia?" I ask in a strangled voice. "How the hell would they even find us?"

"No fucking clue."

Getting out of here is sounding better and better.

Keeping his hand wrapped around mine, Preston starts walking us back to the van and the cabin.

My pulse won't stop going haywire. Even though we're not exerting ourselves, I'm struggling to catch my breath.

Preston studies me with a side glance. "How are you holding up?"

I put a hand over my thundering chest. "Oh, you know. Just panicking."

Stopping, he brings me in for a hug. God, he really knows how to dish out some comfort. With his arms wrapped around me, it's hard to think about anything outside of us. Concentrating on his warmth and scent, I breathe until I feel better.

Pulling back, I give him a nod. He nods back. Just like that, my strength is replenished. A little.

Once we get back to the spot we were in before, we spy on the second guy who's outside now. He looks a lot like the other guy, only he isn't completely bald. His dark hair is buzzed short, just like the stubble on his face.

Pacing on the porch, he holds his phone up, waving it around in an agitated way. He barks a few words into the house that I don't understand.

"Russian," Preston supplies, and my heart knocks against my sternum when I realize what that means. "I can't tell what he's saying, but I think we both but know who sent them."

CHAPTER 21

Preston

Fucking Ivan. Of all the people hunting us, it had to be the Russian mafia.

But how, though?

Out here in the middle of nowhere, I should be untraceable for everyone.

I suppose he could've dug back in my foster care history. He could've seen that I aged out with the Marshalls, leading him to believe we're still on good terms. All he'd have to do is look up properties belonging to them, and boom. We're caught.

Long fucking shot, though. It'd be a lot of effort to send his guys across three states just on a hunch.

Ultimately, it doesn't really matter how Ivan figured it out. The fact is, we're in deep shit.

The guy on the porch curses at his cell phone, then bangs it on the railing. He tries to dial someone, but he gives up when it's clear there's no signal. Yeah, reception out here is a bitch. That'll work in our favor.

Rosalie shivers next to me, her shoulder quaking against my arm.

We really need to get this girl a suitable coat. Something insulated. My leather jacket isn't meant for near-freezing temps.

Slipping off my flannel button-up, I drape it over Rosalie to give her another layer.

As she tugs it across her chest, she eyes my exposed arms. "What about you? You're only wearing a T-shirt."

"Cold doesn't bother me," I downplay it. Because although I don't mind the nippy weather right now, I'm not invincible. Hypothermia would get to me eventually.

No matter. Soon, we'll be in the van, and we'll be speeding away from here.

"See that chump?" I ask Rosalie quietly, tipping my head toward the guy on the porch. "We'll wait until he goes into the house. Then we'll make a run for it to the van."

Biting her lip apprehensively, Rosalie's blue and green eyes peer up at me with fear. "What if they see us?"

"We'll stay low—we'll be partially blocked by the vehicle, and it's not very far. I'll get into the passenger side first and slide into the driver's seat. You follow me. Then, we're out of here."

I'm trying to sound as upbeat and positive as possible, and it seems to help. Pressing her lips together, Rosalie gives me a determined nod.

A few seconds later, the guy goes into the cabin.

And that's our chance.

"Now," I whisper, rushing forward.

Reaching behind me, I open my hand. Rosalie's soft fingers slide against mine and latch on. Staying bent at the waist, we burst from the trees and make a beeline for the van. Thankfully, I left it unlocked so I don't have to waste time fumbling with the keys.

Keeping my eyes on the house, I open the door, dive over the passenger seat, and scramble behind the wheel. While I'm sliding the key into the ignition, Rosalie gets in and shuts the door as softly as she can.

"Seat belt," I order, not bothering to put mine on because I'm too busy starting the van and shoving the gearshift into drive.

I peel out through the yard, making deep tire tracks in the

grass as I whip a U-turn. Gravel kicks up when I speed down the lane, forming a cloud of dust behind us.

In the rearview mirror, I see the men run out of the house. The one without the sunglasses bounds down the steps like he's ready to chase us on foot.

"Brace yourself," I say as the RV comes into view. "This is gonna be bumpy."

There's a wider gap between the road and the trees on the left side. I'll have a better chance at scraping by if I go that way.

Slowing a bit, I veer off the lane and hope the ground isn't too soft from the rain yesterday. If we get stuck in mud, we're fucked.

We creep by the RV without any issues with our tires.

We're almost in the clear when a third man steps out from behind the RV, putting himself right in my path. For a second, I consider running him over, but he holds up a fucking AK-47.

And points it right at Rosalie.

Gasping, her hands tighten on the armrests.

I slam on the brakes. We jerk to a stop literally two feet from the man. He doesn't even flinch. Like a psycho, he keeps an almost bored expression on his face, as if he's prepared to get hit by a car just for a chance to stop us.

"Preston?" Rosalie's voice wavers. "Do we have a backup plan for this?"

No. I don't. I was in such a hurry to get Rosalie away from here, I didn't consider the possibility that there were more men hanging back.

Prowling, the armed man dressed in black slacks and a black Henley takes slow steps as he rounds the van and keeps his aim trained on my woman.

All it takes is a second to shoot someone. One second.

I could floor it, but he could hit us from behind or blow out our tires.

I've witnessed enough violence to know when someone will follow through with a threat. And the asshole in front of us *will* pull that trigger. There's a cold determination in his brown eyes.

Unlike the other guys, this one has a short blond haircut that reminds me of a military style, and I realize we're facing someone who's trained with weapons and combat.

I hold my hands up in a show of surrender.

In hindsight, I wish I'd driven by on the other side of the RV. At least then Rosalie could bolt into the forest and have a fighting chance while I tackle him. With how close the vehicles are, she can't open her door. She's trapped in here.

"I'm sorry, baby," I rasp.

"Is it over?" Sounding more scared than I've ever heard her, she grabs my arm. "Are we caught?"

Impatiently, the man motions with the gun, wanting us to get out.

I slowly lower my hand to the door handle and pull it while speaking quietly to Rosalie. "I can try to negotiate. Now's the time for words. I'll talk to these guys. Maybe they can be reasoned with."

As we shuffle out, I make sure Rosalie's partly behind me, but I keep my hands visible so I don't look like a threat. "If you let me call Ivan, I can explain. Rosalie's not well."

The man's jaw ticks. "If the girl's sick, she should be with her dad." American accent of the southern variety, which means he's probably not one of Ivan's tried and true goons.

"She doesn't want to be with him."

"I don't give a fuck."

Footsteps on gravel approach quickly from behind. Spinning, I see the guy from the porch.

He raises his gun, and I pin Rosalie against the van to protect her.

Without hesitation, he pulls the trigger.

I grunt as my shoulder gets punctured, and within a split second, I realize I haven't been shot by a bullet. There's a needle-like dart sticking into me.

A tranquilizer.

Another one is fired off, and it hits my thigh.

So much for talking it out.

"No!" Rosalie must think I'm about to die, because she shoves me back and puts her body in front of mine.

She takes the next dart. Her body jerks when it pierces her stomach, and from the 'oh shit' look on the man's face, I'd say he knows he just made a big mistake.

"Rosie, baby." Turning her to face me, I yank the needle from her abdomen.

Touching the spot, she whimpers.

"You crazy girl," I scold her. Under any other circumstance, I'd never call Rosalie crazy. It's a trigger word for her. But fuck. She was ready to take a bullet for me. Framing her face, I touch my forehead to hers before the sedative can takeover. "Why'd you do that? Why, baby, why?"

"He was shooting you."

My arms are suddenly pulled behind me. Immediately, metal clicks around my wrists. Just because I can, I whip my head back and feel a crunch when my hard skull meets something soft.

While the American guy starts yelling in my ear about having a broken nose, the other man tackles Rosalie.

It feels like everything is happening in slow motion as I watch my worst nightmare.

Dropping to my knees, I'm helpless while Rosalie screams, scratches, kicks, and elbows.

I've seen her fight like this before.

In fact, I've been on the receiving end of it. I remember how she ran from me that first night. It's kind of funny how she thought she could take me on in a chokehold. Unfortunately, she was no match for me, and she won't win with this guy either.

My thoughts are fuzzy. My limbs are heavy. I'm going to lose consciousness soon. We both will.

I'm bigger than Rosalie, but I got double the dose she did. Would've been triple if she hadn't gotten in front of me.

She's being affected by the tranquilizer, too, but at a slower rate. Either that, or her will to struggle is stronger than mine.

She's wild, bucking and biting as she fights a battle she knows she'll lose.

My crazy girl. Never loved anything the way I loved her. Never been loved back with the same ferocity either.

And I failed her. I failed my beautiful, fragile, innocent wife.

I fall face first to the ground. The damp grass pads my landing.

Then everything goes dark.

CHAPTER 22

Rosalie

The constant rumble of the RV is somewhat soothing as I lie bound on the bed in the back room. My hands are tied in front of me with white fabric, and my ankles have zip ties around them. There's also a gag in my mouth.

It didn't start out this way.

When I woke up a couple hours ago, I wasn't restrained. Immediately, I got up and yelled profanities at the men. I demanded to be with Preston, and when I saw that he was uncomfortably passed out on the floor of the kitchen with his hands cuffed behind his back—and he had two more darts stuck in his leg to keep him unconscious—I threw a fit.

I broke some mugs and kicked a cabinet until it cracked.

The two Russian guys tried to calm me down, so I bit both of them. Apparently they felt threatened enough to tie me up.

I don't know what time it is, but it's dark out, which means we must be pretty far from where they took us.

The guy with the shorter beard—who I've learned is called Nico—appears in the open doorway. "We're getting dinner."

I glare at him.

"Do you want anything to eat? To drink?"

I don't nod or shake my head. Narrowing my eyes, I mentally tell him to go fuck himself.

Unfortunately, I'm not telepathic and he doesn't get the

message, because he climbs onto the bed and removes the fabric from my mouth. "Are you going to be a good girl now?"

"Fuck you." I snap my teeth at his hand, almost getting his finger in the process.

Expecting him to be mad, I flinch a little because I'm sure he's going to retaliate with violence. But he doesn't. Instead, he laughs.

I'm so taken off-guard by his reaction that he has time to slip the gag back into place without risking injury.

"She's Ivan's daughter, all right," he announces to the other guys before leaving to join them up front.

He's totally unaffected by my behavior. I can hear him talking and chuckling with the other Russian guy. I didn't catch his name, but I've been calling him Shades in my mind because he hasn't taken his sunglasses off this whole time.

Maybe Nico and Shades don't want to hurt me. Either that, or they've been ordered not to. They could've, but they haven't. All the bumps and bruises I've acquired are due to my own refusal to be subdued.

The American one, on the other hand… I don't like him. His name is Donovan. It seems like his job is just to drive, but every now and then, I swear he glowers at me in the rearview mirror. I've been a pain in his ass, and I've done damage to his RV.

Good.

Before the day is through, I hope to make all three of these goons regret taking on the task of retrieving me.

Wiggling like a worm, I scoot toward the end of the bed and look out the door. Preston's still on the floor with no signs of waking. I'm worried he's cold and uncomfortable. The least they could do is give him a blanket.

Honestly, I'm more concerned about him than myself.

I might have Ivan's protection, but Preston doesn't. He's

going to be in trouble, and it's all my fault. If I'd just gone to my father in the first place, none of this would be happening.

The RV takes a slow turn, and then we come to a stop in a parking lot. Through the windshield, I can see streetlights and lit-up signs for stores and restaurants.

Now that everything is still, I'm aware of how sick I feel. Whether it's motion sickness, withdrawals, or the fact that I haven't eaten in hours, I'm not sure.

So when Nico comes back with a sack of burgers and fries, my mouth waters and my stomach makes audible noises at the smell.

Then there's a painful twist somewhere in my abdomen.

Never mind.

It's not hunger.

I'm going to throw up.

Making urgent noises behind the gag, I shake my head at Nico.

"Don't bite me," he says, carefully pulling the fabric out of my mouth.

I promptly puke on his shiny black shoes.

Stepping back, he barks out a few harsh-sounding words. I don't know that they mean, but I'm guessing he's cussing up a storm.

"More trouble than they're worth," Donovan calls from the driver's seat. His voice is a bit nasally because of his messed-up nose. Preston did a number on his face. There's a lot of swelling and bruising.

I heave a few more times, spitting what I can onto the floor, but when it's clear my stomach has nothing left but bile, my body finally stops rejecting what little fluids I have in me.

Still disgruntled about his shoes, Nico grabs a bottle of water from the little fridge in the kitchen. He brings it to me and holds it out.

My throat burns from throwing up, and my mouth is a desert thanks to the gag, but I refuse to take the water.

I want it. I could grab it with my tied-up hands, but it feels wrong to accept anything from the enemy. I might be harming myself in the process, but declining his help is the only form of protest I have at the moment.

"Come on," Nico insists softly before glancing at Preston. "He would want you to, you know? If he were awake, he'd tell you to drink something."

He's right. I can see it now—Preston waking up to find me dehydrated and vomiting. Pissed that I didn't take better care of myself when I had the chance.

Wrapping my shaking fingers around the plastic, I take the bottle and lean up to sip it.

Nico's shoulders slump as if he's relieved. "There you go. We'll be there soon."

The RV gets going again.

In the next twenty minutes or so, I slowly finish the water while watching Preston for any signs of waking. When we pull up in front of a downtown street lined with concrete buildings, his foot moves.

My eyes dart to the bad guys. They're not watching him. If he could just have a few more minutes, he might come out of it and I can talk to him. Look into his eyes. Hold his hand.

Unfortunately, he doesn't get more time to wake up because Donovan shuts off the RV. He and Shades get up from their seats and go over to Preston. Lifting him by the shoulders and ankles, they haul him out the door.

"Where are you taking him?" I shout after them.

Panicked about losing sight of Preston, I squirm farther off the bed. I might land in my own puke, but I don't care at this point.

Nico approaches with a knife. "Do you want to be a good

girl and walk, or am I going to have to throw you over my shoulder?"

If agreeing to be good will get me out of here faster so I can stay with Preston, I'll do it. "Walk. I'll walk."

Seeming satisfied with my compliance, Nico cuts the zip ties from my ankles. He leaves the cloth bindings on my wrists and helps me stand. I'm stiff and achy, but I loosen up the more I move.

When Nico and I make it out of the RV, I study my new surroundings as I step onto the curb.

I'm not sure what this part of town looks like during the day, but at night it's pretty creepy. Decrepit brick buildings line both sides of the street, and a lot of them look unoccupied. There's trash littered on the sidewalks. Several of the streetlamps are burned out, so entire sections of street are cloaked in shadows.

The guys carrying Preston are across the street, and they're heading to a closed shop. Old vacuums are lined up inside the dark windows, and there's a sign that says, *Jesus saved you. We'll save your vacuum.*

What the fuck? I thought we'd be going to a fancy office or a warehouse. Anything mafia-ish. This is just bizarre.

It's probably a front. If someone is dealing with illegal shit, a vacuum repair shop would be a good way to disguise it.

Preston almost gets dropped on his head when Donovan struggles with getting the glass door open.

"If they'd let me help, I could make sure Preston doesn't get hurt more than he already is," I tell Nico, yanking my arm from his grip.

Ignoring me, he fusses over my messy appearance. He removes a leaf remnant from my hair and straightens my clothing. Wanting to make me look presentable, I assume.

Batting his hands away, I march forward, determined to be close to Preston. But an arm hooks around my waist before I can get very far. Not more than a second later, a vehicle speeds past the RV, just a couple feet from me. It's so close, the whoosh of wind makes my hair fly around my face.

Then I notice the vehicle is familiar. It's our van, and it's being parked here. There must've been a fourth man in the group to retrieve our stuff. Probably to erase any evidence that we were at the cabin.

I don't want that. The past couple days with Preston were the best of my life, and I don't want our time together in our little heaven to be wiped clean as if it never happened.

"Careful," Nico barks, jostling me a little. "You'd be roadkill right now if it weren't for me. Didn't anyone ever tell you to look both ways before you cross the street?"

No, actually. I could count the number of streets I've crossed on one hand.

I start to laugh. And for some reason, I can't stop. Hysterics take over, and Nico grumbles while half-dragging me along with him.

He mutters something about me being crazy, and for some reason, it's freeing. For once, it doesn't hurt my feelings. Because being insane just might be the best defense I have.

If I found a knife and stabbed Nico, no one would be surprised. On the contrary, it's expected of me.

Mentally unstable. Armed and dangerous.

Maybe I'll live up to my mother's claims after all.

As soon as we get into the shop, I look for sharp objects. There's a cup full of pens at the register. It's totally morbid to think about, but all the crime documentaries I've watched have taught me the soft, vulnerable places on the body where I could do the most damage. The throat. An eye.

But my attention is quickly pulled away from thoughts of murder to concern for Preston. Donovan and Shades are still carting him around, but a third man has joined their efforts.

"Wherever he's going, that's where I want to go, too." I point ahead with my tied hands.

Nico doesn't respond, but he guides me in the same direction everyone else is headed.

After passing a few rows of vacuums, we arrive at the top of the staircase at the back of the store. Wherever it leads, it's dark down there. It smells, too. Musty, like the basement at my house.

The exit to my right is open. Outside, I can see a poorly lit alley and a dumpster. I could kick Nico in the balls and make a run for it. He's getting comfortable with me, but maybe that's because he doesn't think I'll leave Preston.

And I won't.

Down we go.

There's a room at the bottom of the stairs. The guys bring Preston in there and unceremoniously dump him on the concrete floor.

Ouch. He's going to feel that later.

"Do you have to be so rough with him?" I gripe, taking one step at a time as Nico holds onto my elbow as if he's escorting me like a gentleman.

"I'm not supposed to answer questions," he replies in his thick Russian accent. "I bring you to your father. That's it."

Sighing, I let him lead me, but instead of going straight, we take a left. Much to my horror, he tugs me past the room Preston's in. Digging my feet in, I resist and start to fight.

"Igor!" Nico shouts. "Some assistance here."

So, Shades has a name. After shutting the door and locking Preston in, Igor joins Nico in dragging me down the hall.

"I want to be with Preston!" I yell over and over again.

Kicking my legs and punching with my joined hands, I manage to get a couple good blows in. I knock the sunglasses off Igor's face, and now I see why he wears them. His left eye is missing, and the injury looks recent. The skin is red, swollen, and oozing a bit.

The gruesome sight gives me the motivation to struggle harder.

If losing an eye is an occupational hazard of working for my father, I want nothing to do with him.

But eventually, I'm overpowered. I'm achy, tired, and weak from hunger. My feet are captured, and my chest is squeezed in a bear hug as distance is put between me and the one person who makes me feel safe.

CHAPTER 23

Rosalie

I don't like being locked in rooms alone. There's a clock on the wall behind the desk. It's not a grandfather clock, but still. The *tick, tick, ticking* is chipping away at my composure. It feels like the walls are closing in.

It'd be different if Preston were with me. He'd make everything okay. I don't know why they want to keep us apart, as if we're some kind of dangerous duo. It's not like we'd be able to do much damage.

For one, Preston's unconscious. Well, with how much time has passed, he might be awake now, but he won't be at full strength. And two, these men have power in numbers, handcuffs, and guns.

Then again, maybe they don't plan on keeping Preston alive.

I can't accept that. I can't even think about it.

Wishing Nico had left me in my cloth bindings instead of trading them for handcuffs, I frown down at my new restraints. I've tried to slip my hands out of the cuffs at least a dozen times, but the metal is just too tight, and now my wrists are all red. The chain has been looped through the arm of the leather chair I'm sitting in. A very sturdy chair that's bolted to the floor.

I suspect I'm not the first person to be shackled here. Seems like they want their guests to stay put until the boss arrives.

Resting my head on the wingback, I study the office.

Everything is so cold and lifeless. Sterile. There's a stainless-steel desk in front of me, but nothing's on it. No papers, pens, or pictures. I suppose they wouldn't want to give me anything to fight with.

Two high windows are covered by bars. There's a wall of wooden bookshelves to my left. The florescent lights above me illuminate spines of encyclopedias and classics, but most aren't written in English.

The floor is just cold, gray concrete.

It's weird to think this could have been my life.

If my father had wanted a role in raising me, would I have played here? Would my photo be on his desk now? Would he have been kind and gentle, or would he have ruled with an iron fist? Would my presence have made a difference in this scummy basement?

It needs a remodel, stat.

The jingle of keys gets my attention. Turning in the chair, I peek at the steel door. There's a loud metallic click as the bolt slides back, but before it can open, I recoil and decide to hide for a little bit longer. Bringing my knees up to my chest, I loop my shackled arms around them.

Footsteps make their way across the room, and when a man comes around the side of the chair, the first thing I see is a cream-colored suit and a black tie.

I focus on that tie, shiny like silk.

My father can force me here, but he can't make me look at him. He can't make me talk to him.

Unnerving stillness and the annoying ticking stretch on for long moments in a battle of wills. Seems my father is playing the same game I am. If I got my stubborn streak from him, I doubt he'll break first.

Damn it, curiosity gets the best of me.

I lift my gaze to his face.

I swallow my gasp, gulping hard as I look at eyes that are almost identical to mine. His right eye is blue. His left is green.

But he's not looking at my face. His attention is trained on my chained wrists.

He glances at someone I can't see behind the chair. "What has happened?"

"I'm sorry." I think it's Nico. "Please, Ivan. You have to understand. She was difficult."

"Of course she was difficult," Ivan replies angrily. "You knew it wouldn't be easy, but you promised she wouldn't be harmed."

"She jumped in front of Ethan. Got shot with the tranquilizer. She was already violent before she passed out, and—"

"You shot my daughter?" The deadly calm in his voice is chilling.

"It was meant for the guy," Nico protests, almost whining.

And because I'm mad at the entire situation and I feel like being a bitch, I pipe up, "And that Donovan guy pointed an assault rifle at me."

Ivan scowls in my direction, then his murderous sneer is aimed at Nico. "Where the fuck is Donovan?"

"Said he had to go see a doctor friend. Ethan broke his nose."

Pouring fuel on the fire, I add, "I haven't eaten all day either. They kept me bound and gagged for the entire trip."

I can't see Nico, but he makes a choking sound. "I offered you food. You threw up on my shoes instead."

"She got sick, too?" Ivan's rage is palpable.

Scary, scary man.

I can actually sense his anger vibrating through the air.

Cracking his knuckles, he strides over to the other side of the desk. He pulls the top drawer out and slips something onto his right hand. It looks like four thick rings all attached to each other.

Brass knuckles.

Ivan charges Nico, and I hear a thump, a squish, and a crack as he hits him a few times.

Nico grunts with pain.

Part of me is like, *yeah, kick that guy's ass*. The other part doesn't like the thought of anyone getting beaten on my behalf.

Is this the fate that awaits Preston? Or has Ivan already dealt with him?

The thought is enough to make me nauseous again.

"Okay, okay," I say, exasperated, and the punching stops. Without looking back at the damage Ivan has done to Nico, I wave my hands dramatically, clinking the chain loudly. "I get it. You're this big bad man and no one should cross you. Could someone just get me a sandwich or something?"

"I'll do it for you, miss," Nico immediately offers, probably glad as hell to have a reason to get away from Ivan.

"Fine." Coming over to the desk, Ivan drops his brass knuckles. They clank loudly when they hit the metal, and I flinch. There's blood on them, but he doesn't seem phased as he takes a black handkerchief out of his pocket and wipes off his hands. "Go to the deli down the street. Get her one of everything. While you're out, give Donovan a call. I want him here."

"Where's Preston?" I ask, earning an annoyed look from my father.

"In deep shit."

"If you hurt him…" I try to stand up, but the handcuffs prevent it.

Glowering at the cuffs, Ivan comes around the desk while getting a key from his suit pocket. He unlocks them, and I rub my wrists after the metal falls away. Without any respect for my personal space, he picks up my hand and inspects the raw skin.

"I apologize for this. They weren't supposed to restrain you."

"Guess I didn't give them much of a choice."

His lips tick up with a ghost of a smile. "My daughter, finally with me."

"I want to be with Preston." I snatch my hand away. "I need to see that he's okay. I can forgive a lot of shit, but I'll hate you forever if something bad has happened to him."

Ivan must see how much I mean it, because he waits a few beats, then gives me a nod. Typing out a quick message on his cell phone, he sits behind his desk.

I expect him to pepper me with questions or try to get to know me. Instead, he sits quietly with his hands coolly folded over his stomach.

Maybe this is how he interrogates people. He just stares at them until they crack and start blabbing like I do.

"I didn't want to come here," I blurt, needing to segue into begging him not to punish Preston the way he did Nico.

"That much is obvious."

"It's not Preston's fault that he didn't bring me to you. I asked him to take me somewhere else. Somewhere far away."

"That wasn't your order to give. You're not the one who hired him, darling."

I bristle at the darling comment. "But I did marry him. As his wife, I think I'm a little more important to him than you."

Ivan's face gets dark. "You did what?"

Just then, the door behind me opens. Somehow, I know it's Preston. I can feel him near me.

Now that I'm not chained to the chair, I jump up and turn around. Igor, with his sunglasses back in place, is assisting a groggy Preston. Before he's even three feet inside the room, I'm running to him.

He engulfs me with one arm.

"Baby, I'm so sorry," he whispers into my hair. "So sorry."

"Don't," I whisper back. "You didn't do anything wrong. You're alive, and that's all I want right now."

Just being close to him makes all my pains seep away, but my worry for him increases. His skin is ice cold. Shaking off the flannel I'm still wearing over the leather jacket, I drape it over his shoulders. I manage to get one of his arms into it, but his other hand still has a handcuff on it, and Igor isn't letting go.

Suddenly, Preston and I are being separated. There must've been another thug behind Igor, because someone's firmly guiding me back to my chair while Igor chains Preston to his.

No one breaks out the handcuffs for me again, but by the way Igor places himself between our chairs, it's clear Preston and I are supposed to stay apart.

A wave of sadness causes a strong physical ache in my chest, and I fold in on myself with a whimper.

Splaying his hands on the desk, Ivan leans forward and studies me before straightening up. Slowly, he walks around the metal furniture between us and casually leans against it while using a softer tone with me. "What's wrong, darling? Are you feeling unwell because of the trip?"

"She's detoxing, asshole. You pumped her full of tranquilizer when her system is stressed." Preston spits at Ivan's feet. "Mother fucker."

Instead of reacting with rage, Ivan's eyes go wide and his face pinches with something close to regret. "She's on drugs?" he asks him, then focuses on me. "You're on drugs?"

"I'm not talking to you until you let me be with Preston."

"Don't you know his name is Ethan?" Ivan says almost mockingly. "He's got you fooled."

"I know who he is. *I know him*. And to me, he's Preston."

Ivan and I stare at each other, our two-toned eyes locked.

Steepling his hands against his chin, he looks from Preston to me. From me to Preston. Then he nods his permission.

I'm out of my chair so fast, I practically fall onto Preston's lap. I touch his leg where he was shot with the darts. "Are you hurt? Did they hurt you?"

He puts his free arm around me. "I'm all right. Sore, but I'll live."

"I'm the one who should be sorry." I kiss his cheek, his temple, his lips.

A throat clears.

Right.

Ivan.

"What have you been using?" he asks me. "I might deal drugs, but I don't want you hooked on that shit."

I laugh humorlessly. "Well, my mother doesn't agree with you on that. Co-parenting would've been a disaster. No wonder you stayed away."

"I don't understand. What are you saying?"

"I'm saying, she's been feeding me pills for the past six months. It seems she wanted me to be addicted." I suppose I don't need to explain the hospital trip that resulted from my accidental overdose, because Ivan already knows about that. So I briefly mention it, then I tell him about the doctor who showed up at my house afterward. I tell him how I thought I was taking prescription medicine for my anxiety—only to find out they were painkillers. "Preston's been helping me." I look back at the man I love and lightly scrape my fingers over his stubble. "He doesn't want me on them either. He wants the best for me."

"I want the best for you, darling," Ivan interrupts our moment, but he does look a tad uncomfortable to be witnessing so much affection between Preston and me.

"Well, you failed," I fume at him. "It's your first day on the job—and I'm no expert at what dads should be like—but I can say with certainty this isn't the way to do it." Angrily waving my hand, I indicate the entire fucked up situation.

Ivan winces.

He's surprising me.

He's not supposed to be soft or sorry. I've been preparing myself to deal with his wrath, not his remorse.

"That's all I've ever wanted," Ivan rasps, "is to find you and make sure you're safe and happy. I… apologize for the way my men handled it."

Brushing off his half-assed apology and his attempt to pass the blame to someone else, I say, "Speaking of finding me… how did you do it?"

"There's a tracker in your arm," Ivan replies casually.

At first, I think he's joking. But when he continues to stare at me with his serious face, I make a noise of outrage. "Excuse me?"

"A nurse gave you a shot at the hospital—"

"Yeah, a flu shot." I remember that. While my mom was in the bathroom, a nurse came in and gave me a vaccine.

"No, darling. That was a lie." Ivan's back to being unapologetic.

My hand slips into the leather jacket and goes to the place on my inner bicep where I got the injection. After I get into my shirt and do some prodding, I find a hard little bump under my skin. It's so small. I probably would've never figured out it was there.

A fucking tracker. That's something neither Preston or I thought of as a possibility.

"How could you convince a nurse to do something like that?" My voice is rough with emotion.

"Simple," Ivan answers. "I offered to put her son through college. It's amazing what people will do for their children."

"That—that's—" Sputtering, I glare daggers at Ivan, but he's unaffected. In fact, he's downright smug. "That's a violation of my rights!"

Preston's been quiet during our exchange, but his body has tensed up, and I know he's pissed off on my behalf.

"Donovan doesn't have the best reputation, but his tracker technology is unrivaled," Ivan continues. "He'll be punished for pointing a gun at you, just as Nico was for sedating you. Please know that everything I do is because I care. This world is rough. I want to shield you from it."

"I think overprotectiveness is what got us into this mess in the first place." Getting to my feet, I bravely step up to my father. He's got a foot of height on me, but it doesn't stop me from giving him a piece of my mind. "Mom had the same idea— keep me locked up so I'd never experience anything in the outside world. But by isolating me, she deprived me of all the good stuff, too. She kept me from you, and you let her." I point my finger at him. "Why swoop in and rescue me now? All this time, you knew where I was, and you let me sit there and rot in that house. Why didn't you come get me? If you're so powerful, you could've just—"

Ivan cuts me off with a wave of his hand, looks to Preston, and asks, "What have you told her?"

"As much as she can handle right now." There's a warning in Preston's reply. I'm not sure what that warning is, but Ivan seems to understand.

Surprisingly, he backs off. Pursing his lips behind his steepled fingers, he gives Preston an appraising look. Almost... respectful.

"What?" My head whips back and forth between the two men before my eyes land on Preston. "What were you supposed to tell me?"

"I think what we have here is an instance of miscommunication," Ivan says smoothly, smiling as he spreads his hands like he's conversing with friends instead of people he abducted. "Let's take this meeting to a more comfortable place, shall we?

I would like to invite you both to have dinner with me at my home."

I doubt we're allowed to refuse. But as long as Preston and I can stay together, I'll go without a fight.

And that's how we end up at a brick mansion that makes my mother's Victorian estate look like a gingerbread house.

CHAPTER 24

Preston

The first thing Ivan did when we arrived at his house is separate us.

But not for the sinister reasons Rosalie suspects. She put up quite a fight when a grandmotherly maid named Helga started guiding her away to go take a shower and clean up, but I promised her it'd be okay.

Not just because she got filthy in the woods, but because Ivan and I need to have a conversation without her listening.

I'm no longer restrained, and Ivan's thugs are absent, but I can't let my guard down around him. This man is a killer.

I keep that in mind as I follow him into a lounge of some sort. There's a warmth and sophistication about the room. It's masculine, with its built-in bookshelves, a wet bar, and the case of expensive cigars. It's dimly lit by crystal wall sconces and the fireplace to my right. An expensive white fur rug is spread out on the glossy wood floor. It's big. Probably a polar bear or something. Various antlers are mounted to the wall, and I wonder if Ivan hunted them himself on some luxurious safari.

But I'm not charmed by shiny light fixtures, high-priced alcohol, or trophies. Ivan's riches are laying on a foundation of drugs, money laundering, and blood, and that makes them tainted.

He hands me a glass of bourbon.

I don't tell him I don't want it, but I accept it and set it on the mahogany side table next to the fancy-ass leather chair I'm sitting in. I wouldn't put it past him to slip a sedative into my drink.

As if he knows my line of thinking, he smirks, raises his glass, and takes a sip. "You know what I've learned in my lifetime?"

"What?"

"The world is a very gray place. The difference between right and wrong is sometimes split by a hair."

"If you're trying to justify your actions today or any other time, you can stop. I don't care if you didn't mean to cause Rosalie harm—you still did it."

"I wasn't talking about my intentions or wrongdoings. I was referring to yours."

"Ditch the subtleties and riddles, Ivan. Just tell me how you really feel."

His jaw ticks. "I did things your way, Ethan. I gave you time to extract my daughter the way you thought was best. And how did you repay me? You took her from me. When I first learned you had run off with her, I realized I was wrong to place my trust in you." This is the moment I think Ivan's going to lose his cool. Instead, he surprises me. "But after hearing the way my daughter speaks about you… I've changed my mind. I shouldn't have assumed you'd hurt her. You've been good to her."

"I love Rosalie," I tell him honestly. "I'd do anything for her. Even keep her away from you."

"Rosalie," he repeats with a smile, letting my snide comment slide. "Which brings me to my question. Why didn't you tell her who she is? That she was kidnapped?"

"She's dealing with a lot. She's…"

"Fragile," he fills in for me, and I nod. He shakes his head. "She might surprise you. I sense a strength in her."

"I err on the side of caution."

"Probably smart." The flames from the fireplace light his face. He looks so much like Rosalie it's kind of freaking me out. "Listen, I might be a bad man, but I'm not unreasonable. I understand why you didn't want to bring her to me."

No shit. "I left the decision up to her."

"Do you always let your women have your balls?"

I suppress a laugh. I don't think Ivan's trying to be funny. He's so deadpan and direct.

Shrugging, I answer, "She's the first girl I've ever been serious about."

"How serious?" With his elbows on his knees, he leans forward. "Would you give up your life for hers?"

"Without hesitation," I confirm. "I hope it doesn't come to that, though, because she needs me. She doesn't understand the world like you and I do, and I want to be with her every step of the way. We want a future together."

"I figured, since you married her."

"She told you?"

"I think she was trying to convince me not to kill you."

"And what have you decided about that?"

Silence stretches between us. Ivan's expression is blank as he stares me down with his mismatched eyes, and I hold his gaze, refusing to cower. I'm sure some men have pissed their pants from that look, but maybe I take comfort in the fact that he'll have to face Rosalie's wrath if he touches a hair on my head. She'd give him hell.

"Someday, will you—" Ivan's hard mask slips as his gaze drops to his hands. "—will you tell my daughter the truth about her past? Can you try to make it easy on her?"

He's talking like Rosalie and I are going to get the future I'm asking for. Like he isn't going to blow my brains out for disobeying him and running off with his money and his only living relative.

"You're letting us go? What's the catch?"

Ivan chuckles. "You mean, why are you not dead where you sit?"

"A guy does wonder these things."

"You're the best person for my daughter. I can see that."

"But?"

"But nothing. I admit my plan wasn't completely formulated when it comes to her. When I found out about her, all I knew was that I wanted her with me in my gray, morally questionable world. But after that? Keeping her safe? My options are limited because being my daughter makes her a target for all my enemies. I considered making her stay here, but that would make me no better than Loralee. Or I could ship her off to a private school in Switzerland. I also thought about marrying her off to one of my associates—a man I know would protect her."

I growl at the last part. The thought of Rosalie being given to some guy is enraging.

"Easy." Humor tugs at Ivan's mouth as he holds out a hand. "She's already done that, which makes my decision simple."

"What decision?"

"I want you to take care of her. Make her happy. I love her, Ethan. I would die before I let anything happen to her. It seems you feel the same, and that's the best outcome I could possibly hope for."

I search Ivan's face for a sign of deceit, any hint that he might be toying with me. I find none. I don't have time to be too elated about it, though, because a distant crash comes from somewhere in the house.

Ivan tilts his head. "I think it's dinner time."

Another crash, along with some yelling.

I wince. "And I think Rosalie might be done with the shower."

Both of us hurry out into the foyer, and Rosalie's screaming can be heard from somewhere behind the wide curved staircase.

"I did what you said!" *Crash*. "Now where's Preston? You told me he'd be here." *Crash, crash*. "I swear if he's hurt..."

Trailing behind Ivan, I follow him through a swinging door. The kitchen is just as grand as the rest of the house. Marble countertops. Stainless steel appliances. A restaurant-grade stove.

Rosalie's in a standoff with the maid. Her hair is wet and wild, sticking to her sneering face. Wearing just a pink robe, she's planted by an open cabinet, and she's got a stack of plates in her hand. There are sharp shards of destroyed dishes all around her bare feet.

"Baby," I rasp, walking forward. Rosalie's eyes light up at the sight of me, and she looks like she wants to run to me. I shake my head. "Don't move."

After removing the plates from her hands, I scoop her up. Broken pieces crunch under my shoes as I carry her away from the mess.

Ivan seems unfazed by her fit or the fact that she isn't dressed properly. Elegantly sweeping his arm out, he asks, "Shall we eat in the dining room?"

Rosalie turns up her nose. "I'd rather eat in my room with Preston."

"Let's hear him out." I kiss the top of her head.

She narrows her eyes like I just betrayed her. "You want to spend time with this guy after what he did to us?"

I can admit when I'm wrong. Yeah, my assumptions about who Ivan is as a person were right. He's a criminal.

However, I largely underestimated his love for his daughter.

I'd thought his drive to find her was fueled by pride and a sense of ownership. Maybe he couldn't stand the idea of someone else raising his kid. But it's not like that at all.

He and I aren't too different when it comes to her. We'd

both break the law just to make sure she's safe. We'd compromise our very souls for her happiness.

He went after us the way he did because he didn't know my intentions. He didn't know how much I love her.

Now he does, and he wouldn't hurt me if it meant hurting Rosalie in the process. I'm sure of it.

"I think there's been a misunderstanding," I tell her, and Ivan nods in agreement before leading us into a big room with a long eighteen-seat table.

A dim glow comes from a chandelier with fake candlesticks. Old paintings—no doubt expensive originals—hang on the beige walls. Mauve curtains frame the tall windows overlooking the backyard where there are some trimmed bushes and gardens lit up by solar spotlights.

Ivan pulls out the chair at the head of the table, and I place Rosalie in it. I sit adjacent to her, and Ivan takes the seat across from me.

Food is already spread out on domed dishes. When I remove the top from my plate, it's a gourmet meal of filet mignon, mashed potatoes, and roasted vegetables. Steam wafts up, and my mouth waters.

"Normally Helga would cook for us." Ivan waves his cloth napkin at the food before covering his lap with it. "But tonight I had Igor stop by one of my favorite restaurants. I hope you like it."

"How do we know you're not going to drug us?" Rosalie accuses, looking torn as she shoots suspicious looks at Ivan and longing glances at the steak.

"Darling, if I wanted you unconscious, I'd just call Nico back with the tranquilizer gun."

It takes me about two seconds to realize Ivan's joking. His lips twitch before he bursts out laughing. The man can joke. Who knew?

"Please, eat," he requests sincerely. "The sandwiches you ate on the way here were merely an appetizer. And I know it's late, but after dinner, I have a doctor coming to check you over."

Rosalie frowns. "A doctor? Like a real one?"

"Yes."

I give her a tight smile as I cover her hand with mine. "It's not a bad idea."

"Which part?"

"The food and the doctor."

"You trust him?" Rosalie asks, talking about her father like he's not in the room. Ivan's jaw ticks, but it's the only outward sign that he's annoyed.

"When it comes to you? Yeah," I answer. "I really do think he wants what's best for you."

"Then he should've let us go. He shouldn't have sent his thugs to hunt us down like dogs. He shouldn't have put a fucking tracker in my arm."

"I can deactivate the tracker," Ivan interjects with sad eyes. "In fact, once you've had time to recover from this ordeal, I'll have my doctor remove it all together. Rosalie." It's the first time he's said her false name, but he does it with sincerity. "You have every right to be angry. I did what I did because I was desperate. You have to understand—I didn't even know about you until you were four years old, and then I didn't know where you were. You had… vanished. Imagine waiting and worrying for as long as I have."

Rosalie blinks at the new information. Information I withheld from her for a reason. "So you've never met me before? Even when I was a baby?"

"No, darling."

"My mom told me you left us."

"I didn't. I couldn't have, since I was never with you in the first place."

"So my mom kept me a secret from you?"

We're getting dangerously close to the truth and Ivan knows it.

He just nods and says, "I searched for you for years. I couldn't find you, but not for lack of trying. If you hadn't gone to the hospital this past spring, I still wouldn't know where you were."

Seeming to come to a conclusion—a wrong one, but still one that makes sense to her—Rosalie sighs. "So my mom hid me to keep me away from you? From all this?" She waves a hand around at the house, but it's clear she means Ivan's job.

"Among other things," Ivan confirms. "Loralee Pearson isn't… sane."

"You got that right." Snorting, Rosalie loosens up a little, pointing her fork at Ivan. "It's a good thing you tolerate crazy chicks because I'm no picnic myself."

"Darling, you're not like her. You do know that, yes?"

"Yeah, I'm realizing that."

"Well, I'm not like that woman either." Ivan can't keep the contempt out of his voice. "I'm not going to hold you captive. All I've ever wanted for you is a good life. If that means caring for you from afar, then I can do that."

"Afar? Like, you don't want me to stay?" Rosalie's face is skeptical as she cuts her steak. She doesn't believe him, and for good reason. Ivan's done nothing to gain her trust, but I can tell he wants it.

Sighing, he suddenly looks tired. "I know you shouldn't be here. My lifestyle is dangerous. I can't offer you the independence and the adventures Etha—I mean, Preston can. But I'd like to help you both, if you'll let me. Let's make a compromise we'll all be happy with."

"Deals usually come with stipulations." Sitting up straighter, I say, "I'm going to need you to elaborate."

"In light of the recent discovery that you're married," Ivan gestures to us, "I'm going to extend an opportunity. I can give you the means to be comfortable. Money."

"Illegally obtained money," I deadpan.

"Gray money," Ivan contradicts.

"What's the difference?"

"What would you say if I told you I donate forty percent of what I make to charities?"

"You do?" Rosalie asks softly.

Ivan turns his eyes to her. "Yes. I'd be lying if I said my generosity is completely selfless. I did it for you. To find you. I figured it couldn't hurt to be involved with places you might go. Food banks, shelters, schools. Hospitals—every Christmas, I anonymously pay off hefty medical bills for people who can't afford it. It makes me a popular man and gives me a certain amount of influence." He glances my way. "Would you consider me a better person if I made my fortune through something boring, like banking, but kept it all for myself?"

Gray world. He's right about that. We're getting into the messy topic of ethics, and I'm definitely not an expert.

"On my dime, you can get an education," he continues. "A home somewhere far away where you'll be free from danger. More specifically, one of my vacation homes. You can live there cost-free. All I ask is that you keep the place up and let me visit a couple times a year."

Rosalie glances at me. I've seen that look before. The hope in her eyes.

In a silent exchange, we consider the option as we try to read each other.

A twitch of Rosalie's lips. *What do you think?*

I rub my jaw. *It's not bad.*

A shrug of her shoulders. *I wouldn't hate it.*

A subtle nod of agreement. *If that's what you want.*

I look to Ivan. His presentation sounds like a pretty sweet setup, but if we go along with this, I have to lay some ground rules. "There can be no illegal activity in or near the house."

"Of course," he agrees.

"And no one can know where we are."

"Absolutely."

"And if we choose to leave at any point, we're free to go, no questions asked."

Ivan hesitates. His gaze bounces to Rosalie, and I can see a genuine pleading there. He wants this. A connection to family. And he's afraid to lose it.

I think he's about to say yes when his cell phone rings. Picking it up off the table, he answers it. Although it's not on speaker, a frantic male voice comes through.

"Boss, there's an issue."

"What?" Ivan barks, scooting his seat away from the table to stand.

"An altercation between Nico and Donovan. Nico and I tried to bring Donovan in. He resisted. Shots were fired…"

That's all I hear before Ivan's too far away for me to catch more of the conversation, but I watch his body language. He's tense, his shoulder muscles bunched inside his white suit jacket. His knuckles lose color from gripping the phone so tight.

"He's not the only one who can track a person. Tap into his GPS and find him. I'll deal with him tomorrow." Ivan hangs up. Smiling as if nothing's amiss, he turns toward us. "Let's finish dinner and discuss the future."

∽

Ivan wasn't kidding when he said he'd been ready for Rosalie's arrival for years.

She has her own room in this big house, and it's clear that Ivan designed it just for her.

This place is like a time capsule.

The décor is stuck halfway between childhood and something more grown up. The walls are pink. A white dresser has a music box full of jewelry and a few little teddy bear statues on top of it. The matching vanity holds a giant spotlighted mirror, perfume, and a makeup kit. Dresses of various sizes—seriously, 5T to women's large—fill the walk-in closet. Shoes, too. There's a cushioned bench under the window, and when I opened it, I found a few dozen stuffed animals inside along with a child's catcher mitt, a baseball, and a bat.

I never knew someone could be so prepared for so long. And Ivan has been ready for any version of Rosalie. For as long as her father has known about her, he's been willing to accept her at any age, shape, or size.

That's love.

Going along with Ivan's future plans comes with risk—he claims he won't interfere with our lives, but if we're living in one of his houses, we'll be dependent on him. Part of me balks at the idea of accepting such generosity. As a grown man, I want to provide for my family, but the truth is, we're out of options and we need Ivan's help. There are still people out there looking for us, and it's dangerous for us to stay anywhere near Michigan. Getting out of the country altogether is ideal.

Of course, this means flying over the ocean, which will be terrifying for my wife. Nico might need to shoot her with the tranquilizer gun just to get her through the trip, which is scheduled for tomorrow morning on Ivan's private jet.

"Everything's happening so fast." Rosalie rolls over in bed to face me.

"Isn't that how we like to do things?" I tease.

Amused, she hums. "Guess so."

"Tomorrow, we'll get out of here." I pinch a wisp of her

hair between my fingers and feel the cool smoothness. "We'll be so far away, you won't even feel like we're on the same planet."

"The Maldives. Where exactly is that?"

"Southern Asia. It has beautiful beaches."

She shudders. "Why does it have to be by water?"

"A lot of vacation homes are. Plus, I'm pretty sure there's no extradition there. If Ivan needs to hide from the law, it would be a smart place to go." I lightly tap her chin. "I think you could get used to the water. You might even grow to love it. With some therapy—"

"You think I need a shrink? But you said I'm not crazy."

"Don't look so offended, baby." I try to keep my smile reassuring because, yeah, she needs counseling. It could take years for her to work through the shit of her life, but I don't say that. "Lots of normal people go to therapy. Loralee tainted your view of mental health. She made you believe there's either sane or insane, when in reality, there's a vast expanse of everything in between. Your trauma wasn't inherited. Something happened to you when you were young, and it changed you."

"What do you think happened?" Rosalie twists her lips to the side as she studies me. "Sometimes you talk as if you know more about me than I know about myself."

"How about I tell you what our lives will be like once we get to our destination?" I suggest.

If she notices the change in subject, she doesn't call me out on it. "Okay. Will we get jobs?"

"I don't think we'll have to. Not with the money Ivan's giving us."

"Then what will we do all day?"

I push Rosalie onto her back and climb over her. "I've got a lot of ideas."

Her legs fall open, and my cock notches against her hot

pussy. Unable to hold still, she squirms, rubbing herself on my dick.

She moans softly, trailing her finger over my bare shoulder as she bites her lip. "Be specific."

God, she's so perfect for me. Gorgeous. Fiercely loyal.

Always ready to love me.

That's the big one—she shows me love in so many ways. How she puts me first. How she's willing to fight for us. How her body lights up every time I'm close.

Jokingly, I rattle off a couple mundane activities that have nothing to do with sex. "We can go for walks. Drink non-alcoholic pina coladas. Oh." A great idea comes to me. "You could set up with your paints and canvases on the boardwalk and sell portraits."

Grinning, Rosalie playfully pokes my shoulder. "Uh, super fun, and we can revisit that idea another time, but I was thinking something hotter."

"Ah." I nod knowingly. "Sunbathing."

Rosalie laughs. "Only if you're fucking me while we do it."

I still don't take the bait. "That might result in some pretty weird tan lines."

She lets out a cute growl. "Stop toying with me, Preston. I need you now."

Remembering she was just looked over by the doctor, I mentally debate between ravaging her and getting her some Advil. "How was your checkup?"

"The doctor said I'm doing great."

I watch her for a sneeze, but it doesn't come.

"I'm serious," Rosalie insists. "After taking my temperature and my vitals, my father's doctor told me he didn't think I'd need medical intervention to get through my withdrawals. I'm a bit dehydrated, underweight, and likely dealing with a vitamin D deficiency, given my lack of sun exposure. But that's nothing some water, food, and supplements can't fix. The doctor said he'd fly out to the vacation home to check in on me a few weeks once we're settled. Talk about a house call, right?"

"In that case..." I thrust against her, then I start unbuttoning her pink satin pajama top. "I can think of some sexy activities. We'll lounge around naked with the back doors wide open." I circle her nipple before giving it a pinch.

Gasping, she grinds against my cock. "What else?"

"We'll be able to feel the warm breeze on our skin as we fuck in broad daylight." Sliding down, I scrape my teeth over her stomach. "I think day-fucking will be our new favorite hobby. And, baby, I can't wait to watch you ride me."

"Who says you have to wait?"

I halt my descent, and my eyes snap up to hers. The bedside lamp casts a dim light over her face. Her cheeks are pink, and she's giving me that look. So much heat and desire.

Rosalie hasn't taken the lead during sex yet. She's just been enjoying what I give her, learning what I show her is possible.

Now she's going to show me.

Wiggling out from under me, she gets me onto my back. My black sweatpants are dramatically tented, and all she has to do to free my erection is tug the stretchy waistband down.

I watch her as she pushes her own pants off. Straddling me, she lets her unbuttoned shirt slide off her shoulders, and she tosses it to the end of the bed.

I've got the best fucking view.

Some of her brown hair has come loose from the French braid I put it in. Long wisps frame her face, and the braid is draped over her shoulder, just begging to be grabbed.

"Rosie, baby." I wrap my fingers around the silky rope while rubbing her thigh. "Come fuck me."

Grabbing her waist, I encourage her to scoot up so my cock is poised at her soaked entrance.

If she has any apprehension about having sex under her father's roof, she doesn't show it. On the contrary, she takes my hard shaft in her hand and sinks down on me.

"Ohh," she moans, loud and unfiltered as her head tips back.

I glance at the locked door. I suppose whoever Ivan put on watch in the hallway could have a key. If they think I'm hurting Rosalie, they might barge in.

Guess we'll just have to be quiet, but I'm struggling just as much as she is. With a clenched jaw and flared nostrils, I breathe heavily through my nose as Rosalie works my big cock into her tiny body.

Just the sight of my length disappearing into her is enough to make me come, but I hold off.

It's always like this with her.

At first, I thought my lack of control was because I went without sex for so long. Now I know this is just how it is with Rosalie. She's a sex goddess.

Tight and wet. The noises she makes. How responsive her body is to every single touch.

Lowering herself until she's completely impaled on my dick, she winces and sighs at the stretch as she gets accustomed to the new position.

"How does it feel like this?" I ask, cupping one of her tits.

"Different," she pants, looking down at me through heavy-lidded eyes. "Deeper."

Sitting up, I graze my fingertips down her back while kissing her shoulder. "You have no idea what it does to me to see you like this. I'm just so fucking thankful you're mine."

She starts rocking her hips.

I groan.

Bracing her hands on my shoulders, she keeps moving, her motions getting more exaggerated as she slides up and down on me. Her nipples drag against my chest, and when her clit rubs on my lower stomach, she whimpers, "Talk to me. Tell me how much you need me."

To Rosalie, dirty talk isn't always dirty. She really gets off on the lovey-dovey shit. And if I'm being honest, so do I.

"I love you." I kiss the column of her throat. Latching onto a place I know she likes, I suck hard enough to leave a hickey. Then I begin lifting her by the hips, bouncing her on my lap. "God, I love my wife. You make me so damn happy. You're everything to me. You're all I need, but I'm still going to put a baby in your belly."

Her inner walls involuntarily clench at the mention of getting her pregnant.

She wraps her arms around my neck to get better leverage and kisses me hard on the lips before saying, "Well, there's nothing stopping us now."

CHAPTER 25

Rosalie

Morning comes quickly. With only one nightmare to wake me and Preston right there to cuddle me back to sleep, it wasn't the worst night I've ever had.

I'm pleasantly sore this morning. Muscles I've never been aware of are reminding me of what Preston and I did before going to sleep, and every time I move, there's an ache between my legs.

I want a repeat. Soon.

"I got this one for you on your sixteenth birthday." My father pulls my attention back to the present as he brings out yet another dress from the closet to fold it into one of the many suitcases he's giving me for the trip.

I doubt I'll ever wear a gown that fancy, but I smile anyway.

Currently, I'm in black leggings and one of Preston's flannels. Although I have a closet full of luxurious clothing at my disposal, I insisted on being comfortable for the flight. I'm still not sure how I'm going to get through it. Not only have I never been on a plane before, but the thought of being stranded over nothing but ocean for hours sounds like my own personal version of hell.

"Would you like a drink, darling?" Ivan asks, eyeing my

balled fists as I sit on the side of my bed. "I realize you're underage, but a shot of bourbon could help."

"No." I shake my head. "Thanks, though. I'm trying not to rely on substances to get through everything, you know?"

Returning to the closet, he beams at me, and his voice is muffled in the smaller space when he says, "Such a strong girl. I'm so proud of you."

My heart warms at his sincere compliment.

I've already forgiven him for yesterday. It's hard to stay mad when he's being so great. If I had doubts about his affection for me before, I don't anymore. Even though we're just getting to know each other, I can see through his tough exterior. As scary as he was when we first met, when it comes to me, he's a big softy.

I suspect no parent is perfect. Ivan's certainly far from it, but he's the only father I've got. It'll be a while before I think of him as "Dad" but I hope he and I will get there someday.

There's a swirl of longing and regret when I think about everything we've missed. All the father-daughter moments we never got to have.

I imagine he would've been the kind of dad who tucked me in at night and told me stories. He would've given me extra dessert because I pouted. And when I wanted to go to a real school, he would've let me because I begged. Probably a snooty all-girls private school, but still.

In return, I would've been his reprieve from the hard world he's built around himself.

I think we would've been good for each other.

As I touch another silky dress in his extended hands, sudden tears spring to my eyes. "You promise to come see us at Christmas?"

"Oh, Rosalie." He steps forward, and the frilly blue fabric

gets squished between us when he pats me on the shoulder. "I promise. Only being behind bars could keep me away."

I think he's joking. At least, I hope he's joking, but with his line of work, anything could happen.

"Then don't get arrested," I quip, and he chuckles as he goes back to making sure I have every outfit for any occasion.

Thankfully, it's not all formal wear. Opening the fourth suitcase, Ivan piles in some jeans in my size, leggings, T-shirts, tropical-looking tank tops, and flowy cotton sundresses.

Helga's been washing the clothes Ivan's guy collected from the cabin. If we were sticking around longer, I'd probably insist on wearing what I already have. But I have to admit, getting a new wardrobe is nice.

A soft knock comes at the open door of my bedroom.

I perk up because Preston's back from helping the guys load his luggage into the SUV Ivan's letting us drive to the airport. He's wearing a white T-shirt he borrowed from Ivan, his own leather jacket, and some dark-wash jeans Nico gave him. With the stubble on his face and his hair combed back, he looks like a modern-day James Dean.

Another day, another identity.

That seems to be the theme in my recent life.

At least the role I'm playing now has the advantages of private jets and vacation homes. The fact that Ivan's pilot is the one transporting us makes me feel a tiny bit better about the trip. All my father's employees know how much I'm worth. And what it would mean for them if something bad happens to me.

Being a mafia princess is weird.

The final suitcase snaps closed, and two men trail in behind Preston to carry them out.

"Preston. Welcome to the family." Ivan extends his arm, and at first, I think he's going to shake Preston's hand. But then I see the back end of the gun he's offering. "Take it," he insists. Preston hesitates, so Ivan adds, "Please. It would make me feel better to know you have it for protection. It's loaded. The safety is on."

Reluctantly, Preston accepts it and sticks it in the back of his jeans under his shirt. I've only seen people do that in movies. Me? I'd shoot my own ass off.

My husband comes over, cups my face, and plants a swift kiss on my lips. "I'm going to give you a minute alone to say goodbye. I'll be in the SUV."

Nodding, I watch him go.

I hop off the bed and face my father. "Well, this is it, I guess."

"I'm sorry I can't see you off at the plane." Ivan glances down at his phone. "Donovan wants to meet at the mall, and I can see he's already there waiting for me," he scoffs. "The coward is too scared to see me in private."

I give him a look. "Gee, I wonder why."

He snickers and shrugs.

Giving my room another once-over, I thank him for everything he's doing for us. "Seriously. It means a lot to me to have your support." I pick up one of the ceramic teddy bears and touch its textured head. "Maybe once it's safer here, Preston and I can come back. It's funny that this place sort of feels like home already. I think I would've liked growing up here."

Ivan's eyes soften, but he's splitting his attention between me and his phone. His face looks troubled as he swipes up on the screen. "And I would have enjoyed that very much, but you must go now. Loralee Pearson has increased her efforts. There are posts about you and Preston on the internet. How do you kids say these days? Viral. News has gone viral."

Great. Internet sleuths are the last thing we need right

now. Those people can be incredibly tenacious, and for once, I'm glad I don't have any social media accounts.

"Bye, Ivan." A hug doesn't quite feel right, so I awkwardly shake my father's hand.

Stopping in the doorway on my way out of the room, I take one more good look at the home that could've been mine.

But there's no point on dwelling on the past or hypothetical situations. Because I've got a future with the man I love, and that's all that matters.

CHAPTER 26

Preston

I haven't felt this at peace in a long time. We're almost in the clear.

Before we left Ivan's, he gave me backroad directions to the airport. It's a longer drive—about thirty minutes instead of twenty—but I don't mind.

I love hearing Rosalie softly hum to the radio with the window cracked, the cool wind whipping through her hair.

"Can you believe this?" she says for the third time, patting the duffle bag at her feet.

It's full of cash. In addition to letting us keep the stash we already had, Ivan gave us another fifty thousand, with the promise that an account would be set up for us in The Maldives.

"You know what I'd really love to do?" Rosalie holds up a wad of hundreds.

"What's that?"

"Have sex on a big pile of money."

I bark out a laugh. "Are you serious?"

"Yeah. We could spread it all out on the bed and just roll around in it naked."

"As sexy as that sounds, money is covered in bacteria. It sounds like an infection waiting to happen."

Rosalie drops the bills back into the bag. "Party pooper. Don't ruin my fantasy."

"Okay, okay. I would risk E. coli for you."

She laughs.

Unfortunately, our carefree banter is interrupted by an intruder.

I notice a vehicle in the rearview mirror, and I instantly have a dreadful sinking in my gut.

It's a black SUV like the one we're driving. Tinted windows. Blacked-out plates.

Did Ivan forget something? Maybe he had to send one of his guys after us.

"Rosie, check my phone, would you? Any calls or texts?" I try to sound nonchalant, but I must fail because Rosalie looks concerned as she picks up the burner Ivan gave me.

After flipping it open, she snaps it shut and sets it back in the cupholder. "Nothing. Why?"

It wouldn't be completely out of the ordinary for someone else to take this route, but the vehicle behind us is getting closer. Fast. I'm already pushing sixty miles per hour on a bumpy country road that isn't meant for high speeds, so whoever's behind us is booking it.

Noticing the way I keep glancing in the mirror, Rosalie turns to look behind us. Her eyes go wide, because now the asshole is right there, way too close for comfort.

It can't be Ivan. He wouldn't gain our trust just to hunt us down when we least expect it. He wouldn't do that to Rosalie, and he wouldn't endanger her. Plus, if he wanted me out of the picture, he would've done it in the privacy of his own home.

I don't believe this is random either. They're after us.

Choices, choices. Go faster or slow down?

There are no side streets for me to take to try to lose them. We're still ten minutes from the airport.

Suddenly, the SUV speeds up and tries to pass us on the left.

I veer over a little to give them some room, but instead of going ahead of me, the vehicle gets closer, crowding me into the ditch.

"Shit." I hit the gas to get ahead of them and swerve back onto the road.

"What the hell is going on?" Rosalie asks, right before they speed up and ram our bumper.

She shrieks.

"Fuck." My hands tighten on the wheel as I try to maintain control of the vehicle.

Hyperventilating, Rosalie makes a grabby motion at me. "Quick, give me the gun."

"What are you gonna do, baby? Hang out the window and shoot at him?"

"If I have to!"

Grunting, I jerk the wheel to avoid a deep pothole, because if we hit a dip going this fast, we could wreck.

Maybe that's what they're hoping for. Whoever's in that vehicle, they want us to stop, either by choice or force.

There's only one thing for us to do—the unexpected.

"Rosie," I say calmly, even though my heart is racing, "put the cell phone in your pocket."

"Okay." She slips the device into the chest pocket of the flannel.

"Good. Now button it in so it won't fall out."

She does what she's told. "Don't you think we should call Ivan?"

"No, he wouldn't be able to get here in time. I need you to hold on tight, all right? Grab the door handle and dig your feet into the carpet. I'm going to hit the brakes on the count of three."

Bless her, she doesn't question me or protest. She just obeys. She trusts me with everything. Her life, her heart.

I don't want to let her down.

"Three, two, one." I slam my foot on the brake.

Our tires squeal as they skid. We're not fully stopped, but a second later, our pursuer crashes into us from behind. Hard.

Hard enough to make the front end of their vehicle buckle up like an accordion. If we're lucky, they might be injured or unconscious, and we can make our getaway.

Pushing down on the pedal, I try to accelerate, but the SUV just shakes as our tires spin. The smell of burnt rubber wafts up. I floor it again, but we're not going anywhere.

"Our bumpers are stuck together. Fuck! Get out." I open my door before rushing around to Rosalie's side. No one emerges from the other vehicle, but we can't stay here. "Still got the cell phone?"

Rosalie pats her pocket. "Yeah."

Taking her by the elbow, I drag her into the woods lining the road. "If we can get to a concealed spot and call Ivan, maybe I can find out what the hell is going on."

"What about the money?" Rosalie asks, glancing behind us as we trudge through dried leaves. "And all our stuff?"

"We leave it. It'll do us no good if we're dead."

Her body jolts. "Dead? You think we're going to die?"

I look back at the road. I can still see both vehicles through the trees. Steam is coming from under the hood of the one that had been chasing us. Other than that, there's no movement.

I have no idea who we're dealing with, but I hope they're knocked out cold.

I get my gun out. It's been a long time since I held a weapon in my hand with the intention of using it. Flicking the safety off, I point it down while keeping my finger along it, so I'm ready to get to the trigger if I have to.

Tucking Rosalie close to my side, I say, "It'll be all right."

I'm not sure if it's true, but Rosalie believes me. She nods quickly as she clings to me.

My good girl. My sweet yet fiery wife. I hate that she's been through so much in the past few days. I'd thought those difficulties were in the past. I'd thought we were home free.

I'd thought wrong.

A loud bang goes off somewhere. Rosalie shrieks, and it takes me a second to realize my gun has dropped from my hand.

Then the pain registers.

My palm feels like it's been run through a shredder. Looks like it, too. Blood is flowing out of the bullet-sized wound in a steady trickle.

Shoving Rosalie behind a thick tree, I cover her body with mine. Another shot rings out and the bark near my head splinters.

"Oh my God," Rosalie whimpers. "We're being shot at." When she sees my injury, her eyes go wide and her jaw drops. "Did you get shot?"

"Yep," I rasp. "Stay very still."

I peek out, and I only see a blur of black clothing on a tall frame before our attacker is unloading two more rounds that hit the ground near us. I duck back behind the tree.

Those are warnings. If he's good enough to aim for my firing hand and hinder my ability to shoot back, he could definitely hit me somewhere vital.

Tearing the bottom of my shirt with my teeth, I rip a strip off and wrap the fabric tightly around my hand. It hurts like hell, but it's not life-threatening.

"I dropped my gun," I say in a hushed whisper. "We don't have anything to fight back with. You need to be ready to run." Before Rosalie can convince me otherwise, I shout, "Okay, you've got us. Why don't you tell me what you want, and we'll see if we can come to an agreement?"

"The girl," the gruff reply comes from about twenty feet away.

He's getting closer.

He's also asking for the one thing I can't give him. "What do you want with her?"

"There's a large reward on her head. I intend to cash in. She won't be harmed. I promise you that."

"You're working for Loralee Pearson?"

"I work for myself." That's basically a yes. Fucking Loralee.

"What about Preston?" Rosalie chimes in. "What do you want with him?"

"I can get extra money if I bring him, too. Preferably alive, but I'll take him dead if I have to. Reward will still be the same."

"You don't want to do this," Rosalie barks defiantly. "My father is a very scary man. He'll come after you."

The man chuckles. "On the contrary, Ivan Belov should be scared of me. He has no idea what I'm capable of."

Rosalie tilts her head to the side as if she's coming to a realization. "Donovan? Is that you?"

"She's a smarty pants," he quips, confirming her suspicion.

I've only heard the guy talk once before I was tranquilized, but now I recognize the slight southern drawl. "Aren't you supposed to be meeting Ivan?"

"Yep. If only that asshole was as smart as he is rich," Donovan sneers. "Lucky for me, he's not."

I hate that Donovan's right. If he'd known Ivan was watching his location, all he'd have to do is leave his device where he wanted Ivan to think he is.

I suppose Ivan could be realizing his mistake right now. He might be heading this way.

He might be too late.

Rosalie's shaking more than she was before, and I don't think it's because of the cold.

Donovan scares her.

Listening intently, I measure his footsteps. He's slowly and methodically closing in, but there's an unnatural rhythm to his gait. Step, slide. Step, slide.

He's limping. Looks like that crash might've banged him up after all. Which means Rosalie might have a chance at getting away if I can injure him more.

But that means using the only card I have left to play.

The absolute last resort.

Self-sacrifice.

Ever since realizing Rosalie feels the same way about me that I do about her, I've been determined to stay together. Separating was never an alternative I wanted to consider.

Admitting defeat sucks. Giving up the love of my life sucks even more, but I'll do anything to protect Rosalie.

Time to wave the white flag.

Slipping my good hand into my back pocket, I pass my wallet to Rosalie and very quietly say, "Take this. Inside, you'll find a business card for Jen Harding. When I say 'go' I want you to run that way." I tip my head to the deeper part of the woods. "Go as far as you can, then hide and call Jen." Rosalie's looking up at me with big, fearful eyes, and she's trembling as she waits for more instructions. "Tell her you're with Ethan Smith and your name is Melody Parks. Say you're on County Road twenty-one-hundred North about ten miles south of the airport."

"Melody?" Her eyebrows pinch together. "Who's Melody Parks?"

"What's all that whispering about over there?" Donovan asks. Maybe eight feet away now. "Don't do something stupid."

"Just do it," I hiss. "It's very important that you do this. Do you understand me?"

"Why are you talking like you won't be there?" Rosalie asks.

I give her a look, and she sees the pain in my eyes. She starts shaking her head violently, but I put my finger to my lips to hush whatever hysterical rant she's got on deck.

"Listen." I project my voice to Donovan. One last attempt to bargain with him. "We have cash. A lot of it. Why don't you just take that instead? It's more than the reward you'll get."

"Or I could take your money *and* the reward." Fucker won't be reasoned with.

It's clear he intends to leave here with Rosalie. And my dead body, most likely.

Well, over my dead body, motherfucker.

CHAPTER 27

Rosalie

Preston's about to do something very foolish. I feel it. I know it.

Gripping his wallet in one hand, I hook my other around his elbow to hold him back from doing whatever he's considering.

"We surrender," he tells Donovan. "We'll go peacefully."

When my nose starts to tingle, I know it's a lie. What the fuck? My internal lie detector is extended to Preston now? Well, they do say holy matrimony joins you as one person.

I sneeze as Preston puts his hands up. I sneeze again when he slowly moves forward while shrugging me off his arm.

I don't want to let him go, but I don't want to defy him either. He gave me instructions that could save us.

Or save *me*, at least.

Needless to say, I don't agree with that.

What would Harlee Verona do? Would she listen to Preston or would she do something stupid along with him?

Putting his injured hand out behind him, he gives me a 'stay' gesture, making it clear that he's going forward with his plan whether I like it or not. Blood is soaking through his self-made bandage, and it's dripping from his fingertips.

My heart's in my throat as he exposes himself completely

to the man after us. The man who doesn't care if Preston lives or dies.

"Where's the girl?" Donovan asks, and just so he knows I'm still here and doesn't start shooting again, I peek out from behind the tree.

"I'm here."

He doesn't look triumphant or happy to see me. It's worse. He looks resentful. Bitter. He has the same disappointed expression my mom always wore when I did something bad.

Keeping his gun aimed at Preston, he says, "You two have caused me a lot of trouble."

Yeah, I guess so. Preston got Donovan good yesterday with that headbutt. Two little white strips are taped over the gash on the bridge of his red, swollen nose. Dark bruises surround his eyes like a raccoon.

In addition to that, he's made an enemy out of Ivan. I suspect if my father gets Donovan alone, he'll have worse worries than a banged-up face.

He crooks his finger. "Out, girlie."

Preston discreetly wags his hand at me, flicking blood this way and that.

I know he wants me to leave. To run away from him. I just can't right now. Not when a gun is pointed right at him.

"How did you find me?" I ask, stalling.

Donovan smiles, but what should look like a friendly expression is creepy with his dead, dark eyes. "The tracker, of course."

"Ivan turned it off."

"And he thinks I can't turn it back on?" He laughs. "I can find anyone, anywhere. I'm the best investigator there is."

"No." I shake my head. "Preston is."

Donovan smirks. "If that were the case, do you really think we'd be in this situation? Listen, I'm not fucking around. Do you want to end up like the last guy Ivan hired?"

Preston's body jerks, like he's shocked. "That was you? You killed the detective?"

"Who else would it be?" Donovan screws up his face, like he's offended someone else might get the credit for his murder.

"Honestly? Figured the guy pissed Ivan off, and Ivan offed him in return."

Shrugging, Donovan explains, "He was standing in the way of me and a lot of money. I needed this job. Then Ivan went and hired you instead. He put me on the sidelines like I'm his backup plan."

"So you decided to double dip?" Preston asks. "Take his money and collect Loralee's reward?"

"No. I was loyal to Ivan until he made it clear he wants to bash my face in. I did my job—he should be thanking me, but of course nothing is good enough for him. I'm done with this shit. I'm looking to retire. *Today*," Donovan emphasizes. "And I can't do it without Loralee Pearson's money."

During the conversation, Donovan's been distracted, and I notice Preston's using it to his advantage. He's been inching, ever so slowly, toward his gun that's still on the ground. It's several feet ahead of him, though. Plus, it's closer to Donovan than it is to him.

Raising my hands above my head, I start to shuffle from my hiding place. "Okay. Okay, Donovan. You got us. See? I'm coming out. Just don't hurt us. We'll go with you."

My damn nose. It burns as soon as I say the last part, because I know for a fact Preston doesn't intend to make this easy for him.

When I sneeze a third time, Donovan motions me forward with the gun. "Move it. It's too cold out here. I can't deliver you sick."

Suddenly, Preston lunges forward. At first, I think he's diving for his gun but instead, he goes past it, tackling Donovan at the knees.

With a pained shout, Donovan falls backward, and his handgun goes off, sending a bullet to the sky. There's a scuffle between the two men. Preston gets a few good punches in with his left fist, but Donovan's still got a firm grasp on the gun.

"Go, Rosalie!" Preston yells. "I mean it, damn it. RUN!"

Remembering what he said about the business card in his wallet, I do just that. I turn and stumble over logs and leaves as my shaking fingers take out the card and the phone. It's difficult to keep going while tapping the right digits on the cell, but somehow, I get it done.

I press send.

Without stopping my hike, I hold the phone to my ear and listen as the line rings twice.

"Harding," a female voice answers. Her voice is low and gravelly, like someone in the movies who smokes a lot.

I'm out of breath, but I manage to repeat what Preston told me to. "M-my name is Melody Parks." Pant, wheeze. Much to my surprise, I don't sneeze at the falsehood, and after I rattle off our approximate location, I finish with, "A guy is here with a gun. Donovan somebody. Preston—I mean, Ethan Smith is fighting him right now. Ethan's trying to protect me, but he might get killed."

Silence. Thinking the connection got cut off, I check the screen, but the call is still there.

"Hello?" I ask impatiently, stomping over beds of twigs.

"Did you say Melody Parks?" There are some papers rustling in the background, and I don't know why the hell she's caught up on that part and not sending help.

"Yes! Please, hurry," I tell her urgently.

"We're on our way," she says. "I need you to get somewhere safe."

Just then, the cracking blast of the gun echoes through the woods.

I stop.

Turn.

I've gone so far that I can barely see the road, but I know Preston's back there somewhere.

Another shot.

Then another.

I flinch with each one, and it feels like my heart is going to leap right out of my chest.

"Melody? Melody, are you there?" The words coming through the speaker are needy and excited, but this call isn't important.

Not if Preston is dead.

Because if he's gone, nothing matters.

I flip the phone shut and slip it back into my pocket.

I can't leave without Preston by my side, so I stagger in the direction I came from, back toward the danger. I'm already winded from running, but I keep going as fast as I can without falling on my face.

Everything is too silent and still.

Quiet as death itself.

No birds are chirping. There's no wind whistling through the branches.

It's just my footsteps and breathing. Alone. All alone.

As I get closer to where we were before, I recognize the tree we'd been standing behind because a chunk of bark is missing from where the bullet struck.

My knees are weak, and my stomach is churning.

Pressing my palms to the rough surface of the tree, I use it to support myself as I make my way around it.

When I find both Preston and Donovan lying on the ground a few feet apart from each other, I cry out and stumble.

Neither of them are moving.

Did they kill each other?

Tears burn my eyes as I drop to my knees and crawl forward.

Preston's gun is still in the same place he dropped it before, near his foot. He looks like he's sleeping. His lips are pink, and his face is peaceful as the sun shines through the branches overhead.

"Preston?" I whimper, straddling one of his thighs as I kneel over him.

Laying my hand on his chest, I wait for movement.

A breath fills his lungs.

He's alive.

Quickly, I take stock of his injuries.

There's a small pool of blood forming in the mud underneath his hand. The fabric he used to wrap it is so wet it's useless now. A gash above his eyebrow is also bleeding quite a bit. Obviously, he got hit in the head pretty hard.

Wrestling off the new gray peacoat Ivan gave me, I bunch it up and slide it under his head.

When I find more blood on the ground around his left side, I unzip his leather jacket, and I see red.

Bright red, soaking the white T-shirt. The fabric is heavy and sticking to his skin, but I push it up. Peel it off, is more like it.

The wet sound from the fabric makes me want to gag, and when I get to a place under Preston's ribs, there's a red stream continuously oozing from a bullet hole in his abdomen.

I make a noise of despair.

I'm not familiar enough with anatomy to guess where the internal damage is, but I know he's losing too much blood.

"Oh, no. No." Taking off my flannel shirt, I place it over his wound and apply pressure like they would in one of the crime shows. Slow the bleeding. That's the best I can do.

I'm in just a fitted T-shirt now, and the chilly air adds to my trembling. Shaking so hard I'm practically vibrating, I sob quietly, "P-preston, wake up. Please. Please, d-don't leave me. I can't do any of this without you. I love you."

I softly kiss his lips. They're warm, and breath is passing through his nose.

I take comfort in that, but my reprieve doesn't last long.

A grunt comes from a few feet away, and Donovan's arm twitches. He's regaining consciousness.

Readying myself to defend my man, I reach back, grope around, and find Preston's gun. I have no idea how to use it, but maybe the threat will be enough to get Donovan to back off.

When he stands, it's hard to tell where he's injured because he's wearing all black, but the material of his jacket is torn over his shoulder, and it looks wet. Maybe Preston shot Donovan with his own gun during the struggle. Good.

Donovan's also favoring his left leg, and his nose is busted up even worse than before. Blood runs from his nostrils, down his lips and chin.

He snarls at me while eying the gun in my shaking grip. I'm probably holding it wrong, but my finger is on the trigger.

The concept of shooting is simple enough. Point and pull.

"You're not going to shoot me, sweetheart."

"I might." I'm telling the truth. One hundred percent.

If he doesn't see how serious I am, then he's an idiot. He's backed me into a corner. I don't like being cornered.

I've stopped thinking of him as a person. He's just an obstacle in my way.

Armed and dangerous.

Armed and dangerous.

Mentally ill teenager on the loose.

The claims from the news reports come back at me like a cruel taunt. Maybe they weren't so far off after all. I never wanted to be in this position—kneeling over the love of my life, aiming a weapon at someone I want to kill.

But I've been given no other choice.

"You're going to come with me." Donovan lifts his gun so the barrel is aimed at Preston's chest.

One more shot, and I don't think Preston will make it.

Donovan and I are at an impasse. He'll take my soul mate from me, definitely. I'll try to take his life from him, but I might miss.

Hot tears coat my cheeks. "I'm not leaving without him."

"Then you can help me carry his ass to the car. I don't care as long as you hurry the fuck up."

"He needs a hospital. Please."

The flannel shirt is almost soaked through.

With every second that goes by, Preston's life is leaking out of him. The sight of how much blood is around me is jarring. It makes me feel light-headed, and I sway a little.

I can't pass out right now. I can't.

A faint ringing starts up in my ears. I close my eyes, swallow hard, and shake my head.

The ringing gets louder.

It takes me a second to realize the sound isn't inside my mind. It's coming from somewhere else. And it's getting louder.

I know that sound.

Sirens. Lots of them.

My eyes snap open just in time to see Donovan closing the distance between us. Limping, he keeps his gun on Preston. "You don't have a choice. Either come with me or he dies now."

He grabs at my hair to pull me up. My scalp stings as chunks of strands come out, and something inside me snaps.

I'm really fucking tired of everyone telling me what to do.

As I'm yanked to my feet, I point the gun and pull the trigger.

Donovan wails as he drops his weapon so he can clutch his

upper thigh with both hands. I got him in the right leg, dangerously close to his groin. He falls to his ass.

I just gape at him. I actually shot him. I mean, yeah, it's not hard to aim at close range, but still.

A new sound joins the sirens as the *chop, chop, chop* of a helicopter passes over us. My rescue is getting closer, but I can't look away from Donovan's wound. It's spewing blood at an alarming rate.

He lets out a rageful scream as he struggles to get to his feet. With both legs out of commission, he can hardly walk.

Waddling, he makes a slow retreat to the SUV Preston had been driving. I keep the weapon trained on him until he crawls into the driver's seat.

Since the vehicles are stuck together, it's not easy for him to get going. He battles with the gearshift, switching from reverse to drive a few times before the bumpers are finally dislodged.

The passenger side door is still open, and as he speeds away, some of the cash from the duffle bag flies out and scatters.

Preston groans, and I look down to see his face screwed up with pain.

"Babe?" I ask excitedly, kneeling beside him. "Wake up. Please, wake up."

My face is hovering right over his when he blinks and opens his eyes. A relieved sob lurches from my throat.

Grimacing, Preston tightens his lips thin as he grits his teeth. "Donovan."

"He's gone. Just rest. Y-you don't have to talk," I soothe, trying not to be a blubbering mess. "Help is coming. We'll tell them the truth." I try to sound optimistic as I resume pressure on Preston's abdomen. "We'll just tell them we want to be together, and they have to let us, you know? We're adults. We're free."

"Are you hurt?"

"I'm fine."

Even when he's literally bleeding out, Preston's thinking of me. My esophagus becomes impossibly tight as my emotions become too much.

What if this is the last time Preston and I ever speak to each other?

I don't even want to entertain that as a possibility, but whatever I say now, it has to count. "I just want you to know how much I appreciate everything you've done for me. And how much I love you. You're my whole life, Preston."

The sirens are louder. Deafening. So many sets of flashing lights line the road now. Police cars, ambulances, even a fire truck.

Preston's eyelids droop as he gazes up at me. "I love you, too, baby. Never thought I could love something like I love you. Never knew someone could help me love myself. And I haven't given you enough credit, because you're so strong. Did you know that? I think you might even be braver than me. So strong… And you're like a lighthouse, only you shine love on me wherever I am. You're a love lighthouse. It's good… love…"

I think he's delirious. His words are slurred and not making a ton of sense, but he's talking, so I'll take it.

People are approaching us. They fan out, surrounding us from all sides.

Instinctively, I curl over Preston.

The man who's the closest stealthily moves around a tree, and he's holding a gun. That's when I notice a lot of the officers have weapons. They're all looking at us as if we're dangerous. As if we're the threat.

"Don't hurt him," I beg. "He didn't do anything. He didn't do anything wrong."

"Baby," Preston whispers weakly. "Just do what they say."

"Ma'am, we're going to need you to drop the weapon."

I'd forgotten about the gun. It's still in my hand.

I toss it away and raise my arms to prove I'm compliant. As they swarm in around us, my concern stays on Preston. He's still lying flat on the ground, his hand covering the shirt to keep pressure on the wound. His face is too pale. Almost grayish. He's not supposed to be that color.

"He's been shot at least twice that I know of," I announce. "He's hurt, so be careful with him."

Someone shouts for a medic and new people start running this way.

A blur of activity follows. A stretcher is brought over, and I scoot back to give everyone room to help Preston. After a tubed mask is put on his face, hands wrap around my wrists from behind. Two men help me—well, *force me* is more like it—to my feet.

"Ma'am, do you have any other weapons on you?"

"No." I don't know why they bother asking, because they're checking for themselves, patting my ankles and legs, moving their way over my body.

"Do you need medical attention?" The question is aimed at me, but the voice seems far away. "Ma'am? Ma'am?"

"I think she's in shock," someone else says.

"Move! Move out of the way." It's the low, gravelly voice from the phone. Jen Harding. And she's nothing like how I pictured her.

Petite and blonde, she wears a no-nonsense pantsuit. White and pristine. She's going to get it all dirty out here. At least her shoes are ready for action. Combat boots are an odd pairing with her outfit, but somehow, they look right on her.

"Give the girl some space, for God's sake," she scolds, her middle-aged face wrinkling with a disapproving scowl. "And someone get her a blanket."

When she locks eyes with me, her demeanor softens just

a tad. She looks at me in a way that's not quite motherly, but there's a depth of something I can't identify in her eyes.

I think she cares about me, but that can't be right. I've never met her before. Have I?

She offers her hand for a shake, confirming that we probably don't know each other. I just stare at it, but she stubbornly keeps it extended. "Jen Harding, Federal Bureau of Investigation. I specialize in missing children's cases."

I'm a little confused. That doesn't pertain to me because I'm not a child. Besides, I haven't been missing for that long. Yeah, my mom made a big stink about it, but the FBI should really save their resources for more important people.

I finally go to shake Jen's hand, but metal clinks, and I realize my arms are locked behind my back. They cuffed me? I guess I hadn't been paying attention. I didn't even notice the metal go around my wrists.

Jen's eyes widen, and she fumbles with a keyring. "You cuffed a kidnapping victim? What's wrong with you? I knew I shouldn't have let rookies come along for this."

"Preston didn't kidnap me," I interject, but everyone ignores me.

"She had a gun," a man argues.

Another officer tries to back up his coworker, but Jen cuts them off with a loud scoff as she unlocks my handcuffs.

"You're not old enough to know who this is, are you?" she asks the young officer to my right. "Melody Parks. Name ring a bell?" She waits for all of one second before answering, "Of course it doesn't. You were too busy playing T-ball while she was living a nightmare."

"I'm not really Melody Parks," I admit, rubbing my freed wrists. "Preston—I mean, Ethan just told me to say that."

A scratchy blanket is draped over my shoulders, and Jen gets in front of me. "Do you know why he told you to say that?"

"No?" It comes out sounding like a question.

She scrutinizes me with her light-brown eyes, and I get a weird feeling. Like she can see through me. Like she can see something I don't.

The hairs on the back of my neck stand, and my body convulses with a shiver.

She tugs the blanket tighter around my shoulders. "I'm going to ride in the ambulance with you, if that's all right."

Absentmindedly, I nod. "As long as I get to be with Preston, I don't care."

Gently urging me to move forward, she puts her hand on my back. "They're already leaving with him."

I see what she means when the sirens and lights turn back on, and the big white vehicle speeds past Donovan's wrecked SUV. Panic floods in at the thought of being separated from Preston, and I resist Jen's efforts to get me to go toward the second ambulance.

"They're going to the same place," she reminds me.

And I relent because I go where Preston goes. Always.

CHAPTER 28

Rosalie

Well, this isn't how I pictured my day.
I'm supposed to be freaking out on a plane while flying over the ocean.

Now I'm just freaking out in a hospital room by myself.

Two officers are stationed outside my door, so I feel a little bit like a prisoner. Not like I want to leave, though. On arrival, I was told Preston is in surgery and it could be a while before he wakes up. Might as well wait.

Hanging out in a bed with TV, meals, and nurses on standby in the meantime isn't so bad. The IV and the heart monitor are probably overkill.

I've had a battery of tests done to determine if I have whiplash or a concussion from the crash. Other than being cold, shaken up, and sore, the doctor hasn't found anything seriously wrong with me. They still want me to stay the night for observation.

My mom is probably shitting her pants.

By now, I'm sure she's caught wind of the fact that I've been found, so I've made sure everyone knows I don't want her visiting. The last thing I need is my suffocating mother hovering over my bed. If she comes here, hopefully Jen will be around to intercept her.

I like Jen. I recounted my entire story to her in the

ambulance, starting with how strict my mother has always been and how I waited until what I *thought* was my eighteenth birthday to make my escape. And how Preston was there to help me—I really emphasized that part, because they need to know he didn't take me against my will. I left out the fact that he was hired by my father. Painting him as a good Samaritan just sounds better.

Speaking of Jen.

A knock comes at the door and she pokes her head in. "Oh, good. You're not asleep." She's got a thick beige folder in her hands as she pulls the visitor chair over to the bed and takes a seat. "There are some things you need to know."

She's so solemn, it makes my concern spike. "Preston's okay, right?"

"This isn't about Preston. It's about you."

I calm a little and link my hands over my stomach. "Okay."

"What's your earliest memory?"

What a random question. "Um..." I shake my head. "I guess a petting zoo at my house?" I tell her about the time my mom hired the traveling zoo for my birthday. "Or what I thought was my birthday," I add. "She lied about that."

"Loralee Pearson lied about a lot of things," Jen says wryly. "Before I start telling you everything, I want you to know there's a counselor here at the hospital for you to talk to until we can set you up with a permanent therapist."

There goes the therapy talk again. "Listen, I'll talk to someone if it'll make everyone feel better, but I'm not crazy. My mom lied about that, too. You know she's dishonest, so why would you believe her?"

Instead of reassuring me of my sanity, Jen goes on, "I've dedicated my life to finding missing children. More often than not, I fail. Those failures keep me up at night."

She looks exhausted as she runs a hand through her

shoulder-length hair. It's feathered and frizzy, like she tried to tame it with hairspray, but she couldn't stop touching it. An anxious habit. Her job really gets to her. Maybe she cares too much.

"I know a thing or two about trouble sleeping," I tell her, so she knows I can relate.

We share a small smile, then she opens her folder and places a picture on the bed next to me.

It's me.

I know it as soon as I see the blond hair, the two-toned eyes, and the cleft in my chin. But I'm young here. Just a baby. My wispy curls aren't even down to my shoulders yet, and I'm a little pudgy.

"Eleven months old," Jen clarifies, tapping the photo. "Have you ever seen a picture of yourself at this age?"

Now that I think about it, no. I haven't. All the pictures around our house were of me as a toddler or older.

I flip the picture over.

Jen points at the name scrawled on the back. "Melody."

"What's this Melody stuff?" I glance at her. "Did my mom have my name changed?"

Taking out her phone, Jen hits a couple buttons and sets it on the table next to the bed. There's a business-like air about her as she says, "I'm going to record our conversation if that's okay. We might need it later for legal purposes."

"Legal purposes? Do I need a lawyer? People are supposed to request a lawyer during an interrogation, right?"

Jen gives me a reassuring smile. "You're not being charged with anything, Melody. You're the victim here."

I rub my temples because the name is starting to stir up strange feelings. "Can you stop calling me that? It sounds weird."

"All right. All right, Rosalie. What I'm about to tell you is going to be upsetting. If you need me to stop, say so."

My palms are sweating. My heart is racing. I feel like life as I know it is a ticking time bomb, but I nod anyway.

Apparently Jen knows my history well enough to recite it by memory, because she doesn't look down at her papers when she starts to tell me my beginning. "You were born on September 25th nineteen years ago to a woman named Mara Wick. She was an exotic dancer. She had some issues with substance abuse, but it would seem she stayed sober during the pregnancy."

"Wait," I interrupt her. "Are you telling me my mother used to be a stripper with a different identity?"

"No, I'm saying Loralee Pearson is not your biological mother."

"She—" I blink. "She never told me I'm adopted."

My mother and I look enough alike that I never questioned our relation. There were even times when I felt like I saw parts of myself in her. We have similar noses. We're both blondes with fair skin. She's short like me.

Plus, the mental illness issue... Oh, *fuck me*. Even that's a big pile of bullshit.

It can't be hereditary because we're not related.

Jen pushes on with the story. "After you were born, Mara started using again. Heroin, mostly. She died of an overdose when you were four months old. The authorities were called to her apartment because the neighbors heard a baby crying for the entire day. Since the father was unlisted on the birth certificate and Mara had no immediate family who would take you in, you went into foster care."

She pauses, giving me a moment to process everything she said. Once she stares at me for several seconds and realizes I'm not freaking out, she continues, "You suffered from an abusive situation in one of the foster homes when you were two years old. You were caught stealing cookies from the pantry, and when the parents questioned you about it, you denied it. They knew you were lying, so they held you over the sink, put a cloth on your face, and poured water on it. It seems this was their go-to method of punishment."

My nose starts to burn, and I rub it. "Waterboarding?"

Jen looks surprised with her raised eyebrows. "You remember it?"

"Not really." My damn nose does, though. I rub at it some more. "Did they do that to me a lot?"

"Yes, for a few months, until one of the older kids in the home reported it."

The mystery of my inability to lie and the sneezing suddenly becomes clear. Because every time I try to picture myself as a little kid in the situation Jen described, my body responds. It's weird how some part of my brain has been conditioned, but I have no memory of the events.

I sneeze but wave at Jen to keep going.

"After that, you were adopted," she confirms.

"By my mother."

"No, not by Loralee Pearson. When you were three, you became part of the Parks family. They had been fostering you for several months, and they said they knew from the first day that you were meant to be their daughter."

"I don't know anyone by the name of Parks." I laugh nervously. "Are you sure my adoption file didn't get switched? You must be mistaken."

I feel like Jen's telling me a story about someone else. Not me.

But she's not done yet, and it keeps getting worse.

"You disappeared the following fall when you went camping." She heaves out a sigh. "The thing is, the campsite is twelve miles from Loralee Pearson's residence. We actually interviewed her, and she gave us permission to search the woods on her property. You were so close the whole time. Search parties combed the area for a week, and you were right there, in that house."

"You must be mistaken," I repeat. Because this can't be real. Because if it is, my entire life has been stolen from me.

And my mother wouldn't have kidnapped me. Would she?

Unfortunately, I immediately know the answer to that. Yes. Yes, she would've.

"In the end, all we found was your shoe. It had gotten caught in some twigs on the riverbank about two miles from where you went missing. Between the water and the cold temperatures, you were assumed dead, but your body was never recovered, so…" Trailing off, Jen shrugs with a wobbly smile. "I never gave up on you. I always thought you were still alive."

Preston knew all this. At least, he had an idea. He had to.

He'd hinted at some unpleasantness in my past, but I didn't push because I was so happy in the present. Maybe I should've pressed for answers sooner, but I never imagined it would be this bad.

And this is really fucking bad.

"I'm going to read you a report from your adoptive parents, okay?" Jen lifts a pair of bifocals to her nose. "Let me know if it triggers any memories. This is a statement from your mother: We were fishing. Melody was near the dock. We use bologna for bait, and she loves to eat it when we're not looking. Mason turned his back for just a second to grab an extra pole, and when he turned around, she was gone. What if she fell into the river? She can't swim. The water's rushing so fast today, and it has to be freezing."

Water rushing. Freezing.

Oh, God.

Jen's voice fades out as a memory pushes forward.

I'm playing with a slice of bologna. It's thin and wiggly, and I fit it into one of the slats between the wood on the dock. It slips from my fingers, and I watch it get swept away. Thinking I can catch it, I lean over the side of the dock and reach…

Splash.

The next thing I know, cold shocks my entire body and I can't breathe. I'm flipped and twisted this way and that under the water. Everything hurts. I break the surface a couple of times to get a breath. There are some shallow parts where I can put my feet down, but I'm yanked back in because the current keeps knocking me over.

It feels like my struggle goes on forever before black nothingness takes over.

I wake to a face. My mom's face.

No, not my mom. Loralee Pearson. She's slapping my cheeks and rolling me onto my side so she can pound my back. I'm coughing, gagging, and spitting water out. I can't feel my body. I can't feel anything.

I gasp, and my chest feels tight, just like it did that day.

The blood pressure cuff on my arm tightens, and the heart monitor starts going crazy.

"Where did you go just then, Rosalie?" Jen's closer to the bed now, and she's clutching my hand. "You remembered something, didn't you?"

Nurses quickly file into the room, stopping me from answering as they fuss over me. One gets out a thermometer and holds it up to my forehead. Another is manually checking my pulse.

"I'm fine," I say weakly, but it's a lie, and I sneeze.

My entire life was just blown up in a matter of minutes.

So this is why Jen knew I'd need counseling.

I was taken. Stolen from my real family. The woman I've called Mom for as long as I can remember is a criminal.

That's why she never let me out of the house.

Not because she wanted to protect me. Not because she wanted to keep me away from my father.

Not because *I'm* crazy.

But because *she is*.

She had to hide me so she wouldn't get caught.

"My life is so fucked up," I wheeze.

"Loralee is in custody," Jen tells me fervently. "She'll never hurt you again."

A mental image of the woman who raised me pops up in my head, only now she's not finely dressed. Her hair isn't in place. No, she's behind bars in a scratchy jumpsuit.

I don't feel any satisfaction. Not even a little.

I don't know what I feel. It's not guilt, because she deserves to be locked up for what she did. But the woman I know won't fare well in someone else's prison.

My, how the tables have turned.

"Can I—" I gulp. "Can I go see her soon?"

"Rosalie, she's not your mother and she doesn't deserve your sympathy. She victimized you for the past fifteen years." Jen pats my hand. "You'll get your justice in court. Why don't you consider writing a statement?"

"A statement?"

"Yes." Jen pauses. "Do you know how to read and write?"

"Of course I do." I'm actually offended, and the blood pressure cuff starts tightening again. "I studied geography and history. I've read all the classics. I even learned algebra and geometry, and believe me, I didn't want to. I hate math. My mom—I mean, *Loralee* wanted me to be smart."

"Okay, okay. Just making sure. Think about writing a letter to Loralee about your feelings and experiences. A testimony."

"The patient needs to rest," one of the nurses says firmly to Jen.

Jen nods, but before she can turn to leave, I grab her wrist. "Did Preston know about all this?" My gaze drops to her folder. "This whole time, has he known everything?"

She shrugs. "You'll have to ask him that."

Oh, I will. The man has some explaining to do, but I won't be too hard on him. I can't. Not when he took bullets for me. "When will he be out of surgery?"

"Soon," a nurse responds, and then I'm offered some reassurances and a sedative.

Wanting a break from everything I just learned, I accept the medicine, and instead of a pill, the nurse injects something into my IV. The effect is immediate.

My eyes get heavy. As the room empties, I let myself sink into the blissful calm.

Jen left my baby picture behind. It's right at my fingertips. I don't want to look at it.

Instead, I envision Preston's face. I think about his smile and the way he rubs the cleft in my chin. I remember the way he holds me when I have a nightmare.

Most importantly, I imagine our future together. One that will be a hell of a lot better than my past.

When I wake up, it's dark outside. The lights in the room have dimmed, and Ivan's sitting in the chair Jen was in before. His elbows are on his knees and he's hanging his head.

Still groggy from the medicine, I blink at him, wondering if this is real or a dream.

"Are you allowed to be here?" I ask, and Ivan's head whips up.

He smiles. "I'm family, darling. Plus, the staff love me here. I basically paid for the new pediatric wing four years ago."

"Yeah, but you know cops are swarming the halls. FBI, Ivan."

His lips twitch with amusement. "I'm aware."

"Aren't you worried they're going to arrest you?"

"For what? Visiting my daughter in the hospital?"

"No," I scoff. "Just the dozen crimes they probably know you've committed."

His face becomes thoughtful. "Law enforcement and I have a long history of… understanding each other."

"What does that mean?"

"They leave my business alone, and I help them catch worse men than me when they need information."

My eyebrows go up. "You're a snitch?"

"An informant." He makes a sour face. "Snitch is such a childish word."

"Tattletale," I tease, making him grin again. Leave it up to my father to try to make something morally questionable sound sophisticated. "What time is it?" I look around for a clock. "Is Preston out of surgery yet? Can I see him?"

Ivan scoots closer to the bed to cover my hand.

"Darling." He swallows. "They thought it would be better for family to tell you the news…"

"What news?"

"Preston didn't make it." Four words. Flat. Matter of fact.

In a short time, I've gotten better at social cues and reading people. Body language and facial expressions are fascinating.

I'm still becoming familiar with genuine compassion, and it's weird to see it coming from a hardened criminal like Ivan.

Some people might think my father is a cold man with the way he speaks, but I see the sympathy in his eyes. The eyes that are nearly identical to mine. I might be imagining it, but I think I even see a sheen of tears there. The only time my mother—err, Loralee—ever cried was when she was trying to manipulate me into feeling bad for her so I'd comply with whatever she wanted me to do.

I snatch my hand away from Ivan's. "That's not true. That can't be true."

"I'm sorry. He—"

Flinging back the blankets, I swing my legs off the bed. Getting up too fast is a bad idea because it makes my head spin, and I have to grasp the side of the bed to steady myself.

Ivan stands. "What are you doing?"

"Going to find Preston."

He grabs my shoulders. "He's gone. His internal injuries were too—"

"You're wrong. Preston can't die."

I know I sound irrational. No one is invincible. But to think that the man who rescued me, the man I married, the man who's shown me more about life in the past several days than I've known in my entire lifetime… is just gone?

I can't accept that.

"It's a conspiracy," I claim, shoving Ivan away and ripping out my IV.

I barely register the sting on the back of my hand. Blood leaks from where the needle had been, but I don't bother trying to stop the flow. It drips from my fingertips as I get to the door, and it smears across the handle when I wrench it open, making the metal slippery.

The two police officers startle when they see me. Jen is sitting in a chair across the hall. She shoots to her feet and calls for a nurse.

"I need to see Preston," I demand. "Now."

As Jen approaches, she puts herself between the guards, blocking my way out. "Rosalie, you need to get back in the bed."

"Not until I see him! It's not real."

Not real, not real.

Tell me something real, babe.

Any second, I expect Preston to push his way into the room and say he's fine. He'll tell me he loves me, and that we're going to be so happy together. We're going to be a family.

Instead, in a group effort, the officers crowd me, forcing

me backward. Ivan's behind me. He's saying something softly, probably trying to calm the situation, but everyone's just pissing me off. A nurse comes in, making the room feel ten times smaller with so many people around me.

They're not going to let me out.

I panic. And I get really angry.

Going over to the vitals monitor, I shove it to the side, knocking it off its wheels. It hits the floor with an ear-splitting crash. Next, I attack the IV stand. I throw it so hard it makes a dent in the wall.

I'm still bleeding. Red drops and streaks decorate the floor and other places in the room. I think about the red that soaked my shirt when I held it to Preston's gunshot wound.

He lost so much blood. Too much.

Maybe they're telling the truth.

No, no, no.

I don't even realize I'm screaming the words until multiple hands drag me backward, and the air is nearly knocked out of me when I'm pinned onto the bed. My yelling gets cut off, and like an animal, I growl and thrash.

More nurses pile in.

At least four of them are restraining me when the doctor comes into view with a syringe. I try to scoot away from him, but I can't. Someone's got my arms and legs locked down with a freakish amount of power. You wouldn't think the petite nurses are that strong, but apparently, they train for this shit.

"All right, Melody," the doctor says calmly, and the name sounds all wrong. "Let's make you feel better." He shines a light in my eyes, then wipes my upper arm with something cold. "This will help."

There's a slight sting as he pierces my skin with the needle.

"I'm sorry," Ivan says as he stands back and lets the staff work. "I'm so sorry, darling."

I want to tell him to fuck off. I want to spew obscenities and hateful words. Anything to make the heartache leave my body.

But my tongue won't work.

Gasping sobs work their way up my throat, but I don't feel like I'm the one making the sounds.

I don't feel like I'm inside myself anymore. I'm detached. Floating.

And I'm so tired.

My mind is foggy. My limbs are heavy. My thoughts scatter, ebbing and flowing like a rushing river.

During my struggle to stay conscious, I realize the nurses are working on getting my IV back in on my right hand while my other arm is strapped to the bedrail with a padded cuff.

Jen and Ivan are at the foot of the bed, talking quietly, but it doesn't look like a hostile conversation. If anything, they're friendly. Isn't that funny? My father, big mafia boss, chatting it up with an FBI agent like she couldn't arrest him tomorrow for all the shit he does.

I'd never tell on him, though. Even if they questioned me for hours, I'd keep my mouth shut. Because he's the only family I have left.

He's the only family I have left.

Because if my mother abducted me, she's not really my mother. And if Preston's gone, that means I'm a widow.

A tear rolls down my temple.

I thought I was lonely before. When I was trapped in that house, in that attic, I thought that was rock bottom.

I was wrong.

This is the lowest low. I might as well be drowning all over again, and this time, there's no one to pull me out.

CHAPTER 29

Two Months Later

Rosalie

One place I can't follow Preston? Into death. Well, I guess I could, but I know how he felt about suicide, and to be honest, dying isn't all that appealing to me either.

No one around me seems to believe me, though.

Everyone hovers now.

I was kept at the hospital for five days on suicide watch after I found out Preston had died. Talk about being treated like a mental patient. Admittedly, alternating between crying hysterically and thrashing against my bed restraints wasn't a good way to get anyone to trust my state of mind. I think they were one step away from tossing me into a padded room.

But eventually, exhaustion and a constant flow of sedatives won. I became compliant. I ate when they told me to. I watched TV. I allowed visitors to come see me. A doctor removed the tracker, and I took medications without an argument.

Most of it is a blur. I think my mind couldn't cope with the sadness I felt, so I've blocked a good portion of it out.

Once Jen and the hospital staff believed I was well enough to leave, they released me to a family I don't remember. The Parks.

Legally, I belong to them, and Ivan said Bridgette and Mason are better for me than him. They can give me stability, and they didn't hesitate to welcome me back into their home. Ivan still calls me once a week, but he's giving me space because he wants me to have some normalcy.

Preston wanted that for me, too.

Normal. Boring. Basic.

I live in a suburban world of block parties, North Face jackets, and Starbucks now. I even have a Facebook account, and I'm up to a hundred and thirty-four friends. Casey recently got an account, too, and I think she did it just so we have a place to chat.

I've gone to movie theaters. I've been to stores entirely dedicated to selling makeup. I've eaten fast food until I feel sick, and I've wandered the aisles of grocery stores without anyone telling me I can't put chips and cookies in the cart.

For so long, that's what I thought I wanted, but now that I'm in the world, I realize it's not all it's cracked up to be.

Not without Preston.

I miss the cabin and the bubble we were in when it was just us. The squeaky mattress. The scratchy radio with shitty reception. The crackers and soup.

Most of all, I miss feeling whole. Preston and I fulfilled something in each other. Something we were both desperately craving.

A love lighthouse. That's one of the last things he said to me. I didn't understand it at the time, but now I know what he meant.

The way I loved him was so bright and obvious, he had no choice but to recognize it.

In his last few days, I gave him that.

And he told me I was strong. Brave. I hold onto that fact like it's my lifeline. And maybe it is. When I need strength to keep going, I remember how good we were for each other, and how much faith he had in me.

Bringing my hand up to my chest, I absentmindedly toy with the lighthouse necklace I never take off. I'm also still wearing my wedding ring, which hasn't gone unnoticed by pretty much everyone.

The media's been a bit of a shitstorm.

Once word got out that Melody Parks had been rescued, alive and well, the news had a field day with it. When a child who's been missing for fifteen years is found, it gives everyone hope. Hope that all the missing children out there aren't gone—they're simply misplaced.

Big white vans have been camping out on the streets in front of the Parks' home as the reporters wait for a chance to ask me questions. About my time in captivity. About my escape. About Preston, the mysterious man who helped me.

Yeah, he's a hero, and the world knows it. I haven't said much, but I made sure to tell them that.

But the private details—like my short-lived drug addiction and my off-the-books marriage—are not public knowledge, and I don't intend to make them so.

Even Harlee Verona reached out. She found me on Facebook, and she said she wants to set up an interview. If I were going to spill my life story to anyone, it would be her.

I'm just not ready yet.

This is the first time I've been out of the house in a week. I could blame it on the reporters, but really, their annoying presence is just an excuse to hole up and veg out.

Unfortunately, I can't claim to have a headache forever, and there are certain appointments I have to go to. Mainly my therapy.

"Look at this." Bridgette hands me a pamphlet to the local community college, which was conveniently sitting among the magazines on the side table in the waiting room. I wonder if she planted it there on purpose. "Once you get your GED, you could apply."

Nodding, I give her a forced, noncommittal smile. "Maybe."

Turns out, the "education" Loralee gave me wasn't legit. The information I learned was correct, but none of it counted toward actual scholastic records. As far as the system is concerned, I have no high school diploma. No grades or transcripts to speak of.

I scored high during my assessment tests, though, and I've been working with a tutor to catch up.

"Or you can go to a state college," Bridgette continues. "If you don't want to attend class in person, you can take your courses online. You can do it from anywhere in the world."

"Where would I go?" I ask numbly.

"Or you can stay at home for as long as you like." There's hope in her blue eyes as she says it, and I know she longs for the daughter she lost.

I'm not her.

I don't know the Parks, and they don't know me.

Granted, it doesn't stop them from trying to be good parents. Man, they try. Bridgette gives me too many choices—*so* many choices—like she's showering me with mass amounts of freedom. Mason just gives me space.

It's probably difficult for them to take in someone as traumatized as I am. When they adopted me, they signed up for a cute toddler who they could raise the way they wanted. Instead, they got a grieving adult with more angst than a teen soap opera.

"You can study anything you want," Bridgette suggests, continuing with her list of options. "Ivan has offered to pay for your tuition. Of course, we'll chip in what we can. You know we kept your college fund going."

She keeps talking about that college fund. I think she wants to drill it into me that they never gave up on getting me back.

I wonder if she realizes I don't blame her for what happened. I should probably tell her that. Maybe I will today. After all, isn't that the point of family counseling?

So far, Dr. Fairmont and I have met one-on-one three times a week, but I agreed to let Bridgette sit in today because I can sense her mounting frustration with my lack of motivation.

Despite acquiring more makeup, I haven't worn any since before Preston died. I don't paint anymore. I no longer listen to songs on repeat.

I eat when I'm told. I shower when I'm reminded. I put effort into my schoolwork.

Honestly, I'm doing the best I can, even if going through the motions is all I can manage.

As I look around the waiting room, I wonder what the doc will want to talk about today. Before each session, I always have a less sensitive subject locked and loaded, but I think Dr. Fairmont sees right through my strategy to avoid heavier topics.

Sometimes she brings up my childhood. Other times she asks about the more recent stuff.

I won't talk about Preston. It's the one conversation that's off limits. She knows that, but she still pushes by asking about the future. Sure, that's her job, but I have no interest in making plans without my husband.

My bucket list is something Preston and I were supposed to do together. That little piece of paper is still folded up inside my fanny pack. Even though I bring it with me everywhere I go, I haven't opened it to look at the checklist. It's just too painful.

The week after I got home from the hospital, I started my period. And I had a breakdown because I wasn't pregnant. I'd been holding onto the hope that maybe I could take a piece of Preston with me through life. I could have his child.

Now there's nothing left of him but memories and an urn full of ashes they gave me at his small memorial. As his wife—even if we never filed the paperwork—his remains rightfully belong to me. I'd been heavily medicated on Xanax through most of that afternoon, making the day seem like a bad dream, but it's not hard to remember the faces in the crowd. Because there weren't many. Jay came to pay his respects. Ivan showed up to support me.

The better part of the day was meeting the Marshalls. Although they didn't see Preston often, they were devastated to lose him.

Preston's with Krystal now. That's what they said, like it should comfort me. It doesn't. It pisses me off. He should be with me, damn it. He belongs here. With. Me.

"Are you all right?" Bridgette asks timidly.

She's staring at my hands, and I realize I'm squeezing the pamphlet to the point of destruction. It's all twisted and crumpled.

"Sorry," I mumble, smoothing it back out on my thigh.

Fidgeting with her purse, Bridgette smiles. "What I'm trying to say is, the sky's the limit for you, Melody."

I wince at the name, and she notices, then immediately apologizes.

I tell her it's fine. It's hard for someone to understand why I don't want a name anymore. Not just that name…

Any name.

I don't want to be called anything. Not Melody, because that's not who I am. Not Rosalie, because any version of Rosie reminds me of Preston. Rosie Doll died when he did.

I still have times when I think he's alive. At night, sometimes I dream about him. It usually starts with a nightmare. Even though I know the source of my drowning dreams is from an actual event, it hasn't made them go away. Sometimes when I'm cold and thrashing, I think I feel Preston's arms around me. It's so real, but when I wake up, he's not there.

One time, I swear his side of the bed was warm and I smelled his scent in the air.

Looks like I've gone a little crazy after all.

I started antidepressants seven weeks ago—the legit kind, prescribed by a real doctor—and they're helping.

Well, they're making me numb.

I don't feel joy, but I'm not crying all the time either.

I didn't even shed one tear when Loralee hanged herself in her jail cell just after the new year. When she was arrested, her lawyer claimed insanity as their defense, and she was supposed to have a psychological evaluation to prove it. She probably could've avoided prison by going to a mental institution, but I guess she thought death was better.

In the end, she was just as selfish as she's always been. She couldn't even stick around long enough to give me closure. I'll never get to ask her about the day she took me. I have nowhere to direct my anger over the entire ordeal.

I took Jen's advice and started drafting a letter to Loralee. Although I'll never get to read it in court, I figure it can't hurt to get my feelings on paper. My progress has stalled a bunch of times, though, and the waste basket in my room is filled with crumpled papers. It's just, nothing I write seems *right*.

Dear Loralee, fuck you.

Dear Ms. Pearson, eat shit.

To whom it may concern…

I really would like to finish it. Maybe I can bring that up with Dr. Fairmont today. That's a safe, Preston-free topic.

It's weird that there's no one else in the waiting room with us. Three other doctors practice out of this building, so usually, there are at least a few others in the chairs around me.

It's so quiet in here, I can hear the clock *tick, tick, ticking* behind the receptionist desk. A pretty, middle-aged woman with red hair sits behind it. Maggie. I think that's her name. A call comes through on her phone, and her eyes go to me.

It's time.

Standing, Maggie smiles. "Dr. Fairmont is ready for you."

Bridgette gets up with me, and she pleasantly comments about the homey décor as we file into Dr. Fairmont's office. I nod in agreement.

The room is covered in warm colors. Browns on the walls and burnt-orange curtains. Ceramics and plants are placed near the window, on bookshelves, and on the coffee table that sits between us. My favorite feature is the fireplace. I don't know if Dr. Fairmont burns logs year-round, but it's definitely nice during winter. On the mantel, there's a card with pink and red hearts on it.

That reminds me, Valentine's Day is coming up.

It's the Parks' thirtieth wedding anniversary, and they have family coming from Connecticut, including their daughter, who will be arriving with her husband and kids tomorrow.

Technically, Tennille and I are sisters. Bridgette and Mason adopted her six years before me. I don't remember her from when we were little, but we met at Christmas. We didn't talk much, and I'm not sure if it's because she wanted to give me space or if she doesn't like me.

Maybe she resents me for being such a draining focus throughout her childhood.

That.

I can definitely talk about that.

It might piss Bridgette off.

I sneak a look at my adoptive mother as we sit on a cushy brown leather couch.

On second thought, it's likely she won't get mad about anything I say. The woman is so level-headed and nice all the time. She's a gentle soul. Zero temper. It's incredibly disarming. Riling her up isn't fun. Just the opposite, it makes me feel guilty. She makes me want to be rational.

Being raised by her would've been good. Really good.

Safe.

Filled with unconditional love, understanding, and valuable life lessons.

For the first time since losing Preston, I feel negative emotions that aren't associated with him.

Something like regret.

True longing for a past I didn't get to have.

"Your thoughts seem deep today," Dr. Fairmont says, and I wonder if I'd been talking out loud.

"What?"

"I said hello three times and you just kept staring at my spider plant. Do you have something you'd like to talk about?"

"Actually… yeah. I feel…" I thought my eyes were all dried up, but I guess I was wrong. Tears blur my vision, my chin trembles, and my lips wobble. "I'm sad," I croak out.

Ever attentive, Dr. Fairmont nods. "Can you tell me why?"

I look at Bridgette, and a tear streaks down my face. "You would've been a great mom to me. I think I would've really loved you. And you would've loved me. With you and Mason, I could've grown up in a normal way. And I wouldn't even have known it was normal because it would've been all I knew, and I probably would've taken it for granted. I wish I had that." My chest convulses with a sob. "I wish I could know what it's like for life to be so easy that I don't even have to think about it."

"Oh," Bridgette sighs sympathetically as she slides across the couch and wraps me in her arms.

I like how soft she is. She's on the plump side, but it makes her hugs better. More comforting. She wears oversized clothes, too. Lots of sweatshirts. From the pictures I've seen, she's been a little overweight for a long time. I imagine snuggling with her as a kid would've been awesome.

Thinking that only makes me cry harder.

"I'll always be your mom," Bridgette says softly as she strokes my hair. "Since the first time I held you, I've never stopped being your parent. No matter where you are, you'll be my daughter."

Once I've finally gotten myself under control, I pull back and wince at all the tears and snot I got on Bridgette's gray shirt. "Sorry."

"Nothing to be sorry for." She laughs a little, though she's crying, too. "You think this is bad? One time, Tennille brought the stomach flu home from school. I think I was covered in barf from my hair to my feet."

"Ew." I chuckle, then I pluck a few tissues up to give to her.

She wipes under her eyes, taking off some of her eyeliner in the process.

Two months ago, I would've carefully dabbed my cheeks so I didn't ruin my makeup. I don't have to worry about that now.

"You know what the plus side to not wearing makeup is?" I wave my own tissues. "There's no mascara to run when I cry."

"Why don't you put on makeup?" Bridgette asks curiously. "You own so much of it. If you don't know how to use it, I can teach you."

"That's okay," I decline her offer.

"Really, I'd love to help."

"No. It reminds me of—" I stop, realizing I'm about to start talking about Preston.

"Reminds you of…?" Dr. Fairmont asks patiently.

Well, fuck it. I'm already crying. Might as well go big today.

Through a series of sobs, I talk about Jessa. My friend from the card game. How close we became. But really, it was just a ploy Preston had invented to learn when I was leaving so he could be there to help me.

Since I'm already on a roll, I tell them how I'd been watching Preston from my room. The feelings he stirred inside me.

Then I get into our days on the run together.

How every minute felt like this forbidden, high-stakes game

because we weren't supposed to be together. For a lot of reasons. He was older than me. He was hired by my father to find me, not fall in love with me. We were hiding from so many people.

But damn if I didn't want him to be mine forever. Certainly longer than a few days.

"I just miss him." I hiccup. "My childhood was stolen from me. Now my future has been taken, too."

"You could make another future," Dr. Fairmont says optimistically.

"I hate the idea of that," I state honestly. "No life I could make for myself will ever feel right without Preston in it. I guess it sounds bad, but I don't care about my education or a career. It doesn't matter where I'm living. He's the one who made life good. The circumstances were secondary."

"You felt like you could handle anything as long as he was by your side."

"Yeah. That's exactly it."

"Have you made any plans going forward?"

"Not really." I glance at Bridgette. "But I know Preston would've wanted me to do all the things I've always dreamed of. Maybe we could start by getting some more college pamphlets."

It pains me to say it—it hurts to even think about planning out a future without Preston, but I owe it to myself to try.

Dr. Fairmont smiles at me. "This is wonderful. It's a breakthrough."

My eyebrows go up. "It is?"

She nods. "Not only are you talking about Preston, but you're including your family in your decisions. You're opening up and accepting help. Are you still taking your medicine?"

I pat my fanny pack where I keep my cell phone. "Yeah. I have a daily timer so I don't miss it."

The doctor's smile grows, then she grins at Bridgette. "I think she's ready."

"Ready for what?" I look back and forth between them.

Bridgette's eyes are shining with unshed wetness, and Dr. Fairmont types something out on her phone. A second later, the door opens with a quiet click.

And Jen Harding comes into the room, with her spiffy clothes and combat boots.

What's happening here?

Jen takes a seat in a leather chair next to Dr. Fairmont. The flames blaze in the fireplace behind them, making them look like heroes dashing out of an explosion to save me.

Keeping her eyes on me, Jen leans forward with her elbows on her knees. "Donovan Vogel, AKA Donovan Fowler, was caught three weeks ago. He was apprehended at the Mexican border."

"You got Preston's killer? Why didn't you tell me sooner?" This whole time, I've imagined Donovan running around on a beach somewhere, sipping icy alcoholic drinks.

"We were just trying to focus on you," Dr. Fairmont provides.

"Well, it might've helped me to know…" I feel my old temper rising, but I push it down. Because I do trust Dr. Fairmont. If she felt it was best for me to learn this news at a later time, she's probably right. "Yeah, okay." I blink a few times, processing what this means. Justice. "Well, good. I hope Donovan gets beaten to death in jail."

"Melo—Rosa—that's a terrible thing to say," Bridgette hisses, her cheeks red with embarrassment at my brutal outburst.

I just hike a shoulder. I haven't completely changed. Sure, I have better control over my emotions, but I'm not a saint like Bridgette. Endless patience and forgiveness are traits I don't possess.

Unaffected by my ire, Jen shrugs. "Right now they've got him in solitary. Donovan's a high-profile case because he's wanted in four countries for assassination. He's a killer for hire, and one of the men he murdered was an important government official. So, witnesses are crucial to his conviction."

"I'm a witness," I say flatly.

She nods. "Yes, you are."

"Is this the part where you tell me you're whisking me away into witness protection?" I joke.

No one laughs.

"Oh, shit," I breathe out. "That's what's happening here?"

"Not exactly," Jen replies. "You wouldn't have to go away forever. We just need to keep you somewhere safe until the trial is over. Keeping a protective detail on you twenty-four-seven isn't ideal."

"The vans outside our house." I gape at Jen. "That's the FBI?"

"Only one of them. The rest really are reporters, and their presence has actually been quite helpful. No one's going to come after you when there are cameras around."

I turn to Bridgette. "So you're sending me away? Is that why you brought up online classes and studying abroad?"

She tries to smile, but she looks sad. "I don't want you to go, but I want you to be safe. This is your choice." She reaches over to pat my hand. "You don't have to testify if you don't want to, but I think it would be good—"

"Of course I'm going to testify," I say a little too sharply. I lower my voice and look to Jen. "Do you have any other witnesses?"

"We do," she answers. "The responsibility won't rest solely on your shoulders. We've been building a case against Mr. Fowler for a while, and you'll have company where you're staying in the meantime."

"Company?"

Maybe I'm seeing things that aren't there, but I swear I detect a twinkle in Jen's eye.

Preston might be alive. He might be in the same witness protection-ish plan, and my heart lifts.

My imagination starts to run wild in the second it takes her to clarify.

"Ivan," she says with a smile, utterly destroying the glimmer of my dreams coming back to life. "He's been staying at his residence in The Maldives, and he'd love to have you there with him."

"Right." I can't help sounding disappointed.

It's not that I don't want to spend time with my biological father. I do. I felt a connection to him the day we met, but Ivan is a reminder of Preston, because he knew him first. Ivan's the reason we fell in love in the first place.

My eyes burn, but before I can start crying, Jen leans forward like she's about to tell me something important. "This knowledge is limited to the people inside of this room and the witnesses. That's it. We're talking top secret. It's very important for you to keep the lid on this. No one—and I mean no one—can know about your location."

"What about Mason?" My eyes land on Bridgette.

"I'll tell him Dr. Fairmont suggested you go to a wellness center in California."

My lips quirk up on one side because Bridgette and Mason seem to have the perfect marriage—one where they don't have secrets. "You're going to lie to him?"

"It's not entirely dishonest, sweetheart. You need sunshine and time to be yourself without anyone watching."

"If you're worried about our sessions," Dr. Fairmont inserts, "don't be. We can continue your therapy over the phone."

Seems like they've thought of everything. Other than the

fact that I'll be going to the place Preston and I should've been together all along, I have no reason to say no.

Maybe it'll be good for me. Like Bridgette said, a place where I can figure out who I am in privacy.

"So." I take a breath. "When do I leave?"

CHAPTER 30

Rosalie

The limo Ivan sent to pick me up from the airport stops in front of a big white stucco house, and I stare at the two-story mini palace.

I'm lucky to be here—I know that. Lucky to be alive. Fortunate to have so much luxury available to me.

I just can't help the painful way my heart twists when I think about how wonderful it would've been to have Preston here with me.

Concrete steps surrounded by tropical vegetation lead up to an ornate wooden door, but I'm not sure why there's even an entrance when double doors on either side are propped open. White curtains billow in the breeze, and I can see past them to the back of the house. The sun is setting behind it, and the bright orange orb hovers above the water in the distance.

Ivan bounds down the steps wearing a casual attire of khaki pants and an untucked white button-up shirt. It's the most dressed-down I've ever seen him. Also the happiest.

He grins broadly as the driver lets me out of the back seat. Before I know it, I'm engulfed in a hug.

"My daughter." Ivan laughs as he sways us back and forth. "How was your trip?"

"Not bad," I reply truthfully.

Much to my surprise, Bridgette already had my bags packed

at Dr. Fairmont's office yesterday, so I literally walked out the back door of the building, got into an SUV with Jen, and left for the airport.

I barely had time to think about what it would be like on the flight, but that's the thing about losing someone you love more than anything in the world. It changes your fears. Alters them. Sometimes eliminates them all together.

Because you know what? If the plane had gone down and I died in a fiery crash in the water, well… big whoop.

If heaven exists, then I'd be with Preston.

And if it doesn't… then at least I wouldn't have to miss him anymore. I'd be sharing eternal nothingness with him, and that thought is extremely comforting to me.

But we didn't crash. The flight went smoothly. I even slept for a good portion of it, and I took some time to finish my letter to Loralee. After several more drafts filled with scathing profanities, I went with a less angry approach. I stuck to the facts, listing all the ways her decisions affected my life. I wrote about the toll she took on my mental and physical health and how she stole my childhood. I told her she's selfish, and I don't forgive her. Not yet. Maybe not ever.

After I was done, I quietly read the letter out loud as if she were sitting in front of me. Then I tore it up and threw it away.

It's over. My closure with her is as good as it'll ever be.

"We're finally together." Ivan pulls back and takes me by the shoulders to look at me. He must see grief all over my face, because his smile fades. "This place has a way of making everything better. You'll see."

After unloading my luggage, the driver accepts a hefty tip from Ivan and takes off.

"You must be hungry," Ivan says, picking up two of the suitcases and starting up the stairs.

Lifting my Hello Kitty backpack, I follow him. "Yeah, I could eat."

"I can make macaroni and cheese."

"Sure."

"I mean that literally." Chuckling, Ivan motions for me to go in first as he holds the door open. "That's the only thing I know how to make."

That pulls a smile from me. "Where's Helga?"

"Leave of absence. The drawback to this witness deal is the secrecy. Normally I'd have a full-time staff to clean and cook, but we'll make do, won't we?"

I nod. "I'm a good cook. I can help."

Knowing my way around the kitchen is a life skill Loralee provided me with. I didn't realize it at the time, but all that baking, making meals from scratch, and scraping by with what food we had available… it comes in handy.

Ivan sets my stuff down on the tile flooring. "Make a list of ingredients you need, and we'll get someone to go to the market tomorrow."

"Sounds good. Which way is my room?" I start to look around, but Ivan waves me off.

"You can put your belongings away later. The sunsets are amazing here. Why don't you go check out the beach?"

Two months ago, such an innocent suggestion would've made me squirm and shudder. Now I just shrug. "Okay."

"I'll get some water boiling. We can eat out on the terrace when I'm finished, darling."

Darling. In the beginning, I thought Ivan was presumptuous for calling me the term of endearment. Funnily enough, I don't mind it now. It might be the only name I don't loathe.

Maybe I should have my name legally changed to Darling. Weird? Definitely. Do I care? Definitely not.

While Ivan makes some racket with pots and pans, I drop my backpack and walk toward the back patio.

I cautiously step outside. The sun is halfway gone, sinking below the glittering water in the distance. Billions of bright orange sparkles light up the endless ripples.

Breathtaking.

The rhythm of the ocean isn't like a river or a creek. It's not a constant rush or even a trickle. It's a soft roar. A soothing whisper, like someone trying to calm me when I'm hysterical.

Shhh. Shhh. Shhh.

The large stone patio butts up right against the beach. Big green leaves and tropical flowering plants frame the stone walls on either side, but the back view is completely open.

Slipping off my shoes and socks, I set them on one of the wooden chairs at the long outdoor dining table. I shed my zip-up sweatshirt and drape it over my shoes. Then I go over to the sand.

My toes sink in as soon as I step on it, and I smile at the way the grittiness tickles my feet. It's still hot from a day of soaking up the sun.

The smell of the ocean carries in the breeze, and I close my eyes as I breathe it in. For a second, I get a whiff of leather, citrus, and spice.

That happens sometimes—I think I smell Preston.

I've never told Dr. Fairmont about feeling like Preston is still around, but she's talked about grief a lot. Said everyone deals with it differently and there's no right or wrong way.

If only Preston could see me now. Shedding my worst fear to enjoy paradise. He'd be so proud.

As I walk forward, I look around at the deserted private beach. In both directions, the sand stretches on for miles. Most of it is flat and undisturbed, but there's an unnatural-looking pile closer to the water. Squinting, I go toward it.

A sandcastle?

There's a single spire about two feet tall, and when I'm just a few steps away from it, I realize it's not a castle.

It's a lighthouse.

I swallow hard.

I barely even notice how close I've gotten to the waves crawling up the beach until one touches the creation. As water tends to do with sand, it makes part of the structure crumble into a wet heap. The tower starts to tip.

"No," I burst out, dropping to my knees to catch it.

When the damp sand hits my hand, it loses its form and falls through my fingers.

Destroyed. Ruined.

I sit still, breathing hard as I wonder if I can possibly put it back together again. I've never played in sand before—at least, not that I can remember. But I've sculpted a little. 3-D art isn't my forte, but whoever made this lighthouse worked hard. I can't bear the thought of it being gone.

Letting the next wave of water sweep over my fingers, I scoop up big handfuls of sand and pile them onto the mound. I pat it and mold it, but I'm getting frustrated because I won't be able to replicate what it was before.

"You found it," an all-too-familiar voice says behind me. My back stiffens as he continues, "I've been building one every day for you. We can make another one tomorrow."

I glance over my shoulder, and I blink, wondering if my eyes are playing tricks on me. Or maybe I'm dreaming again.

Balling my fists, I let my fingernails dig into my palms and I soak up the sting. Sure feels real, but I don't see how it could be.

Preston's standing just feet away from me.

His black pants are rolled up to mid-calf as the water rushes over his ankles and feet. A black T-shirt with the sleeves cut off displays his arms and shoulders. His skin is darker, like he's been out in the sun a lot.

My eyes lift to his face, and my breath catches in my throat when he smiles. That little gap between his teeth is still just as adorable as I remember it, but it's not his mouth that has me mesmerized.

His eyes.

Although they're shadowed, they smolder with a familiar desire only my husband can express with just one look.

CHAPTER 31

Preston

Jen had a hard time getting me to agree to the plan she and Ivan cooked up, but they had the advantage because I was basically on death's door. After my surgery, I was in a medically induced coma for several days. By the time I woke up in a private government hospital, news of my death had spread, and Donovan was still on the loose.

I was too weak to get out of bed, let alone hunt him down, so I was basically at the FBI's mercy. I was counting on them to make things right and keep Rosalie safe.

I didn't want to go anywhere without my wife, and I definitely didn't want to let her believe I'd died. But Donovan has been a slippery fucker for the FBI. He's gotten off on technicalities and walked when he shouldn't have.

We need to nail his ass, once and for all.

"Preston." Rosalie's voice is just a faint whisper in the breeze, but it slides over my skin like a caress.

Goose bumps break out all over my arms, and the hair on the back of my neck stands. Memories of Rosalie exploring my body come to me like they have every minute of every day we've been apart, and they have the same effect they always do.

My nipples prick, my stomach swoops, and my cock stiffens.

She's finally here, kneeling at my feet. She's in tight jeans and a pink T-shirt. She's still disturbingly thin, and I wonder if she's been eating and taking care of herself.

One of my biggest concerns this entire time has been Rosalie's emotional state. In all the pictures Jen has sent, Rosalie's hair is always in disarray, like she barely brushes it after a shower.

The last orange rays of the day make Rosalie look like a golden goddess with her wild strands whipping about. Most of the brown dye has faded, leaving her locks a dark blond. Since it isn't tied back, wisps blow across her face.

Her bare, pale, tear-streaked face.

God, I can't imagine the hell she's been through. It's been bad for me, too, but at least I knew she was okay because I got daily updates from the FBI team.

Didn't stop me from missing her so much it hurt.

"Baby," I rasp out.

"Are you here?" Staggering to her feet, Rosalie takes a step toward me.

"I am."

"You died." Two more steps.

"I did flatline on the table during surgery, but I pulled through. I'm alive, minus a spleen." I flex my hand. "And I just got my cast off last week."

"I went to your memorial."

"I know," I say, my heart squeezing from seeing Rosalie's pain.

Her blue and green eyes flit about my body, as if she thinks I'm a mirage.

A sobbing breath shudders out of her. "Tell me something real?"

"I'm alive. I'm okay." I gently frame her face with my

hands, and she quivers at the contact. "I love you, and I never want to be apart from you again."

Slowly reaching for me, her fingers splay out on my abdomen where I was shot. She pushes my shirt up, and she makes a desperate noise in the back of her throat when she touches the gnarly scar I've got.

"Does it hurt?"

"Not much anymore."

She flings herself at me, knocking the air from my lungs. Wrapping her arms around my middle, she rubs her face on my chest. Soaks my shirt with her tears. She's clinging to me so hard, her fingernails might be tearing holes in my shirt, but I don't care.

I can't get enough of her.

Running my hands up her back, I tangle my fingers in her hair. Tonight, I'm going to weave it into a braided masterpiece. I'm going to taste every inch of her skin and make love to her like it's the first time.

I can tell the moment Rosalie's happiness turns into rage. Rage over the fact that she's been deceived. Anger for how much grief she's suffered.

She goes rigid against me and glares up with red-rimmed eyes. "How could you do it? How could you let me think you were dead?"

"I had to, Rosie."

"You lied." She pushes away from me. "Everyone lied to me."

"Bridgette and Mason didn't. Even your therapist believes I died in the hospital. Jen and her team are the only people back home who know I survived. Well, and the surgeon who operated on me. But he's being called in as a witness, too, so he's part of this."

"I had to go to your memorial, Preston," Rosalie says, her voice full of anguish. "I have your ashes in a fucking urn."

"Not my ashes."

"What does it matter if they're yours or not? I thought they were. I brought them with me to scatter them here." She points to the ocean.

"My death had to be convincing." Even as the reason leaves my mouth, I know it's a shitty situation no matter how I spin it.

If it were reversed and I'd thought Rosalie were gone? I'd be a fucking wreck.

So when she grabs up handfuls of wet sand and chucks it at me, I take it. I stand still, letting her release her frustrations and pain.

Splat. Splat, splat, splat.

My chest, my neck, one handful even comes dangerously close to my groin.

Rosalie's fit goes on until I'm covered in sandy splotches from head to toe and she's worn out.

Swaying on her feet, she sobs, "How could you leave me alone? I went through something horrible, and you just stayed away. You said nothing could keep you from me. You promised."

"And I kept that promise. Even though I wasn't supposed to, I came to see you." Fed up with the distance between us, I stride forward and hug her to me so tightly she can't get away.

"When?" Her chest is heaving so much it's rocking us both.

"After I got out of the hospital," I answer, then explain, "I spent several weeks recovering in a private medical facility. Gunshot wounds are no joke. But as soon as I was released, I evaded Jen long enough to pay you a visit."

"A visit? I never saw you."

"Didn't you look at your list? Right before I got on my flight, I sort of broke into your house when you were sleeping," I sheepishly admit. "Wasn't easy to do with so much surveillance, but I had to see you. I added something to your list, hoping you'd see it and know I was still alive."

Frantically pushing away from me, she unzips her fanny pack and produces the crumpled paper. She stares at it like she hasn't seen it in a while, and I realize how much my absence has affected her.

She gave up on her list. She gave up on a lot of things.

When she unfolds the paper, her eyes go wide at the item I scrawled on it.

Live Happily Ever After—basic bitch status achieved

"You did this?" Rosalie asks, and although it's a rhetorical question, I respond with the biggest truth I have.

"When I told you nothing could keep me from you, I meant it." I scoop her back into my arms. "I wanted you out here with me sooner, but your health had to come first. Your doctor wanted to make sure you were stable with your new medicine and everything you've been through."

"I am. She seemed impressed with my progress."

"See? You're amazing, and we're going to bring Donovan down. I'm the best weapon the FBI has against him. I'm the only one who's survived one of his murder attempts, so my testimony is the most damning information they've got. That asshole will be shocked when he realizes he didn't finish me off." I kiss the top of her head and apologize again as we sway together. "Please tell me you understand."

"I do." She hiccups. "Just stop talking and kiss me."

I don't hesitate to do as she demands. Her lips are salty from her tears, but I lick at her like she's the last drink of water I'll ever have. As our tongues stroke against each other, Rosalie climbs my body like a fucking tree.

She latches onto me, her legs going around my waist. Her fingers spear through my shaggy hair, and her warm pussy presses against my hard-on.

God, I've missed this.

My knees go weak, and I ungracefully drop to my ass. Rosalie doesn't seem to care. Without missing a beat, she keeps devouring my mouth and rubbing herself on me. I recline in the sand, so fucking happy we can finally do this.

"Baby." I chuckle as she kisses down my jawline. "Your dad's within viewing distance."

She harumphs before slowly placing another deep kiss on my lips. "So, what? Are you two besties now?"

"Something like that." I try to shrug, but it's hard with her pinning me down.

I never thought I'd be friends with a mafia boss, but Ivan's actually a pretty cool guy. We've spent a lot of time watching bad reality TV, playing pool in his game room, and soaking up the sun.

He's totally clueless in the kitchen, but with the two security guards Jen posted at the gate of the property, we've been able to have them run errands for us. We've been eating a lot of takeout.

Donovan's trial is still several weeks away. Until then, I hope to take it easy, build a lot of lighthouses on the beach, and make love to my wife.

"We're married," I announce to Rosalie between kisses, because this is the news I've been dying to share with her.

Lifting her head, she gives me a weird look. "Yeah, I know."

"Legally, I mean. Jen has the paperwork. All you have to do is sign it, then you're officially Rosie Walker, wife of Preston Walker."

Tears swim in her eyes as she gazes down at me. "You had our names changed for real?"

"Well, yeah." I sit up and gently grip her chin. "That's what you wanted, right? You said you liked me as Preston."

"Yeah." She smiles and sniffles. "And Rosie Walker sounds… right. It feels right. I didn't think anything would feel right ever again."

We take a break on kissing to just hold each other for a while. The sky gets darker. Stars come out. The ocean becomes more restless, and water licks at our legs every time a wave comes in.

I notice my brave wife doesn't shake when she gets wet. She's changed. Gotten stronger. Conquered a fear. She might not realize it, but she's exhibited true power during one of her lowest times.

She's more courageous than she knows.

Several things are certain about our future. One, she's going to need a lot of reassurance. Two, we're going to be so damn happy. Three, I'm going to fuck her every day.

With my hands roaming Rosalie's waist, I'm tempted to take her in the sand right here, but my woman needs to eat. Her hip bones protrude a little more than they used to, and I can feel every rib.

Ivan has probably retired for the evening, but I bet he put the leftover macaroni and cheese in the microwave for us.

"Are you hungry?" I ask, my eyes locked to Rosalie's in the moonlight.

"Not for food."

Just then, her stomach rumbles loudly, and I smirk. "Liar." My smile drops. "Hey, you didn't sneeze."

Grinning, she lifts a shoulder. "Guess therapy was a good idea. I hadn't even realized how much I needed it until recently, and now that the shadow of grief isn't hanging over me, I can see clearly for the first time in two months. I've worked through a lot of shit."

"I'm so proud of you, baby." I stand, taking her up with me, and she giggles as I carry her back to the house. "Let's eat. You need to be fully fueled for the plans I have tonight."

"Oh, yeah?" She nibbles at my neck. "That sounds fun."

She's quiet for the rest of the trek, but when we make it to the patio, she slides down my body. Gazing up at me with serious eyes, she asks, "What will we do after the trial is over? Once our lives go back to normal? Well, whatever normal is for us."

I smirk. "I believe you already have a list for that."

EPILOGUE

Eight Years Later
Rosie Doll Walker

"Odie, you're filthy." My eyes bulge as I take in the sight of my four-year-old covered in mud from head to toe. Dashing toward me from the forest, her usually blond hair is caked with brown, and the only part of her that isn't coated with dirt is her eyeballs.

Green and blue blink up at me innocently when she gets to the deck of the cabin. "But I'm safe and sound. Daddy said that's all you'd care about."

I sigh. "He's right about that. Did you catch anything?"

Odette smiles, and she's got the cutest little gap between her front teeth just like her father. "I got two. Daddy got a bunch."

Preston steps up the stairs with a five-gallon bucket filled with creek water and our dinner. He's in his rubber boots, wearing muddy jeans and a black tank top, and I swear he's even sexier when he's all grunged up.

Spending our summers at the cabin has become a tradition, and this is our third year hosting an annual family-and-friends reunion in July.

"We'll have enough for dinner," he says, setting the bucket down with a thud. "A good old fashioned fish fry."

"I'll tell Josiah and Cordelia they can stop worrying about going to town to get pizzas."

Preston bends down to kiss me, and he smells of sweat, leather, citrus, and spice. "Is anyone else here yet?"

I nod. "Bridgette, Mason, and a cousin on the Marshall side. They're all out front setting up their tents. Jay, Casey, and their kids should be arriving within an hour."

"Can I go see Grandmas and Grandpas?" Odette hops up and down excitedly, and I'm torn between letting her go or hosing her off.

I want to protect her from everything, even some mud-borne infection.

I'm being silly.

Some dirt won't hurt.

Surprisingly, motherhood has made me understand Loralee Pearson a little better. Because if my child died, I'd lose my mind, too. It doesn't excuse her actions—I'd never take a kid from someone else—but her grief must've been unbearable and unending.

Sometimes I take comfort in the fact that I helped her through it. She needed me, and although I didn't choose to be with her, I gave her fifteen years of relief from her pain.

Having a daughter has also helped me realize how much I meant to Bridgette and Mason when they adopted me.

The pain they suffered when they lost me.

How much I still mean to them now.

The strangers who took me in when I was nineteen and traumatized have become my family. They're the parents I've always wanted, and they're amazing grandparents.

"Mommy? Did you hear me?"

I shake thoughts of the past from my head and answer my daughter, "Yeah, but stay with an adult at all times. Don't go wa—"

"Wandering off in the forest," the cheeky little thing finishes for me. "I know, I know."

I unbuckle her pink harness and let it drop to the deck.

Okay, so I always insist she wear a leash when she's by the creek. I'm not completely comfortable with the idea of my child going fishing around the same age I disappeared. I know Preston will always watch her, but there are some fears a mother can't let go of when it comes to her child.

Knowing we don't want mud tracked into the cabin when we're expecting company, Odette skips down the steps and runs around the outside of the house. I crane my neck to watch through the windows and breathe easier when I see she's been intercepted by Grandpa Mason.

Some of the dirt transfers to his white T-shirt.

Grimacing, I glance at Preston. "They're going to think we've been letting her run around like that all summer."

"That's what cabin life is all about." He plants a kiss on the top of my head. "But I need to clean up. Don't want our entire family to think I've gone feral out here."

I grin slowly. "You are feral."

"I will be tonight." Preston waggles his eyebrows, making me giggle like the girl he once rescued from the attic. "Odie's gonna stay in Bridgette and Mason's tent, which means you and I have the squeaky mattress all to ourselves."

Humming, I cup Preston's hard cock. "Can't wait."

Looking like he wants to drag me into the trees and have his way with me right now, Preston reluctantly slinks through the back door.

Maybe I'll get pregnant again. Today could be our lucky day.

Unfortunately, I've had some fertility issues. We realized it after about eleven months of trying. At first, we thought it was the stress of the trial with Donovan—who ultimately got sentenced to life in prison without the possibility of parole—but even after all the chaos of that was over, I didn't get pregnant.

The doctor said my body fat content was too low and my

hormones were out of control. Also, vitamin deficiencies were a problem. To put it plainly, my system was out of whack.

I needed time.

And time is what Preston gave me.

After getting permission from the Marshalls, we went to live at the cabin for a while. Our little piece of heaven on Earth. The two years following our move here were some of the best of my life. With Preston's savings, neither of us had to work, though we used our free time for school. I started taking classes for a forensic science degree, and Preston studied criminal justice.

Once I got pregnant, we moved back to Detroit to be close to family and hospitals. On a sunny Friday morning, Odette Francine Walker was born. One look at her, and a dormant part of my heart unlocked. I didn't know it was possible to have so much love for something so tiny, but I was obsessed from the moment I laid eyes on my daughter.

Everything made sense because of her.

In the weeks following her birth, I felt an immense gratitude for all the trials and tribulations I'd been through. No matter how hard life had been, it all led me to her.

Since I wanted to be a stay-at-home mom, I quit college a year and a half short of finishing. I plan to go back someday, but at the moment, I'm happy with the way things are.

And if Preston and I don't have any more babies, I'm okay with that, too. Odie is getting older now. Easier. More independent. She's at a fun age, and since she doesn't take naps anymore, we get out of the house a lot while Preston's at work.

A few years ago, he started up his PI business again. He's still freelance, but he works closely with the FBI. Jen has made it her mission to find other kids like me—kids who might've been stolen and cared for, but once they grow up, they have questions. There's a DNA database dedicated to finding them, which was funded by a large donation from Ivan (who I comfortably call

Dad now). Only two matches have been made in the Midwest so far, but that's two cases solved.

Maybe once I've gotten my degree, I can join in.

Stepping inside the cabin, I glance out the front window and make sure Odette's still occupied. Looks like Nana Cordelia has assigned her with the task of setting up the potluck food on the picnic table, so I move toward the bathroom.

Yeah, we have an actual bathroom now.

The cabin had to undergo some renovations when we moved in.

A heavy-duty generator gives us electricity. We have a small television in the corner, and a lighthouse puzzle we finished as a family is framed, along with a bunch of other pictures on the wall.

Of course, the bed is the same. No way in hell I'd replace that old thing.

Quietly, I slip into the small room filled with steam. The tub has been upgraded, and we have running water and indoor plumbing.

Good thing, too, because that means longer, hotter showers.

Snaking my hand past the curtain, I find Preston's soapy arm.

I'm immediately yanked in, clothes and all.

"Preston!" Laughing, I motion to my now wet T-shirt and shorts. "I was going to give you a hand job."

He shrugs. "As nice as that sounds, I've been meaning to have a reason to get you out of these."

He unbuttons, tugs, and unclasps. In under a minute, I'm naked, too, except for my necklace. I never take it off.

As water rains down around us, I glance up at my husband. God, he's even more handsome now than he was years ago. The gray has almost completely taken over his head, and it isn't fair how distinguished he looks.

I rub my thumb over his bottom lip, pulling down so I can see the gap between his teeth. "Tell me something real."

We still play this game sometimes, and I'm perpetually surprised to find out new things about my husband. Whether it's sad, funny, or just a random fact, he always answers my request.

Staring down at me with serious blue eyes, Preston wraps a lock of my hair around his finger. I get the feeling he's about to say something romantic, and he doesn't disappoint.

"You saved me, Rosie. In the beginning, I thought I was the hero of our story. But it's you." He kisses me deeply, stealing my breath like he always does. "You're the one who rescued me."

THE END

A note to the reader: Thanks for reading LONER! Writing this book was bittersweet for me because this is the last of the Good Guys series. The idea of "good guy" heroes is what motivated me to start writing, so I'll always have a special place in my heart for Travis, Colton, Jimmy, Ezra, Jay, and Preston. If you haven't read the other books in the series and your interest in Jay and Casey is piqued, read on and enjoy the prologue to MAGIC MAN!

Also, if you like sneak peeks at upcoming books, giveaways, and most importantly, **otters**, you should consider joining my reader group on Facebook! Or subscribe to my newsletter to always stay in the loop.

MAGIC MAN PROLOGUE

Jay

The first time I met Casey Maxwell, I told her two lies and a truth. After all, deception was one of my best talents.

Knocking on the screen door of her doublewide trailer, I stepped back on the rotted wooden porch. I studied the faded yellow siding while mentally rehearsing the answers to the questions she would ask.

She'd be curious about the stranger on her doorstep with a mysterious wad of cash, and I had the lies locked and loaded on the tip of my tongue.

Seconds ticked by, and I knocked again.

I knew she was home.

I knew a lot of things about her I shouldn't.

Like the fact that she'd turned sixteen two months ago, her favorite color was blue, and she worked at the diner down the road. She rode her blue bike everywhere because she couldn't afford a car. She got straight A's in school, and she lived in this piece of shit trailer with her mom. Her dad had been out of the picture since before she was born.

And, if she hadn't gotten knocked up by an abusive psycho, she would've been going into her junior year at Brenton High School at the end of the summer.

I heard the rattling of locks before the door opened a little. One apprehensive blue eye peered at me through the crack.

"Can I help you?"

"So," I started, my tone jovial as I raked a hand through my hair. "Last night was a shit show, huh?"

A quizzical quirk of her eyebrow was the only agreement I got, and I could read the sarcastic comment running through her mind.

Ya think?

My assessment of the events that led me here were accurate—an illegal fighting match at an abandoned farmhouse, bloodshed, and the biggest drug bust this small corner of the world had seen in decades.

And Casey was at the center of it all.

Although my memories from the past twenty-four hours were hazy, I remembered seeing her last night. Out of place, too young to be there, heavy makeup meant to make her look older.

After her boyfriend got knocked out, she'd fallen to her knees next to him and quietly admitted she was having his baby.

"Jaxon didn't even tell me where he was taking me last night." Casey's jaw worked with annoyance. "I'm not a fan of violence."

Well, she was dating the wrong guy then.

She probably didn't even know what a bad guy Jaxon Meyers was.

But I did.

Casey wasn't the first vulnerable girl he'd pursued. At least that fucker got the ass whooping he deserved, courtesy of my buddy, Jimmy.

Jimmy had been blood-thirsty on behalf of his girlfriend, Mackenna. She'd been a victim of Jaxon's abuse years ago. The bastard almost killed her. In the couple months since Jaxon got released from prison, he'd been harassing Mackenna with threatening letters.

And apparently also getting a sixteen-year-old girl pregnant. Busy guy.

"Hi, I'm Jay." I offered Casey my right hand.

Without opening the door further, her skeptical gaze landed on it, then flitted back up to my face. No handshake then.

She was afraid of me. Good girl.

I dropped my arm. "I'm a friend of Jaxon's."

That was the first lie. The words felt wrong coming out, but I needed Casey to trust me enough to accept the gift I wanted to give her.

"What does he want?" Her voice was hard. "I'm not bailing him out. Even if I had the money, I wouldn't do it. If I'd known he was dealing drugs, I wouldn't have been dating him. I'm not that kind of girl, so if he gets out you can tell him to stay away from me. I already told him it's over."

Okay, so maybe being friendly with her ex wasn't the right angle to play. Unfortunately, it was the only angle I had.

"No bail for him," I reassured her. "Thanks to the meth the cops found in his pocket, I don't think Jaxon will be seeing life outside bars for a long time."

A relieved sigh left her and some of the worry vanished from the one eye I could see. She opened the door wider, and then I had a full view of her heart-shaped face.

That trust I was seeking? I could sense Casey's defenses coming down a little.

But I wasn't innocent either—not when it came to drugs. I'd been selling and using for years, and it was only a matter of time until I got caught.

After the fight was over, all hell had broken loose when we'd heard the sirens approaching. High on painkillers and panic, I'd tried to outrun the police.

I just wasn't fast enough.

My biggest regret was almost taking Jimmy down with me.

Instead of pulling my car over and keeping my cool like any sane person would've done, I drove into a ditch then took off on foot into a cornfield, leaving Jimmy behind to deal with the consequences.

While searching my car, the cops found my stash and took Jimmy in for questioning. It was probably a good thing he was oblivious about my 'pharmaceutical occupation.' He gave his full cooperation and walked out of the station a free man.

I wasn't so lucky.

There was a warrant out for my arrest, and it was the final nail in the coffin of my downward spiral.

After this last good deed, I was going to turn myself in.

I'd been on the wrong path since I was too young to know better, directed there by the one person I should've been able to look up to. I was my father's son. He'd made sure of it, and now I was going to suffer the same fate as him—a dark, lonely cell.

In an attempt to redeem myself, I'd promised Mackenna I'd find some things out about Casey, because when she'd heard about the baby situation, she was concerned.

Hence, the reason why I was at Casey's house.

I told myself it wasn't because I wanted to personally check on her. It wasn't because I wanted to catch one last glimpse of her before I went away for a long, long time.

Because no matter how pretty she was, I wasn't a pervert. I didn't fuck around with girls who were four years younger than me.

I only had one thing to offer her.

Extending my arm, I held my palm out, facing up. "Here, Jaxon wanted you to have this."

Lie number two.

Casey stared at my empty hand, then glanced from side to side like she was questioning her own sanity. "Um, there's nothing in your hand."

"Oh, silly me. I forgot to do this…"

Closing my fist, I turned it over. I tapped the back of it with my fingers, then opened it again. Seeming to appear out of nowhere was an envelope. The white rolled-up paper uncurled, and Casey's eyes widened in wonder.

It was a magic trick I'd perfected. An illusion. An entertaining sleight of hand.

Snatching it quickly, she made sure our hands didn't touch. When she looked inside, she frowned, then speared me with a glare.

"This is four hundred dollars. Jaxon didn't win the fight." She tossed it back to me. "If it's his drug money, I don't want it."

I just shrugged because she wasn't entirely wrong—it was drug money, only it wasn't Jaxon's. It was mine.

I held it out to her again. "Please? For the baby."

"Shh!" Quickly glancing behind her, she clamored out onto the porch and slammed the door behind her.

Stepping close, Casey ran a hand through her dark strands.

The space suddenly felt much smaller with her out here. I could smell the fruity scent of her hair in the breeze.

Needing distance, I stumbled back ungracefully, leaning my ass against the unstable railing.

Casey crossed her arms over her light-blue tank top and she quietly muttered, "My mom doesn't know yet, okay? She might kick me out when I tell her."

Shit.

It'd been a long time since I'd cared about anyone but myself, but for some reason, the thought of this girl alone and scared made me feel weird.

"All the more reason for you to take this." I shook the envelope.

Indecision warred in her mind as she toyed with her

necklace. A small prism hung from a silver chain, and she ran it back and forth as she considered my offer.

I studied her face for signs of recent crying, but there were no splotches on her cheeks. Her eyes weren't red or puffy, and I respected the determination shining in her crystal-clear blues.

Without the makeup, everything about Casey screamed of youth.

Innocence that had been stolen too soon.

Her rosy cheeks were slightly rounded, and her body was thin. Her hips lacked curves, and her denim shorts hung loosely on her slender frame. Her lips weren't overly full, but the shape was attractive. The corners naturally turned up, like she wore a constant smirk. The arm that was lodged under her breasts pushed them up, creating cleavage that was extremely distracting.

I smiled a little when I looked down at her knobby knees.

She was totally rocking that awkward stage between childhood and maturity, and hints of the woman she'd grow into peeked through.

Someday, she was going to be a knockout.

And I shouldn't have been thinking of her that way.

Averting my stare, I waved the envelope again and the tense muscles between my shoulder blades relaxed when she reluctantly took it.

My mission was complete.

"You have red hair," she blurted out, then blushed the prettiest shade of pink. "I just didn't notice it last night because it was dark, but in the sunlight, it's really obvious." Flapping a hand toward my head, she looked down at her bare feet and rubbed her toes together. "Sorry. You know what color your hair is. I just don't know any ginger guys."

Throwing my head back, I laughed. She wasn't saying it like it was a bad thing. Just a light-hearted observation.

Trapping her bottom lip between her teeth, Casey tried to contain a grin while lifting her shoulders in an awkward shrug. When her smile won out, dimples appeared in both cheeks.

Aw, fuck, she was cute.

Gazing at her, I imagined the what-ifs.

What life could've been like in an alternate universe where I wasn't a fuckup. A place where I took the straight and narrow, did well in school, went to college. Got some job with a suit and tie. Another world where Casey wasn't too young for me, and I wasn't too messed up to be good for someone like her.

One last glance at her knobby knees put me back in my place, and the tremble in my fingers reminded me of the hellish drug withdrawal I was about to experience.

"Well, good luck with everything." I nodded my head toward the trailer, hoping her mom would be supportive. Then I added, "Keep your chin up and your standards high. You hear me?"

The amused twist of her lips sobered as she hugged her middle. "I hear you."

"Promise," I demanded.

"I promise."

When I turned away, I trailed my hand over the rough wood of the railing as I soaked up the last remnants of my freedom.

Wind rustled the tall maple trees surrounding the trailer park. The sky was a perfect cloudless blue. The summer breeze smelled like fresh-cut grass and cornfields.

I'd miss all this.

Just as I made it off the bottom step to the cracked concrete, Casey asked, "Will I see you around?"

I hadn't expected that question, or the hopeful expression on her face when I glanced over my shoulder.

I gave her a sad smile. "No."

And that was the truth.

OTHER BOOKS

The Good Guys Series:
TRUCKER
A Trucker Christmas (Short Story)
DANCER
DROPOUT
OUTCAST
MAGIC MAN

The Good Guys Box Set

The Night Time Television Series:
Untamable
Untrainable
Unattainable

The Night Time Television Box Set

Standalone Novellas:
His Mimosa
Sweet Dreams

Between Dawn and Dusk Series:
Between Dawn and Dusk
The Fae King's Curse
The Fae King's Dream
The Fae King's Prize

ABOUT THE AUTHOR

Jamie Schlosser writes steamy new adult romance, romantic comedy, and fantasy romance. When she isn't creating perfect book boyfriends, she's a stay-at-home mom to her two wonderful kids. She believes reading is a great escape, otters are the best animal, and nothing is more satisfying than a happily-ever-after ending. You can find out more about Jamie and her books by visiting these links:

Facebook: www.facebook.com/authorjamieschlosser

Amazon: amzn.to/2mzCQkQ

Instamgram: www.instagram.com/jschlosserauthor

Bookbub: www.bookbub.com/authors/jamie-schlosser

Newsletter: eepurl.com/cANmI9

Website: www.jamieschlosser.com

Made in the USA
Monee, IL
08 October 2021